Acknowledgments

I must first of all thank Connie Sansome who introduced me to the perils of self-publishing. She reckoned not with my incapacities and was always generous with advice. Her fine book, Minnesota Underfoot, taught me much and is an excellent introduction to the great, easily accessible geology sites of Minnesota.

Jean Mohrig first read the book and offered some good ideas.

My wife, Marie, proofread the text with care and diligence. Proofreading is a tiresome, but necessary task, requiring concentration through a fog of boredom. Blessed are the proofreaders for they weed out error.

My daughter, Karen, gave me many a tip on using the Internet, including directing me to a good HTML teaching program from Case Western Reserve. T.E.Metz and especially his wife also, on the Internet, helped me to learn this task.

My son, Niels, was my general advisor on computer things and aided in the construction of :

our Website [http://www.sonic.net/~nielsj/NOMECOS.html].

Any book is the product of one's whole life experiences. I recall all those good teachers who pushed a reluctant, unstudious boy to learn to write and read good English. I have so many debts. How can I repay those I cannot recall? They are gone now but I call on them through time and space. If I write well, it is due to Sara, Alethia, Mary, Warren. And I am ever grateful to those who taught me natural history Charles, John, Maurice. And I must thank those who made me understand science and get some rigor in my discourse, Park, Cole, Wright.

I am certain to omit someone significant. For example the high school teacher who flunked me in Chaucer. Thank you Miss Dick for teaching me a lesson and thanks too to those librarians and friends who pushed a book into my hands and said Read!

But I am responsible for all and any failures of the book.

Adam Smith, Bird Watcher

by *Paul Jensen*

First Edition

Nomecos Publishing, Northfield MN

Adam Smith, Bird Watcher, published by Nomecos Publishing
Post Office Box 382
Northfield, MN 55057

Library of Congress Catalog Card Number 97-91873
ISBN: 0-9657763-0-1
Printed in the United States of America

First Printed 1997

Cover by Scot Covey; [scovey@Carleton.edu]

Chapter 1 Feedback

***P**olidry* stared at the secretary. She was rumored to be the power that be. An old woman! No! If so, the old boy really is slipping. Maybe he won't be around long enough for me to butter him up! Still, chance to talk to the Big Cheese, get somewhere, straighten out the old fool. If possible. Anyway, really meet the guy, impress him, maybe get a better job.

"Mrs. ah Amansis, he said he'd talk to any employee who had sound ideas about the environment."

"Young man you must realize...hold on. That could be an important phone call. Yes Mr. Volter, yes Mr. Volter. Yes? well maybe…" Mrs. Amansis was impatient; she grimaced; her job would go if this fellow won out. She snuggled the phone to her ear, slumped, and tried to pick out the 'important things' in the caller's chatter, covertly watching the kid as he scanned her office. Polidry was leering at her pictures, then began to giggle at her wall samplers. Young squirt! Her kids thought they were old-fashioned and funny, too. Why not? Still, what kind of world was it now? Better then.

Polidry read 'Home is where the heart is', snickered. Gawd! The only thing missing on the wall was 'God bless our home' or maybe 'Mother'. Obviously the old lady was not too bright. Geraniums on desk not businesslike, but human. Could the old boy really want this old fart around? Gabbling on the phone like an old goose. Showed that change was needed.

I have to spare the boss this. "Mr. Jobert is very busy, sir. I could make room for you tomorrow." She lifted the phone away from her ear, and listened for the explosion. Polidry listened and easily heard the words, "You will do no such thing. I am coming in there and I expect to talk to Jobert, you hear! I am on the Board and I expect a minimum of courtesy, you understand! You can act the doorkeeper when I'm not around. It could help if you blocked that door when all the slobs and creeps come in but, no, you don't do that, do you! Don't pull that crap when I call, understand!"

"I'll tell him you are coming in shortly, Sir."

"Right now! You hear!"

"I'll bring it to Mr. Jobert's attention."

"Good-bye!" Volter's phone headed for its cradle. "God-damned old bag! Gotta get her out of there."

Polidry grinned; they knew about the old girl. The fascist must have slammed the phone into its cradle.

Mrs. Amansis tossed her head. An old bag, indeed! If she had to work for someone like that, better to retire. That visit in Florida was just great. But have to wait to help the Boss. Maybe he could fight it out. She turned to the youth, wondering should she let the Boss take him apart. Really not nice. Still.

"Well now, Mr. Polidry."

"That was one of the fascists, wasn't it?"

A political. "No. Just an angry Board member. Mr. Polidry, I'm afraid Mr. Jobert is too busy. I can set a time for later in the week."

No, she isn't going to fob me off. "Mrs. Amansis, Mr. Jobert says always do things now. That's what I would like to do."

"I see." Yes, he needed a lesson or two. "Mr. Polidry, you must realize Mr. Jobert is busy. And has Board members coming in, meeting tomorrow."

"I'll only take five minutes. Be gone before they show up."

Mrs. Amansis eyed this innocent; the Boss could, would eat him for dinner. "Well now you just wait. Maybe I can talk him into seeing you."

∞

"That boy Polidry is here to see you. Mr. Jobert, he is one of those political agitator kind of people. I tried to get rid of him but couldn't. He insists you invited him in; or at least someone like him. There are lots of those. Too many. And Volter called. I tried to put him off. He was shouting! Can you imagine?"

"Patience, Mrs. Amansis. With the kid, not with Volter. He's beyond redemption; the kid isn't. He's stimulating if a bit naive and he is an honest, bombastic advocate and a true zealot. Can be a dangerous type but Polidry, no, just young. We must give him a chance to expatiate on his ideas. Perhaps we can improve him. Anyway he's stimulating and I need him for relief. Send him in."

"Mr. Jobert, don't pull his leg too much."

"A little humor will help bring him into the real, complicated world."

"He thinks that is where he is. And that you are the ignorant one."

"And so I am. Send in the missionary; this savage waits."

"Boss. Be nice. Ask him to sit down. And Boss. You've got all the Board showing up tomorrow. The call from Volter was not friendly and he's coming in very soon. Today. These are notes I typed up from your comments last time."

"Good idea. I'll need them. You are a jewel! And Mrs. Amansis, this little session will relax me. Don't worry I'll be ready for the Bear. And the others tomorrow. OK. I'm ready for the kid. Send him in."

Jobert sat back, anticipating the bit of relaxation. He looked out the window at the expanse of plant. This is the house that Jobert built… of great ideas and solid foundations; and sweat. Nobody, but nobody, is going to ruin it. He looked around the room. People said the office was a cold mausoleum. Bah! Who cares. That strange creature the wife thought was so good designed it. But not my grouse picture-lousy art, good memories, a good evocator of hunting in the glorious north woods. The forest, the birds, the aspens, ah...the best of times.

"Come in, come in. Grab a chair. Now what's the news from the Save the Environment Movement?"

"Uh Sir." Now why do I grovel for this capitalist? "My name is Polidry."

"Sir not necessary. First name?"

"Doesn't really matter does it, Mr. Jobert."

"Oh yes it does. Can learn a lot about a person from his first name."

"Jacob. I hope it is enlightening." Damn don't mock him; mustn't do that; dammit! gotta schmooz the old boy.

"It is, it is, but I doubt it. More likely somebody on the Board."

"Sir?" the old bastard is shy some cards in his deck.

"Alright. Let's start. You had something to tell me about the environment."

"Yessir." Again! what's the matter with me! Where to begin? "Change is coming the oceans are rising fisheries are failing mercury is everywhere and so on, and so one disaster after another." Damn, damn words,words. Slow down, idiot, talk so he can understand you. "The environment is sending a message. And there is worse to come. There will be hurricanes unmatched in history numerous disasters never before encountered." I'm doing it again! Slow down; he's only a money guy. "I could go on and on. We have to have strong regulatory bodies to keep industries and farmers and others from damaging the environment. We must stop the locating of dumps near poor people, the air pollution around slum areas. And so on. We must forestall catastrophic changes. Ordinary people won't notice until too late. We have to stop the exploiters, enact government regulations." That's better. Polidry took a deep breath. Jobert jumped in.

"People do notice, do react. I know a lumberjack who now regrets cutting down all the big trees."

"If the government had stopped that, he wouldn't be regretting it. And if he had been a little more intelligent he wouldn't have taken part in the destruction."

"He had to make a living. And you'd be surprised how smart he is. But let's talk about little things. Ever notice how things change slowly, Poly, ever notice how things change bit by bit locally? A good bird watching spot disappears under concrete or houses? Lots of people involved. Who's guilty, Poly?"

He wants to talk bird watching! Jesus! "Uh my name is Polidry. I don't watch birds. That's for…" watch it! they say the old boy's a bird watcher..."uh some other time. If the government had established regulations, that wouldn't have…be happening, and that lumberjack, even if he has some brains, goofed and helped get himself into the fix he's in... wouldn't be in the fix he's in. He would still be cutting trees and producing wood for the people's houses. Nor would what happened with all those people have happened."

"He was making a living. Not so smart? I'd bet he reads a dozen books a week. Up there nature makes readers out of people. Not much else to do on winter nights. There isn't even a six o'clock in the morning train. And he, everybody has to have a place to live. People act in their own self interest, don't you think?"

Six o'clock train? He's nuts! "Yes, the capitalists uh I mean the upper classes in this society. But not ordinary people."

"Why not?"

"Because they share things. What we need are people who can arrange things so that everybody gets a fair share."

"Really! hmm, no self interest by the arrangers?"

"Ought not to be."

"Ought and is are two different things. Don't you think you would be swayed by self interest?"

"No. Better to have laws on the books forcing people to do what is right."

"You think having laws on the books will force people to obey the law? You ever break the law, Poly?"

"Maybe traffic laws."

"Why do you obey those laws?"

"Well I might get caught."

"No affect of the right thing to do?"

"Of course."

"Ah so you do what you must, not so?"

"Must? I don't understand. No, I can do what I want. But that's not the same. Make real laws and make 'em obey them. Doing things by plan can prevent the wholesale destruction, the bombing of our environment."

"Bombing? Still it helps if you feel as though you ought to, must, obey the law or rules, eh?"

"Of course." must? what's he talking about? Example-what? uh-er ah, "let's see…you take a bomb-all that energy could be used to make something useful if only the process could be slowed down and damped."

"So how do you do that with a bomb?"

"That's just an example. Uh I don't know...," Jobert waited, watched patiently, staring until Polidry became uneasy, and felt compelled to say something, anything, "uh except to reconstruct the bomb so things go slow."

"Deconstruct?"

Mrs. Amansis entered and placed some papers on Jobert's desk,. She stopped and for a moment watched the kid getting his trial by fire. And retreated to her office to encounter Tim.

"Love of my life. Give me a big hug. What brings you here?"

"Hello, beautiful." Tim Mirave came up to give her the hug.

"Oh Tim you are a sight for sore eyes. A what is it? a jackpine savage! You even smell of the North Woods. Good golden leaves and green needles."

"Funny, I thought people thought we just smelled."

"If only that wasn't an ice box up there in winter, I'd move up there and marry you."

"You are desperate! Too many Suits?"

"Now Tim! That's just civilized people; that's not the problem. It's Volter and the Board. They're getting restless and irritated; they could drive him out, you know. Oh well. I'm so glad you have come. The Boss is in there being very mean to one of our ardent environmentalists."

"Good for him. Guy will learn to get his arguments together before bearding the Boss."

"Well anyway, go in and help him. I mean the victim. Go on in. But not too long... Volter is due in and the Board is showing up tomorrow. The Boss needs to review things. You won't keep him long?"

"No, just going to tell him the grouse are up."

"Do it so he'll want to go up there. He needs that. He's wound up tight today."

"Ah, fun." Tim entered Jobert's office. Jobert looked up, smiled and waved him to a seat. "Big stuff up north, Ed."

"I want to hear about that later. Tim! you are a sight for sore eyes. A human being! What could possibly have gotten you out of the North Woods away from cerulean skies and silence? I'll bet it's beautiful up there now."

"It is. The loons are still yodeling, the mooses are silently slinking through the brush, and the leaves are just beginning to turn."

"Wonderful! Tim Mirave, meet Mr. Jacob Polidry."

Oh God, the Boss's oddball bird watcher. Heard about him. Couldn't that damn secretary have kept him out?

"Glad to meet you."

Tim nodded.

"Tim we're having an environmental discussion. Talking about how to have a controlled bomb explosion."

"Mr. Jobert, I...."

"What you want is negative feedback," Tim volunteered and then wondered where this conversation had started. He walked to the window, looked out on the sea of glittering tawdry cars and monotonous rooftops.

"Oh, but Mr. Polidry wants to be positive. Don't you, Mr. Polidry?"

"I don't know…I…"

"Accentuate the positive, eliminate the negative?"

"Uh, are you kidding me?"

"Unh uh. Just an old song on the point of this discussion."

"I'd as soon drop the bomb idea."

"Oh nooo. It's suitable to the topic. Tim, how can we slow up a bomb?"

"Put in some kind of negative feedback. Something that inhibits increase."

"There you have it, Polidry, a positive slowing of the bomb."

"Uh yes. I mean no. I mean yes that's right."

"Glad to see you're so decisive. Give me a positive example."

Positive? the old boy is off his rocker.

"Yes, of negative feedback."

"That's when something slows down the rate of something else, I think."

"An example."

Tim stepped in hoping to ease Polidry's ordeal, "Use as an example….let's see…increase of people begins to damage the environment so that the environment begins to inhibit further population growth."

"I suppose so but it's really environmental destruction I want to talk about…that and how government can do something about it. That Malthusian business is fascist bunk."

Jobert intervened, "Still, you will agree that something decreasing population growth would help?"

"I suppose so."

"Good. So what you really want to do is to accentuate the negative, eliminate the positive. Not so? Won't you land somewhere in-between?"

"No sir. Government regulations would prevent that." This guy is nuts.

Tim volunteered, "The process could slow and become constant."

"Let's talk about the environment." These clowns are baiting me.

"That's what we are talking about. How about love?" Jobert smiled.

"Sir?" Now what!

"Inhibitor, don't you think?"

"I'm not expert on love, Mr. Jobert."

"Ah, a shame. There is something worth spending time on. Your mother love you?"

"I uh uh think so."

"Well, good to be neutral. Can't always tell. Have more like you, did she?"

"Yessir. I have two sisters, one brother."

"Aha! Love feedback positively on number of kids?"

"I suppose so."

"As in Africa. Uganda is it? Eight children per mother."

"That was due to colonialism. Regulations could stop that."

"Really! Um four kids in your family?"

"Yessir."

"Four kids maybe one too many. Discourage your mother from any more?"

"I don't know."

"Negative feedback from numbers eh?"

Is there any way to get away from this crap? "Possible."

"Regulations? The government in the bedroom. Which branch would you recommend? Interior?"

"Could we get back to the environment, Mr. Jobert."

"Hmm, government as feedback on family size. Now there's a negative feedback for fair. Everybody hate everybody; soon nobody just you. Don't you think?"

"I suppose." The old boy's confused.

"Of course. Mother didn't think you were just any baby. X more babies a good idea, maybe."

Polidry started, "Uh fathers …"

Jobert interrupted, "Very perspicacious of you. Takes two to tango. Pop wants kids...then more kids, right? Right. Two to tango. Should we bring in Granpop and Granmom or maybe the zeitgeist?"

Mrs. Amansis entered, placed papers on Jobert's desk, retired to a corner, observed the discussion. Jobert's picture caught her eye. The Boss liked hunting scenes preferably with dogs. Her eye wandered to the other wall. Mrs. Jobert's imposed modern art caught her eye. She giggled. Jobert's eye wandered toward her catching her thought, smiled. Jobert preferred things solid, natural, like the oak desk he was sitting on the edge of.

"Mr. Jobert, could we get back to feedback proper?"

"Love improper feedback? hmm."

This was too much for Mrs. Amansis who choked and said, "Pardon me…a frog in my throat." Tim Mirave turned his gaze to her. She grimaced, gestured in despair, giggled quietly..

"How about resources? poverty, bad government controlling population?"

"Yes, have to take account of those things but..."

Tim saw a hawk circling outside the window, straightened, became fixed on the wheeling hawk. Jobert watched him cross the room, followed his gaze, saw the hawk and immediately asked what it was. Polidry was disgusted; he was just going to make an important point. Why pay attention to this creep?

"Ed, it's a peregrine falcon."

Ed! Jobert's in his pocket.

"Ah, wonderful. But what can he get to eat here?"

"Lots of pigeons or maybe a robin."

"Poly here thinks the government can solve our environmental problems. Don't you, Poly?"

"Yessir, who else?" careful! humor the old bug.

Jobert started again, "The powder lasts forever."

"What powder? damn bombs!"

"The powder of positive thinking."

"I don't understand?"

"You did mention bombs didn't you? and feedback? Surely you've heard of the historical figure Norma Vincent Peal who has moved many a man. Powder involved probably."

Mrs. Amansis snorted again…powder! choked, strangled, coughed, retreated further into the corner, took out her handkerchief, dabbed her eyes, hid her face. She giggled silently, helplessly and fled the room.

"Mr. Jobert, I'm at sea."

"Ah, of course. I apologize. Words of an old man. You are too young. Let's talk more about that steady state stuff. Tim, can you help us on this?"

"Yes. Like an equilibrium but with wanderings from a certain value which is subsequently returned to."

"A state that's steady. Hm? Never occurred; not in the history of this world; or probably any other world. What do you think, Polidry?"

"Steady state means conditions." Show the old bug I'm not ignorant.

"Ah, like turnover of employees here?"

"Well, yes. I suppose so. I'm more interested in the environment."

"Female?"

"Well, I..."

"Interesting topic. The undulations in the number of female employees here should interest you. How would you characterize their turnover?"

Polidry was now thoroughly confused, grabbed the first thought, "The number of females ought to equal the number of males. Affirmative action. Justice."

"Wouldn't you prefer a higher turnover for the females? Get a good look at the supply. Important to guage the future, not so? ... or would that be unjust?"

"Could we return to the topic?" Easy, easy don't get hot.

"Right. Tim, help us."

"Do you think that hawk hunting out there could be experiencing some kind of feedback?" asked Tim.

Bird watching again! "I suppose he could. I'm not interested in birds."

Tim plowed ahead, tossed in another question. "OK. Now he can eat a robin or a pigeon. Which should he do, Polidry?"

Jobert covered his mouth, sat back, wondered what Tim would elicit. Polidry looked puzzled, his expression disdainful. Heard about this boss's pet. Ignorant hippie. Clothes trashy. Huh! "He should go out in the country where there's food."

"He's here; must eat."

"I don't know."

"I'll make it easier. Suppose there are more robins than pigeons?"

"I suppose he should eat a robin then."

"Is there feedback?"

Jobert watched the interchange between Tim and Polidry. Tim's worn checked wool shirt and patched work pants contrasted with Polidry's conventional blue striped suit oh so carefully chosen to fit the office milieu. Tim was real; Polidry pretending. Tim was watching, constructing Polidry; he would quickly know him. Polidry talked at Tim. He wouldn't know Tim. Tim was to Polidry an object to be talked at, then out of sight out of mind.

"I don't see how."

"Hawk control the rate of growth of both populations?"

"Yes, I suppose that could happen. I don't see the relevance."

"By complicated feedback? Figure it out."

"OK. Yes. It could be…" searching frantically, "The hawk eats the more common one, leaves the other, uh, let's see uh, negative feedback by absence of stimuli from the less common prey."

Tim continued, "Absence of stimuli producing an effect? A better stimulus would be the too numerous pigeons. OK. Let's take another example. Say you have a crowd of robins or pigeons. There's a hawk around. Everyone wants to be in the middle and not get et. Outside guy becomes lunch. Very selfish. Right?"

"Like I said, natural history is not my game. Frightened pigeons or robins act different. I don't know what would happen."

"Could that selfish behavior have a good effect?"

"I suppose." Hw can you turn off this hick?

"Watch the robins the next time a hawk comes by."

"I'm not interested in robin behavior." Why did Jobert turn this guy loose on me?

Tim continued, "So the hawk eats the more common bird. The less common bird can attend to producing more babies. Thus the system becomes more steady even though its components shift behavior or color or what have you. Not so?"

"I suppose so."

There was a sound of a crashing door in the outer office.

"Oh! Good Afternoon, Mr. Volter. Can I help you? Sir! Sir!"

The door burst open and Volter entered followed by Mrs. Amansis, "Mr. Volter is here, Mr. Jobert." Volter snarled and walked around Jobert's office pausing to glare at Polidry, cast a malevolent look at Mirave. He prowled the room like an angry forest bear, listening.

Polidry started again, "But, Mr. Jobert, all of that stuff has nothing to do with preventing the destruction of forests by a big timber company, say, or air pollution by a big factory, the locating of dumps in minority neighborhoods, conservation of resources and preservation of the environment. Human population growth is a separate problem."

Mirave said, "Population doesn't affect any of those things? Not at all?"

Volter grunted in disgust. "Crap, crap!" at the conversation, occasionally halting as though ready to tear the room apart. He snorted, his nose vibrating.

Jobert interrupted, "Wouldn't it be desirable to have a system which stays constant but in which things vary in response to circumstances? Say the number of children goes up and down but always comes back to a replacement number."

"How would you get a great park like Yellowstone from something like that?"

I got 'em.

"First class question, Polidry. OK Tim, how?"

"Not easy. Lots of greens hollering and working through channels."

"So you agree with me. Government must decide some things. Environment is one of them. We need to get political control. I am trying to talk seriously." Polidry was triumphant.

"Right. Poly. And so are we. And you deserve to be heard and to hear. Tim, what do you say to that one?"

From the outer office came the sounds of a feminine voice excitedly greeting Mrs. Amansis and describing some wondrous birds and scenes.

Volter scowled, swore, expressed despair and said, "Oh my God, that's my wife. Any other way out of here, Jobert? That door?"

"Sorry, Volter, that's my private washroom; no exit. You could hide there." Jobert tilted his head, and half smiled, brows lowered, eyes squinting, face, nose, one cheek twitching, looking mockingly in a saturnine manner at Volter.

Volter snarled, "You'd like that wouldn't you! I don't hide from anybody, Jobert! Even my wife."

The door swung open, wide, and in bustled Mrs. Volter followed by a desperate Mrs. Amansis signaling that Mrs. Volter was out of control. Jobert nodded slightly.

"So there you are, Henry," said in a disgusted tone. She turned to Jobert immediately, "Edmund, guess what! I bought the most beautiful bird, a hyacinth macaw. The most marvelous bird. You must come and see it at our summer place in the Absarokas. We've got all kinds of birds there."

Jobert glanced at Tim who grimaced and shrugged his shoulder in despair and asked, "Must be snow there by now. Who's tending to the bird?"

"Oh our servants there. Juan and his wife will take good care of it and of our whole aviary. They love my birds."

Volter rolled his eyes. "They damned well better...she!...gesturing at his wife paid $40,000 for the damned bird."

"Oh Henry, it's only money."

He snorted. "That I damned well worked hard for. She paid the price the guy asked. Could have screwed him down, way down."

Tim observed, cynically agreed, "You could have, Mrs. Volter; the bird was smuggled in."

Volter spoke triumphantly, "I knew the guy was a crook. You could have threatened him, got him way down."

Tim added, "You could, either of you, have reported him to the police."

"So somebody else gets the bird!" Volter sneered at Mirave. "You are some piece of work, Mirave."

Tim shrugged, said, "That I am. But it's the law," and turning to Mrs. Volter asked, "Where is your place in the Absarokas, Mrs. Volter?"

"We're right up against Yellowstone Park; it's a beautiful spot. Oh! of course! I've heard of you! You're Edmund's expert bird watcher. I must ask; there's a bird that sings in our wet spruce woods- the most beautiful song- it sounds like somebody composed it."

"A hermit thrush, Mrs. Volter."

"I thought so-that's what the book said. It was like being serenaded by an angel."

"Some angel! Still we've doubled the value of our investment. Imagine! Only because we're up against the Park like that. People are crazy. The place crawls with mountain lions. We're trying to get the state people to get rid of them. And get them to put in blacktop on our dirt road. Need some pressure to move those damn people."

Mrs. Volter said, "The idea of those lions scares me."

"Can you imagine the damned government hunters came up and wanted to go right through our property. And some tourists too. Damn people think they own the world."

Tim decided to tweak Volter, "It is a public park isn't it? People love the park."

"We do too," said Mrs. Volter. Oh we do so love the Park. That thrush!"

Tim asked, "Do you keep your land in good shape? It is up against the Park. You could damage the Park."

Volter growled, "Listen, that's our land and we might just develop it. It's our private property. Understand! Ours to do what we will."

Tim said, "But you ought to take account of the Park in what you do, shouldn't you?"

Mrs. Volter nodded, "We will, we will. We've .made our touring road in a long graceful loop up to and along the edge of the Park. It looks wonderful! It's not like that awful church and all that traffic through the Park. People, people, people-they wreck everything don't they? They shouldn't be permitted in."

"People, roads, wetlands, parks, some do better... others, most, do worse, finally everybody does worse," said Tim, gesturing in despair.

"Tim you are right. There is the problem."

"People are better than that. With the right political system people would do what is right." Polidry said this as a self-evident truth. Volter snorted.

"How about finding a way to enlist people's selfish behavior in the service of the public good?"

"Wouldn't work. they'd be strong in their selfish behavior, weak in the public stuff, stuff that leads to the public good."

"Well said, Polidry." Polidry relaxed for the first time in the discussion. He'd made a good point.

Jobert said, "Um you said Government must decide things. Could you reinforce the behaviors leading to the public good with some kind of general law about the market? Suppose you provide a market advantage to the public good uh ...say everyone who keeps his bit of wetland wet would gain a permit to charge bird watchers to see the wondrous creatures of his wet spot, see some rare birds?"

"They ought to have that right anyway."

"Polidry, I'm with you there," said Tim.

"There I'm not so sure. I want my patch of land all to myself. Well, how about they could donate those permits to enable the public authority to buy more wetland on the market?"

Jobert cocked his head, looked quizzical.

"OK."

Tim added, "The government would be charged with maintaining a market fully competitive."

"Well, Polidry, you win. The government does have its uses. I think we all need to do a lot more thinking. Mr. Polidry, it has been an interesting talk." Jobert rose, stepped to Polidry, shook his hand vigorously. Tim waved his hand from his seat at the window. Jobert continued, "I advise you to think more about it as I shall. Especially about feedback. The next time you come in, be prepared to talk about feedback in detail. Maybe we could arrive at a meeting of minds. Now I've got some work to do." Polidry looked puzzled; he was disgusted; had he got through to the old bastard? He didn't want to meet that fascist giving him the dirty looks again. He bolted.

Volter growled and started to leave, pulling his wife after him, then stopped, "Taking our land, our property. Socialists! Jobert, get better employees."

"Good-bye Volters. See you tomorrow."

Jobert did not like to be in the same room with Volter.

Volter stopped, turned, erupted, "What in the hell are you doing talking to an idiot like that one?"

"Oh he's amusing and he is somewhat thoughtful. In time he will mature and get more reasoned and subtle in his arguments. He may even be on to something."

Mrs. Amansis came in, placed papers on Jobert's desk, listened.

"He's a jackass. The day I let someone like that in my office, you can call the straight jacket people. I'll be fit for the booby hatch." Volter a burley man, unfittingly dressed in a Saville Row elegant, shiny suit again began to shamble about the room, more like a dressed up circus bear rearing to look at the audience. His wife looked long suffering. Jobert lean, melancholy, dressed in a neat but simple dark blue suit, stood aggressive, alert, at the edge of his desk watching this pacing, amused, waiting. The air now was vibrating with animosity. A mutual antagonism was almost palpable. Mrs. Amansis thought that it was like two bears prowling and bawling at each other in that nature film. Mrs. Amansis shuddered and slid quietly out the door breathing a sigh of relief in the benign air of her quiet office.

Volter watched Mrs. Amansis leave.

"You ought to get rid of that old bag."

"Best secretary I've ever had."

"You keep some odd people. What's this guy doing here anyway?" He glared at Tim. Tim answered, "Just delivering a message." then sat immobile, indifferent to Volter's animosity.

"A clown like this jerk" gesturing toward Tim "can be dangerous to keep around. His loyalties are to the suing, picketing crowd. People like him are all opposed to growth. You know that."

"Some of 'em anyway. I have my doubts too. But Tim isn't part of that crowd. The fellow who just left, yes."

"Bah. He was at least wearing a suit. Might even be normal. You have doubts. That's crazy. Growth is what makes us prosperous. It's the housing starts that signal that the economy is on the way up and that we make money."

"Yes and it's also when someone will screw up my woods where I hunt and that's a problem."

"Nah! Join the Carolina Hunt Club. It's exclusive, and there are 5000 acres of land to hunt on. And they guarantee that you get some quail or whatever it is you are hunting. They'll guide you to the right places. Make sure the birds go by you. The clubhouse is terrific too, first class meals and drinks and lots of good quality, business company. What more could you ask?"

"I can think of things. Volter, to ask a question like that is to show a phenomenal ignorance of true hunting." Was explaining to Volter worthwhile? Maybe get through to him. Try. "To hunt is to become free in nature. It's not just blowing things away. When I'm out there with my gun and dog, my body is working smoothly and I'm floating in both body and spirit. I am alive in a way city people can never know. I can sense the hum of life, the calls of the grouse, the falling leaves, I know what my dog is going to do next. I am a part of nature. To shoot the bird, to kill, is a part of it yes but not the central part. I'd as soon shoot a roadside sign as shoot something that someone else has driven by me."

"OK I can recognize that. Still we need progress."

Volter had grudgingly conceded some ground.

"And what is that?" Tim asked, evoking another snort and disdainful look from Volter.

Jobert continued, "Anyway, all those housing starts going on forever will eliminate those nonpareil moments. I know that economists insist that housing starts and growth are necessary for prosperity. But there is a contradiction there and that bothers me."

"Is that why you are letting the company slip?"

"The company isn't slipping. We've got good products. Things are a little slow now but that will change soon. And Tim informs me that the North Woods Lab has some very positive findings. We're going to have some very valuable products from that lab soon."

"Seeing is believing. You keep telling us all the great things that are going to come from that lab. So far it's a grouse hunting lab... nothing else. We ought to close down that lab and attend to our proper businesses. I warn you I'm going to ask a lot of hard questions at the Board meeting. You and I don't get along. We both know that. But where business is concerned it's not a matter of like or dislike; it's a matter of what is good for the company and I have to tell you I think you are no longer good for the company. I think it's time you retired. That is about as honest as I can get. You are warned."

"I appreciate that. Ask away, threaten. I tell you I don't retire under threat. I built this company. You didn't. Nor did the stockholders."

"Our fire will be friendly."

"That's the kind that kills unexpectedly. I'll be wary."

"All of this will come up tomorrow at the Board meeting. If they saw this freak here," Tim bowed "they'd wonder why in hell he is on the payroll. Mirave! is that your real name?"

"It's his name. And I'd tell them why. He does his work. Tim's valuable. And he knows it."

"A pet like him will make them question your wisdom if not your common sense."

"Tim is the voice of reason He can detect the nonsense no matter its source. I recommend that you find someone like that to talk to, to advise you." Impossible!

"Never! You can be sure I'll be at the meeting tomorrow. Well, I've more useful things to do than talk about this guy. I will see you tomorrow. Come on, woman." Volter shambled out, his wife shrugging, tossing her head, following. He slammed the door as they left.

"What do you think, Tim?"

"People like the Volters is what I'd rather not think about. They mean well; they move where nature is so nice. And they help wreck the thing they moved there for. Make it into a suburb."

"There's one thing about Volter; he will do his level best to prevent this business from collapsing including eliminating me. Can't fault that. That makes him a valuable man. But tell me, Tim, what's the key to the environment problem? What's the key?"

"Self interest. What you gotta do is arrange it so that everybody does what is right."

"So what will make them do that if what they are doing is more fun?"

"Dunno, dunno. Feedback maybe. And just letting 'em know what is happening and hope they respond in time by doing the right thing. That business of hyacinth macaws! Guess how many people will be out in the woods hunting for one at that price. Not to mention scientists or collectors who want one and then the guy who wants to be known as the person who shot the last hyacinth macaw."

"Yes. And about the kid, about Polidry?"

"Hard to say. He could come around; but might be one of your Suits."

"We hope the former?"

"Yes."

"Ah well. What are you doing down here?"

"Dextra needs some supplies fast. She says she's on a real streak of success...uh hydrogen in gallons. And I wanted to visit the dunes. So here I am. And I wanted you to know that the grouse population is at a peak."

"I appreciate that. I'll be there to walk the woods. Where are you off to?"

"Back north right away."

"Still in that cabin?"

"Yeah."

"Little crowded. Won't have any kids in there."

"No. But don't think that question will come up. Although…" Tim hesitated, then stopped.

"Romance? You?"

"No! Well I'm on my way."

"Lucky you. I'll be there in grouse season. Don't tell 'em I'm coming. Like to hear what's going on without preparation. Dextra, hmm, a good choice. Yes, Mrs. Amansis, I know. I've got some work to do, Tim. See you in grouse season."

Chapter 2 Jobert's Folly

"Mary, Edmund Jobert hunts every fall. I'm also sure he will go through this place so thoroughly that I'll learn about things I didn't know existed. He's an exacting CEO and he will examine us like a stamp collector with a magnifying glass. He will miss nothing. Well, we need a stirring up. Running this kind of a lab full of so-called geniuses is not the same as running a factory."

"Mr. Drysdale, he said he just wanted to look around."

"And he will, Mary, he will with a searchlight."

"What are you going to do about those weird ones, Felix and Dextra?" Mary was expressing the grave doubts of the American Legion members about the 'oddballs' the laboratory had introduced into the north woods. She didn't include them with the 'ornery' natives from back in the swamps; they were just ordinary. For sure these 'scientists' were a real collection of oddballs.

Henry Drysdale shrugged and said, "Those are Jobert's personal geniuses and he knows what to expect there; and they are smart, Mary, they are smart. And Mary, you'll excuse my saying so but my weirdoes neatly counterpoint your swamp rats. They are both birds of a feather, if differently feathered. Well, alert the staff... everybody! Type up a notice that he's coming tomorrow. When I say alert, I mean both Dextra and Felix, and the accountants, everybody better know to a T what they are talking about. Mumbling does not impress Jobert. Ah, they know that better than we do. Now I'm off to go over the books; he'll be sure to look at them. Glatz better be able to defend every expenditure."

"Mr. Drysdale, the other research people ..."

"Right! he's sure to ask them where we are in the projects. Tell them that. They must be prepared. Oh, and Mary, call my wife- tell her what's up- I'll get home when I get home."

"So there's a lot more to this visit than grouse hunting."

"He loves grouse hunting but he never forgets his duties nor will I."

∞

“My daughter Alice is up here! What’s she doing here? Ah, the environment movement, of course! Henry, I can’t tell you how delighted I was when I heard that she had joined the environmentalists. A good cause and a distraction from a lousy love affair. How did she know I was here? A first class grapevine?”

“She’s doing a project on the bog next to our labs; something about protecting it and setting it aside for future generations. I have to say, Mr. Jobert, she is surrounded by an unbelievable collection of odd people, some hairy, some unwashed, some chanters, some with strange missions even by their standards, if they have any, and, last but not least, that rabble-rouser, Kraft. He says a lot about you, none of it good.”

“A little charity, Henry. Their motives may be good even if their aims and dress are strange. But Kraft! That bastard! That explains it; she doesn’t know it but she is here through the intrigues and machinations of that creature. You can bet Kraft picked the bog for her. He’s up to something. He’s never had an honest thought. The dissidents who brought down the communist regimes said the lying had to stop. With Kraft the lying is internal and eternal. He’s never had an honest thought in his life. Every word he says is a lie including ‘and’ and ‘the’. That’s a kind of quote, Henry. He was born in falsehood and has been honing his techniques ever since. In college he was a smarm.”

“He was at your school? a smarm?”

“A bootlicking toady. Yes, worse luck. That’s when he became an irritant, a tick crawling up my leg. Not an enemy, a..a skin-crawling presence. Anyway, I never let him get away with any lies. I pointed them out to anyone and everyone. We once came close to a fist fight.”

“Is the man genuinely serious about this stuff?” asked Drysdale.

“About his machinations, yes. He’s got a goal- power, I suspect. He was born to produce a lying system. And that he’s good at.”

“But he’s a just an agitator.”

“No, don’t think that. He knows what he wants and will do whatever is necessary to get it. He’ll follow Principle 2 for sure-each person free to do what he must-but ugh-what he must is despicable. And he will never follow Principle 1- pay the cost of his endeavors; he is sure to off-load on someone else."

"On your daughter, maybe. Principles?"

"On my daughter yes that may be his scheme. Those two principles are the basic rules of the new Department of Environment."

"Oh....bureaucrats with principles. Marvelous." Drysdale surprised Jobert with his irony.

"I must say I was surprised when the Solons suggested those as our working rules. Seem a bit philosophical. But good rules- better than most legislative work."

∞

"Can I help it if I'm full of gas?" asked Thor squeezing his buttocks to stop the fart.

"Yeah, you can-you can go outside. No! not again!"

"I can't help it. I know it isn't possible; uh I mean my lab technique, everybody here is first class-nothing gets out of the containers. Still, I feel uneasy; I've never had so much gas. Haven't eaten anything strange, either. Felix! what are you doing? Stop that! now get away from me! get away from me!"

Felix advanced on Thor brandishing a flaming cigarette lighter, a fiendish grin on his face. Thor backed up, circling to the other side of the lab bench. Felix chased him all over the room shouting, "Scientific test of hypothesis, scientific test!" The rest of the lab workers were hysterical with laughter; even Dextra Chirali looked amused. At that moment the lab door swung open and Jobert and Drysdale entered to see Felix catch up to Thor, then brandish the lighter near his pants.

"Really, gentlemen, this is not a kindergarten."

"Sorry Mr. Drysdale. Felix has a strange sense of humor."

"Felix, what fun and games are you up to?" said Jobert.

"Just a little fun, Boss."

"What's the occasion?"

"Boss, Thor here had the idea that he was gassy from infection by our engineered hydrogen-producing colon bacteria," said Felix.

"Oh, Mr. Jobert, I didn't think that. It's just, well, I'm a little uneasy."

"You and Felix could pretend you are gentlemen," said Drysdale.

"Nobody calls Felix Bountz a gentleman," said Felix.

"You need not worry, Felix, not to worry," said Jobert.

"How nonsensical! I mean the infection idea and that Felix is a gentleman. We know both are impossible." Dextra expressed herself in her usual dry language.

"Don't you ever have doubts, Dextra? I can understand Thor-it is Thor, isn't it? Once I was working with radioactive phosphorus and spilled some, something I had never done before; I knew it wasn't serious but I was panicked until I sat down and thought it out. Even the physicists who made the atomic bomb were a little uneasy about the results-even though they knew what they were going to be. A little uneasiness doesn't hurt. Anyway, nice to see you, Dextra."

"Edmund, when I have doubts, I cannot do what I want to do, and as you can see I have in my lab the evidence of my success. I have transferred the required genic material from a methane bacteria to E.coli. It is functioning."

"Tremendous, Dextra, tremendous. I knew you would do it. Your lab must be adequate then, I take it."

"At first the transferred material did not function."

"Ah, the labs are well appointed, aren't they?"

"Then I went back to the methanotrophs to seek the control genes."

"We decided to set up the labs with the latest technology," said Jobert.

"I succeeded finally. At first the control gene was too far from the dehydrogenase site. We moved it to the right position and everything worked."

"Ah, nice to hear the equipment is good."

"We had all the equipment we needed to do the job."

Jobert was amused; Dextra took for granted a state of the art microbiology lab. This shining, instrument filled room was a far cry from the labs he'd seen when he was a student. And far more expensive.

"Good. Felix, gags like that could be taken seriously by people. No jokes on that topic, eh?"

"OK, Boss. Good news; we have Dextra's bugs in a working large chemostat."

"Good to hear that."

"Even more..."

Drysdale interrupted, "Later, Mr. Bountz. Gentlemen, and you, Miss Chirali, you all know Mr. Jobert. If you can interrupt the fun and games, he wants to know exactly what you have been accomplishing. So! a conference on your work in the coffee room in one hour. Mr. Bountz, put the lighter away and join us there. You especially, Miss Chirali. In an hour, then."

"That Chirali is single-minded isn't she? Mr. Jobert, is Bountz ever serious? He dresses like a-a playboy," said Drysdale.

"And I- I dress like- let's see- a roll-up felt hat, red-checked wool shirt, corduroy pants and boots- like what- a woodsman? Oh yes. A little tomfoolery doesn't hurt. Loosens them up. Don't get in his way when he's working on controls and computer control of a system. He'll walk over you. You've been working with him. You must have discovered that. His results disappoint you?"

"No, no. Never. He seems a bit sex mad to me; but he is able and works hard."

"Henry, people like Felix and Dextra are driven by monomaniacal brains dedicated to accomplishing one end. They concentrate like a cat about to spring. They also have huge egos; they really think they are sprung from the brow of Zeus."

"Brow of Zeus?"

"Look it up. They think they are self-created; I doubt that either has ever acknowledged the influence of a teacher, parent or anyone else. In that they are like all top scientists. Felix is an inveterate joker and a genius, my genius. But remind him again that jokes like that one can be taken seriously by the outsider. Just tell him to stop. Any bad apples, Henry?"

"Maybe. There's our chief accountant, Glatz. Wherever he is, there always seems to be dissension. He is a constant complainer. He goes through a room and it's like a disturbed ant's nest."

"Ah. Like a shark going through a school of fish."

"Yes, something like that. I've thought of getting rid of him but he is good with the books, always up to date."

"Can you keep him away from the others?"

"Not easy. What bothers me most is that he spends a lot of time on the computer. I asked him about it. He says he is checking and improving the accounting programs. It may be so but there is something about him. Ah, nonsense- just different."

"Watch him."

"I must also protest about Tim Mirave. He seems to believe in nothing except maybe watching birds. Was he some kind of error made by the head office?"

"No. He's my idea. He's our loosener. He looks at everything in a different way. He doesn't believe in progress. I ran into him at one of my daughter's things. He was totally rational, something I couldn't observe in most of her gang. Listen to him. He will always give you the unvarnished truth. More than the truth! He'll keep you on your mental toes. And I did want somebody around who will keep track of the environment and that he will surely do."

∞

The first in the conference room was a lab worker who retreated to a corner, slumped in his chair, and seemed to go to sleep; the next was a resolute young fellow who sat at the center side of the table, set out his note book and pencil and looked expectant. Between these extremes there were social groups, the jokers, the cynics, the tired, each located according to his psyche's need.

"Now let's hear what these lab people have to say. Henry, you run the review."

"Come to order! Alright, we'll start at the top. Every one of you is going to get the chance to explain what you are doing. We'll start with Miss Chirali. Miss Chirali, describe your work up until now including the failures."

"Mr. Drysdale, Edmund. I do not fail. I'll start with our new bacterium, a major success. Edmund, I was at a meeting in San Francisco and was introduced to an archaeologist who had been working in New Guinea. Just one of those casual, ostensibly interested, introductions which happen at scientific socials. He talked about all the dig layers and the stuff in them, on and on; but then he mentioned a soggy sample from the bottom of a midden. Gas was coming from the midden. It burned, he said, explosively. He filled some vials with air-free samples from the midden and sealed them, refrigerated, and sent them home. Very intelligent. When they opened one vial, some gas came out.

"I asked whether they had an unopened sample I could look at. Yes, in the refrigerator. They were delighted to have someone like me look at the stuff. Anyway I didn't have anything to do that evening so I borrowed a lab. I treated the stuff with care- no oxygen- and, lo, there was this giant bacterium living in it. I assumed it was a methanotroph and established a couple of sealed oxygen-free cultures to bring back with me. And that archaeologist's find is our gold nugget. It produced copious hydrogen for us in our usual closed system. But it is not an easy bacteria to handle. We've worked out its requirements. A hint of oxygen and it dies. I've now transferred its hydrogen-producing genes to E.coli, our gut bacteria, the bacterium that makes fecal matter stink. Those transformed E.coli are producing hydrogen and will do so as long as we supply food stocks. Not as much as the original bacteria but in quantity. Still, if we can solve the technical problems with the original we could do much better. And I think we can without, I might add, potentially infecting us as Thor feared. Our greatest success is going to be our pesticide-degrading bacteria. Burt can tell you about it."

"Very good. Now Burt, how goes the engineering of the toxin-degrading bacteria?"

"We are making progress. We can zap methyl isocyanate with one of our engineered species of bacteria! Also we are gaining in the ability to degrade organophosphate pesticides. We have two major remaining problems, culturing and preparing large quantities of bacteria for environmental use and the engineering problems of application in real environments. Until we solve these we cannot apply them to large spills. We have every reason to believe we can solve the problem. Our engineers are also working on techniques for injecting bugs into deep anaerobic uh oxygen-free spills."

"Mr. Jobert, Felix is having some success in the mass culturing process," said Drysdale.

"Felix, describe our state of affairs with that."

"Yes, Boss, Mr. Drysdale, we have a sound well- working chemostat- that's a constant state culture container- controlled by our computer programs responding to a dozen sensors to maintain a steady state. We can harvest at a high continuous rate. We have one problem. The transformed bacterium tends to stick to the walls, slowly clogging the system. We have, we think, solved that problem with occasional sonic vibrations of the walls of the container vessel. This works sometimes, sometimes not. We think we see the solution. We can harvest, induce spore formation, and freeze-dry the bacteria continuously for commercial production. We are working with the engineers to perfect a system of gathering and pressurizing the hydrogen continuously. Even so, production is good when the system is working. Maintenance and growth of the New Guinea hydrogen bacteria is more difficult to control. If we solve some problems, and I am sure we will, I think I can see going commercial."

"Don't underestimate the problems of scaling up."

"No, Boss, that's something I would never do."

"Alright. Thor next."

"Well, we are still having trouble....."

∞

Edmund Jobert listened, surveyed the table, well satisfied with the crew. Get good people; that's the fundamental rule. Well, for once I picked a good leader. Henry is just right. Clearly they respect him. No familiarity. Henry's nature. Everything nicely organized. Jobert's Folly, indeed! What a variety of people to staff a research lab! Why are they here? What's the point of it all; Tim would say why not paint pictures, pump gas, become a hermit, get away from these irritating fellows? But the work gets done. And all of them, when a big success happens, transported to another plane where the glow of success reduces all the irritations to triviality. There's Thor, the many-fingered adept lab tech who can juggle five or six test tubes, a pipette, a flask, a mouth to transfer a solution or medium to plates or tubes or whatever, meanwhile carrying on a conversation with a lab partner. And Dextra Chirali, an experimentalist always thinking up new ideas and ways to test them. Wonder what moves her? Dresses like an old maid, hair in a straggly bun, dun shirt and ill-fitting blue jeans, sneakers. Then there's a system whiz like Felix- sex moves him and what else? Always a gay shirt, a decorative watch on wrist, part computer jock, part designer, producing or adjusting programs to analyze data or run experiments through interfaces. And then there is the bumbler, at least in the eyes of his fellows, who still manages to get things done. And the instrument perfectionist working his device to its limit. There are chatterboxes and silent Sams and whistlers and hummers, and the compulsively neat, papers piled in squares, carefully and fully aligned and the disorderly, desk a sea of paper, who seem to get things done anyway. And of course the sly, the cunning, the practical joker, and.. and the lost. Yet with the right leadership, work gets done, analyzed, papers written, reports made to the edification and criticism of their peers. Important to keep things loose and interesting. Obviously Drysdale not inhibiting even the most free characters. Sure, all of the coruscating, venomous, and malicious remarks of social life are here and jealousy, envy, all of the trashy emotions slashing away at the social fabric, a constant undercurrent turbulence of random looks, careless remarks, moods, all undirected but finally destructive. But, still, work gets done. The researchers vary from sweet to noble, to sly to downright evil. And the work gets done. And then there is the destroyer, the malevolent person seeking to destroy others. If you can spot them and, if they are not indispensable, get rid of them immediately. They lie in wait like some poisonous snake ready to strike, a wound sure to fester and corrupt. Can Henry spot them? Yes. Still, ask Tim if there are any such beasts in this jungle. Tim's antennae could spot the animal at the other end of the room. Wouldn't name them unless he thought it absolutely necessary. How could he be so…so…what? so sweet, not cloying, just a ..., just a whole person, the rarest of people, met only three in my life. What circumstances produce such a person?

And Henry Drysdale…formal, dry, ordered, patient, no nonsense. The ideal man to run this crowd. No one of them would ever doubt that he was being treated equably. Each would know his assignment and know when he was doing well or ill.

"What do you think, Mr. Jobert?" asked Thor.

"A good report, Thor. I am pleased by your progress."

"Uh, gentlemen, could I interrupt? My injection machine is working..."

"Later, Teddy. Teddy Sourtis, our inventing engineer. Sorry Ted, we've run out of time."

"I'll want to see that machine later. Congratulations to all and to you, Henry, on running a good show. Henry, better start the process of getting permits to test our stuff outside. See whether they will OK the Renewal Site as a place for experiment. Must already be some pesticides in there. Let the Watershed Chair know what we think we've got and what we want to do. Felix, think about the upgrading of the whole system to a factory scale process. Push those engineers; check them all the way. Just maybe, people, just maybe we have products that will more than pay your own costs- a brave new world. Now Henry and I must go meet with Tim Mirave at the Renewal Site the Watershed Chair required us to construct."

"Sir, Sir, let me introduce myself. I am the Research Lab's chief accountant, Curtis Glatz. It is a great pleasure meeting you. I have followed your work with great interest. You are one of our great entrepreneurs."

"Thank You Mr. ..er... Glatz. Now we must go on this field trip. Good day to you all."

∞

"Henry, books must be kept. Close control of finances is important but I find bookkeeping and bookkeepers uninteresting. Eh Dextra."

"Yes. Mr. Drysdale, I'd like to come along."

"You, Miss Chirali, why?"

"Oh…I'd like to get some samples to check for local methanotrophs."

"Hey, Dextra, the techs did that endlessly," called Thor.

"I still want to go along. There may be one we missed."

"If you like," Drysdale looked doubtful.

"Delighted to have you along, Dextra. Maybe you are like me just a little. Good to see some nature, eh?"

"Yes, Edmund."

∞

Glatz snarled, "Did you hear that? That SOB."

"He didn't mean nothin', Glatz."

"Didn't he? He cut the hell out of me."

"No, you're always inventin' slights. Everybody against you. Lissen! ya come from the swamps like that town-what was it.... Badgerema or something, ya oughtta be grateful to be inna place like this. Company so small din't even have computers up there."

"So I wrote the numbers down nice and clear. And I'm a good accountant. And you..just keep pushing and you'll go hunting for another job! ... I didn't get promoted- could he have been the reason?" Glatz wheeled on the janitor who was pushing a broom against his foot while smiling vacantly, "Toly Quist you push that damn broom up against me once more I'll..I'll .. nuts."

∞

"What the hell is Dextra up to?"

"Thor, she just wants to get some samples, like she says."

"Bolony. Something's up. But what? Polishing the apple?"

"Dextra! not ever, not anywhere."

"Then what?"

∞

"We'll leave the car here. I think you'll like what Mirave has done. I admit I thought he was a foolish pick but he is a hard worker."

"Good. Between us we get the right people eh, Henry. Don't you think so, Dextra? There's Tim over there. Hey, Tim."

"Hello, Tim." Dextra, dry voice, trilling, walked over to Tim Mirave who was looking at a pile of trash on the edge of the bog.

"Dextra is as dully dressed as ever. Interesting greeting, don't you think so, Henry?"

"How so?"

"Not like her. Jesus, what a mess! Tim, how come the trash?"

"The Savages have been dumping here for years. Strange isn't it; they take pride in the beauty of this country and turn around and make a mess of it. Gets my blood boiling. First class positive feedback on me to get the job done. Hard to start but once I see a decrease I have to work that much harder each time. Our first job was and is just getting rid of all these old fridges, stoves, barrels and so on. You'd be amazed at the tonnage removed already. It's no easy job; the bottom is forty feet down and that dead looking mat is floating."

"What's that patch out there? Think I see some flowers," asked Jobert.

"Right. That's really our starting point. It's a hunk of somehow undamaged mat," said Tim.

"Let's go see it."

"It's a bit hairy walking."

"Bah. I've done much worse. Let's go. Dextra, you needn't go out there nor you, Henry. Just stay here."

"I want to go out. Good place for some bacteria."

"Thank you. I'm a dry land person."

"Ha, Ha. Now that's funny, Henry. Let's go."

Tim started onto the mat followed immediately by Dextra who promptly stepped on a mound of moss which began rapidly sinking together with Dextra. Tim grabbed Dextra's arm. Dextra grappled a hold on Tim pulling herself onto the same inadequate mound on which Tim was balanced. Tim attempted desperately to counterbalance Dextra's grip. Unfortunately Dextra adjusted closer forcing Tim over into the bog with Dextra quickly following on top.

"Dextra, better follow Tim's directions out here. He's an expert on bogs. Knows what moves to make. Better get up off him before you sink him out of sight."

"I'd like to but I'm likely to push Tim to the bottom."

"I'd rather be on top," said Tim. "Uh I mean...uh."

"Here I'll give you a hand," offered Jobert.

"Thank you."

"Dextra, let's stay on separate sections of the mat. That way we won't sink each other," suggested Tim.

"Tim, isn't this dangerous?"

"No, Dextra, the mat is buoyant. We'll just float."

"We will float with a lot of bugs."

"Just a few mosquitoes and flies."

"There is no such thing as a few of those."

"Ignore them, Dextra."

"Yes, Tim. Oh, lovely asters. Tell me the plants that are here, Tim."

"OK..Bog rosemary.....leatherleaf... labrador tea... sphagnum and that leaf, there, I think is an orchid; and lots more. It represents what this was originally and what we can bring it back to."

"Let me get over nearer. Now tell me the plants again."

"Get the whole place back to that, Tim. I'll wobble back to shore and talk to Henry. You two take your time."

"That's quite a sight,...you wobbling on the mat with those two. What's going on there?"

"I'd like to know too. Tim's cool, observant demeanor is even more marked than usual. Is there anything?"

"He keeps surreptitiously eyeing Miss Chirali."

"You would too if you had been dragged down to the mat."

"It depends on the woman."

"Henry! you astonish me; now that's funny and even funnier is Dextra falling over and knocking Tim into the bog! She's so well balanced. How come?"

"Who knows?" said Drysdale.

"Here they come. Tim, tell me why does the sight of that broken-down fridge lying in the bog enrage…no, disgust me. Can you explain that? After all, the colors, even the rusting, and the angles, are already there one way or another."

"No, no they are not. Look at it; the fridge fits nothing. Everything you see about the plants, or for that matter, the animals, fits everything else. Look at the intact part of the bog. What you see are harmonious curves and shapes and shadows. Mother Nature has forced economy and efficiency on form and function and on everything from signaling capacity to reproduction... creatures out there are good at what they do. Their leaves are different, the plants are different, because nature insisted. There is an advantage to the shape, the color, the number of branches, their thickness, and everything about the plant. Even the stems, the barks, the heights, the rates of growth, almost everything is advantageous. Likewise with each animal; they are different in uncountable ways and they fit the surroundings. Clearcuts where they remove all the trees are the same; they don't look right; aren't harmonious, a result around here of the subsidies for lumbering from the Forest Service. If they had to pay a true rate for the trees that wouldn't have happened."

"Ha! Tim Mirave as economist. Eloquent! I understand these aesthetic scientific arguments but that doesn't explain my reaction."

"OK. What moves and captures you and me is our intuition of a different world out here, one we know little of... for us to savor and study. Here, we can feast on complexity..collages on top of collages. Notice how quiet it is here. How much silence do you hear in Chicago? And look at the patchwork, a regular quilt of plants. We survived in nature because we can react to all of this."

This peroration moved Jobert, astonished Drysdale, and was received by Dextra with rapt attention. Each in own way was gazing on the bog trying to see Tim's vision. Drysdale spoke up first, "But you can introduce some of the patterns of nature into the city by plantings. Not a bog, of course, but, say, a forest."

"Mr. Drysdale, a forest will soon be reduced to weed trees and forest floor plants, then weeds, then pavement by the mobs unless protected."

"Still, Mr. Mirave, artists can supply some of what you describe. Take, for example, those artists who wrap plastic around islands or across deserts or put shapes on highway slopes.."

"You take them, Mr. Drysdale! They are desecrating nature and should be in prison."

"Ah, Tim, I have felt that way too," said Jobert.

"Very well. A better example. How about what I have seen in Minneapolis where the artist takes a mundane object, a spoon, a maraschino cherry and makes something like a natural history object?"

"Henry, I agree. I think that's great. It puts a little playfulness into the cold streets of the city."

"But nature does that all the time and better, Ed, and with everything. We, on the other hand, build in straight lines with very limited materials and colors. Our buildings are all sharp angles and are bores compared to nature," said Mirave.

"Tim! There's a truck over there. He's dumping trash!" exclaimed Jobert.

"I see him...right...trash. Ed, they sneak in and dump mostly after midnight. They come at two, three, four in the morning and dump. Then disappear on the back roads around a single curve. We caught one who was drunk. He parked behind a bush and was so busy lifting the bottle he forgot to turn off his headlights. Claimed he had been there all evening. Warned him but we couldn't prove anything so we had to let him go. Mostly I think they are the local... trash? no...survivors."

"Tim, this guy hasn't seen us. Let's go get him."

"Uh, we hire people to do that. It may not be safe…"

"Henry, he hasn't seen us. Tim, let's go get him. Come on, Dextra, everybody, run to the car. Tim, you drive. Floor it!"

"Mr. Jobert! ... easy Tim."

"Go it, Tim!"

"Dextra, I need room to drive. Hang on everybody."

Tim rocketed down the gravel road, sliding around corners.

"Mr. Mirave, you're going to roll us off this road!"

"Nah, not now, Mr.. Drysdale. Just brace yourself. Alright, Dextra?"

"Oh yes. I'm hanging onto Tim's arm."

"Not his arm!"

"No, she's stopped, she's hanging onto my leg."

"Safe enough."

Jobert commented, "Who knows? There's the truck. He's taking off!"

"We'll catch him. Hang on, everybody."

"This is ridiculous. Millions of dollars of talent chasing a dumper!"

"Now, Henry. Uh-oh! Bad curve ahead! Wow, like riding a roller-coaster. Where is he?"

"He's gone. This happens every time. They know every little track that can get them out of sight. I'll turn around. Watch out that side, I'll watch this. Must be a track somewhere."

"Stop! I'll walk up this side of the road. Dextra- you over there. Henry, you just watch. We're sure to find the track," said Jobert.

∞

"Tim, I have found fresh tracks," said Dextra.

"Right. Uh, all of you stay with the car."

"No, I want to go along."

"Me too. Henry, you guard the car," said Jobert.

"This is crazy."

"But fun. Let's go."

They followed the tracks to disappear into the trees. Drysdale sighed. If something happens to Jobert I can forget this job and any other job. I could have gotten that job in Silicon Valley and be sitting pretty by now; instead I had to go with Jobert's persuasion. There are no black flies or mosquitoes in Silicon Valley. Near a great city. Hundreds of miles from any decent city here. Solitude would help concentration, he said. Everything available at the computer, he said. Maybe. Still it was a challenging job and well paid. And it looked good for the future; could be a great payoff. There were lots worse situations.

∞

Dextra slipped on a tuft of grass in the middle ridge of the road sliding over to grasp and walk with Tim in the left track. Jobert walked in the other track enjoying the late afternoon air, peering intently into the gloomier and gloomier forest. A bullet whined by. Tim dropped, dragging Dextra with him. Jobert slid behind a tree.

"Ed, the bastard is shooting at us. You and Dextra stay down. I'll get him."

Mirave dashed into the trees soon to vanish in the forest.

"Pooh, I'll go this way. Dextra you stay down. That's an order. We'll whistle when we have him."

Jobert looked for the gunner, shrugged his shoulders, and scuttled, crouching, to the other side of the road to disappear into the woods.

∞

"Tim, take his gun; then give a two finger whistle for Dextra. OK, fellow. That's it. You are under a citizen's arrest. It's a crime to shoot at people."

"Din't shoot at you. Was jus' an accident."

"Tim, any shells in the gun? I see. What do you mean by dumping trash on our property?"

"Always bin a dumpin' place. Evvybody dumps there."

"Ed, there are No Dumping signs all along that edge of the Renewal Site."

"Yeah but that's on'y a week now."

"Ah, so you know about them. Guilty," said Jobert.

He was a little fellow, receding stubble chin, shiny dirty hairline, rabbity. His shirt had an open worn dirty collar frayed at the edges. Every other button down the front was gone. His right sleeve was torn. Cuffs were a mix of dirt and loose fabric. His pants were patched at the knee. Badly scuffed high top shoes peeked out from weed filled cuffs.

"Gennulmen, I'm sorry I done it. I promise not ta do it again. I was just tryin' ta earn some money."

"People hire you to dump?" asked Tim.

"Yup. Real nice people."

"We'll want your name and their names."

"I'm Gilly Lappin. Oh Jeezus, I tell you I won't never get any work again. All I got."

Jobert asked, "Where do you live? No, don't tell us. Get in the truck. Tim, you go with him. Let's go see where he lives. We'll follow."

"Aah, look mister, I'll get the stuff back in the truck. Won't dump again and that's a promise."

"Sure you won't. But first to your home. Let's go. Henry, Dextra you go with me. We'll stay back a little; don't want to eat dust."

∞

"Jesus Christ, look at that yard."

"No need to swear, Tim. We can see it. It's crawling with kids!" said Jobert.

Jobert stared at the yard and wondered: is there a trash person? One who moves into a house, cabin, farmhouse and in a few weeks transforms an orderly universe into a disorderly chaos? Some well-off people surround their houses with cars, trailers, boats, off-road vehicles and pickups but are at least as neat as the collection permits. Others, well off or poor, move in and within a week their homes are a replica of the city dump. There are poorer people who, like magpies, add gewgaws sporadically to their surroundings including wrecked cars, stuffing-erupting car seats, plastic containers, bent tire rims, dirty torn tarps, paper, broken tools. There will be chains and wires and ropes hanging from trees or draped on junkers. Magpies?

"You are Mrs. Lappin?" "Yus." "Mrs. Lappin, are all those yours?"

"I think so. Can't keep count sometimes. That man he come near me I got one."

"One? oh, another on the way."

"Yeah. I'm pregnant."

"A great lover."

"What's that? With Gilly it's bump, bump and I got one like they say in the oven. Always happens. He ain't worth nothin'. Can't do nothin'. But when he sticks me there's a brat. Don't know why he does it. Gotta I guess. Ain't much to me, rather sleep. Waste a time. Maybe dozen kids out there runnin' aroun'. Din't want none a them."

"Ever just say no?"

"How'm I gonna do that. He sneaks up on me when I'm asleep. One thing, Mister, he gotta earn money; relief check ain't enough. Dumpin' is sompin he can do."

"Well, he'll have to stop dumping or start somewhere else. But we are going to turn him in to the sheriff. If we catch him again it's jail for sure," said Jobert.

"Take him. On'y send some food; I get hungry."

"Now woman. Mister, I promise I won't do it again."

"First we talk to the sheriff. He'll decide what to do."

∞

"The camel's nose."

"Huh?"

"The camel's nose. Looks like they are. That guy back there is a charity case. If you hired him to do a job, you'd have to hire someone to watch him. Almost impossible to keep in a steady job. He has all these kids which according to the new rules means he should be heavily taxed. But on what? Society has to support him. If so, why not others slightly better off? If them, ought we not to have some guarantees for every citizen? And so into the controlled prison state," said Tim.

Dextra said, "Oh, Tim, surely not that bad."

∞

Jobert examined the sheriff's office; not fancy, strictly utilitarian. Jobert approved.

"Strictly a working office, eh Henry?"

"Yes. Uh here he is. Sheriff Jager, I would like you to meet our chief, Edmund Jobert."

"Well, the top man. Happy to meet you. Your lab a great addition around here. Now is that Gilly I see back there? In trouble again. Oh my. Gilly, can't you keep out of trouble? Well, what now? Gilly, how'd you and Mr. Drysdale, and Mr. Jobert get together?" The sheriff looking exasperated.

"Weren't my fault. They paid me to do it."

"Uh huh. What did he do?"

"Sheriff Jager, he dumped trash on our Renewal Site."

"Ah, I see. Marko, take Gilly back to his cell. You eat, Gilly?" asked Sheriff Jager.

"Naw. Sure am hungry."

"Get him a meal, Marko. Gentlemen, it's food time. Can't talk until I've eaten. Join me at Nordy's Tavern. Food isn't bad."

"Uh, we should get back. Food here is..."

"Nonsense, Henry, meet some of the locals. Important to communicate with them. Sheriff Jager, we want Gilly to be at the dumpsite to pick up his trash tomorrow morning."

"Day after. Gilly will be there. At the place where he did it. Be there with his truck to pick it up at 8 AM. OK, sir?" Jobert nodded. The sheriff asked, “And I have to ask again what’s a top man doing catching a Gilly?”

“Just a coincidence, Sheriff. I was there; he was there. And then some fun.”

“Be there. Dunno what I’ll do with it,” said Gilly.

“Henry, it’s not a greasy spoon. Local stuff. The food is OK,” said Tim.

“Let’s go find out. Mr. Jobert, I am very interested in what you think is fun. Maybe we could talk about that or the food.”

Chapter 3 All in the muck

"Hydrogen bombs that's what! It's a plot to take away our rights; sterilize us. Who do you people think you are anyway? We got rights too."

"Madam, if I could just explain what we do I am sure you would find that…"

"No you don't! None of your propaganda! Don't care about us people that live around here! Blow us up, walk over our rights! You politicians are all alike."

"Madam, we are not in politics."

"Don't you 'Madam' me. I'll have you know I am a law abiding citizen. We won't stand for you outsiders telling us what to do … "

Midge stared out the window; how long should I listen to this kook? The boss laid it on the line; we are polite to everybody no matter what, but there must be limits. "Uh, Madam..."

"Don't you interrupt me. You kids think you can sass anybody. I'll have you know…....." There's that black, white and yellow bird again. Looks like a parrot. I wonder where it comes from. "Yes, Madam, I am paying close attention to what you are saying. No, I am not trying to irritate you. Please! may I just say we don't, are not going to make hydrogen bombs. We are going to produce hydrogen gas which will be in cylinders."

"Hydrogen, that's what them big bombs are made of. And some of it is going to get loose to poison us poor citizens."

There has to be a limit to listening to weirdoes. "Madam, we are pleased that you called. Feel free to call with questions. You can be sure of answers. We feel the public should know and understand what we are doing."

"Don't you hang up; I have rights." Click.

"Ingrid, Ingrid, the nut has been on the line telling me all kinds of crazy things. She thinks we are making hydrogen bombs. Those research kooks better stop making those trashy jokes about people having gas and somebody lights a cigarette and boom from the hydrogen. Anyway I cut her off in mid-sentence. What I put up with! Uh-oh the boss came in. Oh my, he's got the Jobert himself with him. Uh oh. Bye, bye."

∞

"Henry, what is this story in the papers?"

"They're using us to raise their circulation. Ignore it. You know newspapers like to make stories. And we are an easy target."

"Yeah, I believe that. Still, they had a picture. What was that?"

"Just a little spill, the lees from vat 5, all dead. Somebody left a valve open. Nothing serious," said Drysdale.

"How little? How dead?"

"Only a couple thousand gallons, Thor says. Dead."

"Oh? when did this happen?"

"About a week ago."

"Oh! Henry, Henry, we can't be cavalier about things like this. Get a complete report on my desk tomorrow: quantity, contents, time of day, where it went, what it affected. Understand? What tests were run on the stuff. I want to see it."

"I have not been cavalier. I have required that spills, anything environmental, be promptly reported to me. Tests are already on the way. I'll put what we have on your desk. Mr. Jobert, this isn't serious."

"Sorry. I should have known you would be on top of it."

"Whether serious or not depends on things out of our control, Henry."

∞

"Mr. Jobert, your daughter is on the phone."

"She's calling me. My Alice, my nature bug. I'm afraid to ask; what's she up to? Put her on."

"Dad, you know what you've done to me! You've destroyed my work. We're going to sue the shit out of you."

"Hey, Honey- Whoa! Whoa! Now calmly and clearly, what are you doing here and what is it I have done to your swamp?"

"It's not a swamp; it's a bog. I'm doing a project on the bog. You deliberately spilled some of the bugs from your bacterial vats on my wetlands project. Twelve test tubes of bog gas blew up when we stuck a glowing splint in them. Pure hydrogen and lots of it is coming out of the bog. If someone lights a cigarette there they'll blow up the place. There was a dying muskrat floundering around today. Due to your goop."

"How do you know that?"

"I know!"

"Listen. Where, what part of the swamp is this thing supposed to have happened? I'll come look it over."

"Where! Here, of course. Not a swamp, a bog! You stay away. This is for the courts now."

"Hello, hello. Hung up; she's boiling. I wonder how she is. Skip that. Henry, have you and the staff been in the bog, at the spill site, the site where our pollution bacteria came from? Not! Well, let's have the staff see this spill. Have them at the bog tomorrow morning."

"They will scream. Alright. Mary, send notices to the Suits- ha ha -that's the office heads. Felix gave me that word. He's always a joker."

"The Suits- that's good. And the lab people, Felix and Dextra Chirali especially. Make it 7 AM best time of day, at the bog. Tell all of them and my daughter to meet us at the parking lot. Oh yes, I need my daughter's address; get it. We are going on a bird-watching jaunt to see about your little spill. Let's see. We and Felix have that appointment?"

"Yes, with the technical expert from Control Systems. We'll call you as soon as he shows up. Mary, no other calls unless urgent. Mr. Jobert, it is also possible that the spill may not have been an accident. Somebody may have deliberately opened the valve."

∞

"Ingrid, Ingrid you can't imagine. The supremo, Jobert himself, is going to take all the Suits, including that Glatz, and Drysdale himself into the swamp tomorrow morning. Some kinda spill. Muddy? No. I didn't tell them that-just to be at the parking lot at 7 A.M. sharp-boss's orders. You're right. They deserve it. Yeah, it couldn't be funnier. I wish I could be there. Yeah, Felix and Dextra will be there too; that I can't imagine."

∞

A gentle curl of mist rose from the bog. The early light spattered from the white trunks of the birches. The tamaracks glowed golden in the early light. A goshawk, winged death, slashed through the trees. An owl hooted in the pine grove. Edmund was lost in a reverie, thinking of many mornings tramping the fields, remembering the time when he was a kid, his twenty-two over his shoulder walking through the soaking grass to the brushy field where the bobwhites called. There was a different odor here but, as in the sumac-glowing brush, there was a mingling of many smells, the blend arousing all those primal feelings, a sense of euphoria, all's right with world. The cool air, the quiet, the springy moss, the glistens from drops of dew everywhere, the weaving of shadow and form, the rustle of dead leaves, the sigh of the breeze, all right, all right. He sighed, time and youth gone, but at least he could still experience the tranquillity of a morning like this. How did he get to be what he was and what he did from that beginning? How did he arrive at this transcendent moment? A garble of voices trashed the air. Jobert winced, cringing from this desecration of the moment. Cars pulled up.

"Good morning, gentlemen. You were told this was a field trip, not so? Suits are not appropriate. Well, we are here and must proceed. A glorious day isn't it, Felix. Great to be alive at a place like this."

"If I get my eyes open, I'll try to agree as subserviently as possibly. I'm a B type; I'm a night person. I love the city and, Boss, I would love to accompany you back to the city. I realize there are people who love nature and I can vibe with them but it's not my game. Coming way out into the wilderness is about as much nature as I want. What are we doing here? What are you doing here, Dextra?"

"I am here by request. I have been in the bog with Tim. E.coli could not survive here."

"Felix, try to think of this morning as an experiment in being human and breathe deeply and notice the beauty of the place."

"Sure, Boss, of course."

Dextra said, "I wonder what strange genetic systems are here. Edmund, it is just a little spill, no importance."

Drysdale spoke up, "Miss Chirali, spills must be reported immediately to me. We must have an orderly procedure. The public can easily become excited about nothing or about something."

"More than that, Henry, we have to take every spill seriously. People are afraid of genetic engineering. And even more so when the thing engineered can live in our guts."

"Edmund, that's not so. Our engineered E.coli can not reproduce in our gut."

"Now, Dextra. True if it doesn't revert. Yes, I know, I know. You've blocked that. Maybe so, but when the bug is changed to produce hydrogen they are right to worry. And we must take their phantasms seriously. Dextra, try to think like an ordinary person." Jobert thought that was not possible.

∞

"The greatest farts in all history. Ahhh-here comes a sweater-ahh nice!. Sweaters versus Suits! How totally fitting."

"The greatest farts? Oh. Felix, what.. good morning, Alice. These are your minions?" Jobert beamed. He thought his daughter lovely that morning.

"These are the other eco-naturalists, Dad. And we are all equal."

"OK, escort us to the spill. We can get acquainted later. Thor, you have some containers to get samples?"

"Yes, more than enough."

"We have plenty of samples; you don't need more. And you better roll up your pants, all of you," said Alice.

"Alice, can call you Alice, lovely name. You are not intending to lead us into that, are you?" asked Felix.

"Felix, you mean to tell me that you haven't been into the very source of some of the bugs you are cultivating in the lab? Now what kind of a scientist are you? I suppose you sent a technician. That's setting a bad example. Daughter, lead us through the bog! and, Honey, we like to get our own samples. You come along too, Henry; good experience for you. Hmm, this swamp is like every other swamp. Could be filled in and a gas station put here. Something useful."

"You Philistine! And my father! Oh, stop pulling my leg. Useful! Right now this is a place where water goes into the aquifer to give us good drinking water; that's if you haven't already laced the water with lethal bugs or arsenic or something. In which case you will have the towns of five counties all on your tail. And would serve you right. Alright, follow me."

Drysdale eyed the column of reluctant pants-rolled up Suits and enthusiastic Sweaters and Jeans following the imperial Alice. Should he tell the Jobert there was a better way? No, he's in his woods costume complete with Tyrolean hat today, is enjoying it. I may follow my leader as my duty but I will not wander through that muck after him and that collection of bird-brains-bugs. Just slide into the trees and go round.

"Alice, I can call you Alice can't I? We could be soulmates-aiee-the muck is getting deep. There must be a better path. This is no place for a systems analyst," said Felix.

"This is the way to the spill area. And that is not muck but organic matter, peat.. The color is from the decaying plants. Good for you bureaucrats to commune with this swamp."

"Me, a systems expert, a bureaucrat! The most unkind cut!"

"Us bureaucrats keep things going. Bear up. Systems whizzes are replaceable. Think of what we are doing for the common weal. Achh, I'm sinking too. Shit, the muck is on my pants," said George Ompras. "Gotta roll them higher. That old SOB doesn't care if we ruin our suits."

"Jobert didn't say good morning even," said Curtis Glatz.

"Hell, he's too busy to notice me in the halls, even." said George.

"No, he hates accountants and especially me. That rich bastard has that tramp Mirave as a pet. Mirave is a useless, trashy slob who wouldn't be tolerated by any real plant manager. He's what they used to call a 'hippy', a carbuncle on society. People like us he doesn't give a damn for," said Glatz.

Teddy admonished, "Curtis, George, bear up. He just has his mind elsewhere. He's busy watching birds and, here the man comes. Hi, Tim."

"Hello, everybody. Thought I better be on this expedition."

"Hello Tim," said Alice and Dextra simultaneously.

"Arethusa, Arethusa!" shouted Alice as she deviated to cross the mat, enthusiastic acolytes following.

"Thought the only wood nymph here was my daughter. That's a sight I must see." Jobert staggered across the mat to his daughter, Dextra and Felix reluctantly wobbling after. Tim crossed the mat as though it were a sidewalk. Teddy, as neutral appearing as ever, a typical engineer, hurried over, astonishing the Suits who held fast, looking miserable, their feet soaking up the tan water filling their shoes, and wondering disgustedly at their submission to this idiot walk. Thoughts of golf courses and tennis courts and clubs and bars drifted through their minds. Oh to be somewhere else. Well OK. Chance to impress the big cheese with their willingness to do their duty. A job at Jobert Industries, into the big bucks, maybe a managing position. Appease the old nut.

Alice squatted, her naturalists about her, and pointed to some rather non-descript grass-like structures. One of her minions suggested it was just a grass.

"Oh no. See the old dried flowering stalk. And look at the neat veining, an orchid leaf. A wonderful find."

Shout from a Suit, "What does it do?"

"Do? It does itself. It has solved thousands of kinds of problems to live here."

Shout from same Suit, "Yeah but what good is it? Another useless snail darter?"

"In a way, yes. Must everything be measured by what it does for people?"

"It's not terribly attractive," said Jobert.

"Dad, you should see the flowers, so beautiful."

From a Suit, "Who's ever going to see it here?"

Jobert grinned, "A version of the Bishop Berkeley problem. No beauty unless seen by man."

"Dad, we don't need any philosophy right now. Mister, it's fatheaded to value all these creatures only by what they do for us. If we had a visitor from- what's that star? Beetlejuice? those people would love these orchids even though they might have seen better."

"OK, Hon, what would they see in this orchid?"

"So many things: early in life they make their living from the organic matter in the mat; later they get their energy from sunlight; later yet they unfurl the most contorted, complicated beautiful flower designed to attract the right insect to pollinate it and so on, an endless array of ways of doing things."

A Suit called, "Who cares about that? If they are gone, what is lost?"

Tim thought that deserved an answer. "OK, they go and make little difference, but their presence is an indicator of environmental health. While they are here we know the bog is doing lots of jobs. They tell us things are right. On the day when they blink out of someone's, everyone's, thoughts then we will know that man has blinked out Homo sapiens and let arrive Homo mechanicus, robot man."

"Homo idioticus really and already on the boob tube. So the argument for all this is to keep our curiosity alive." Jobert knew the arguments.

"Yes, Dad, but that's not enough. There's something, more basic, beauty. It's beautiful."

A Suit said, "Hell, we can make our own beauty."

Tim spoke up, "No we can't. We are what we are because we had to respond to line, form, pattern, to shade on shade to survive. Without that ability there is no thought, no reasoning, no anything. They all follow beauty. Our best artists are incompetent compared with the productions here. Have you seen all these abstract sculptures? Interesting but nature does far better."

"Yeah but this mess, this muck, is disorganized," said a Suit swaying trying to keep his balance.

Tim disagreed, "No. Take real life into the city, protect it from people and it will outshine all the artists. A person can stop and feed on complexity, on form, on shadows."

"I like the toot of horns and a cop's whistle," said the same Suit.

"Those are interruptions in a hum of white noise. Here every note, song, movement signals something interesting about to happen."

"Hoo."

"I wrote a bunch of essays on the subject," said Tim apologetically.

"Ha! Another philosopher heard from. And a good one. So the real fundamental reason for preserving this bog isn't its use, value or its functioning but its self and its perception by us."

"Itself, yes. Us, yes. And, Dad, for its use by us."

"Well, Hon, after the Catastrophe, I'm inclined to agree with you. Let's get to the spill; my crew is getting restless."

"About time we move. Soon we'll be under the muck," said George.

"I wonder how much horizontal gene exchange occurs here."

"Out of sight! Chirali up to her ass, you should excuse the expression, in muck and she wonders about genes. Unbelievable! George, you are reassuring. Anyway, what do you know? Boss, what am I doing getting my clothes covered with muck and feeding the mosquitoes in this sinkhole? And sinking! Get me out of here!"

"Felix, those clothes aren't worth that much."

Alice was irritated, "What do you mean a sinkhole! This is one of the best examples of an acid bog in this state. Did you see that grouse that flew up? That tells you this place is a treasure of wild life which you people are so carelessly destroying."

"Dextra, can I give you a hand?" said Teddy.

"No."

"Now introductions. Where's Drysdale? Never mind. Gentlemen, I am Edmund Jobert and this is my daughter, Alice. Alice, meet Felix Bountz, sinking systems expert, and the lady next to him is Dextra Chirali, gene joiner. Next to her is Teddy Sourtis, engineer, inventor. Spence Koch, our all purpose chemist, and Thor Ragnar, our ace lab tech. Then George Ompras, our purchasing agent. You other Suits, thank you for the word Felix, Henry Drysdale will introduce the rest of you later. I don't know all the names yet. Well, swamp doesn't look damaged to me. Anyway, how could you tell? Still I agree- Alice this is a nice swamp. OK bog. I can just imagine a deer nosing out of those trees into my gun-sights."

"Boss, you wouldn't trash an innocent deer?"

"Felix, in case you haven't noticed, animals, people die."

"I don't want to think about it. Alice, introduce us to your beautiful friends."

"I don't like hunting either. This is Diana and this, Gypsy."

"How can you be a naturalist then?" said Jobert.

"Daddy, you made me a naturalist."

"I know that but I wonder if sometimes you aren't sentimental about this reality here. I am no ecologist but I do know that everything out there dies from competition, or predators or parasites or starvation. Hell, all the birds here are predators. They can be nasty, even play with the prey like a cat. I don't know whether you know that death keeps things going. Have you faced that?"

"Yes, I have. But death is not like human death; they don't know it's coming except maybe deer and apes and some others. There's pain and I don't like that."

"The way I feel. I can call you Alice, can't I? I think we are soul-mates. There is a neat Lebanese restaurant in the city with the greatest pita bread where we could talk. That reminds me I'm hungry. Uh, Alice, soulmate, you are leading us right into the deepest muck. Gawd, my foot is going out of sight. I just lost a shoe! Alice, isn't there another path, a nice dry one? How far can we sink? Help! Alice?"

"Pass him this cookie. What does he do?" asked Alice.

"That's my genius systems man. Felix, what the hell are you doing there?"

"I'm stuck, Boss. Alice-dinner? Wow, what was that? This place is dangerous."

"That bird was a camp robber, a kind of jay, Felix. Just getting a cooky for his breakfast. We all got through except you, Felix," said Jobert.

"Our only jay," said Tim.

"Anybody who wants to go to dinner with me has to cross a bog with pleasure." Alice was being mischievous.

"Believe me, it's a pleasure but I'm stuck. And I'm still hungry- that damned bird comes back I'll eat it."

"I didn't realize factory people had a sense of humor," said Diana.

"Wait for Dextra to show you her sparkling wit," said Felix.

"Here's the spill. Notice that all that stinking goop goes directly from your outlet pipe into the bog, Dad. Makes my beautiful bog smell like a sewer!"

"Hello, everybody."

"Drysdale!" (an irritated, disgusted chorus)

"Mr. Drysdale! How did you get here?"

"Simple. I just drove around the bog and came in on the path at the other side. Brought a chair, too. More in the car."

"Henry, you travel your own path, don't you," said Jobert.

"A path!" followed by a rumble of epithets. "We could have walked here along the path!" "Jesus Christ, we could have walked here on perfectly dry ground. Why don't we throw the boss's daughter into the swamp," said Thor.

"Go to it, Thor; go to it. Felix can catch and I'll watch," said Jobert.

"Edmund, you are heartless. That's your daughter," said a laughing Dextra.

"A path! and I'm sinking due to my weighty thoughts about our computer control processes. OK, Suits, go to it. Alice and I can be even better soul mates this evening if we share this smelly muck."

"Weighty thoughts? Hmm? Well! Thor, George, get the seats from Drysdale's car and bring them around here along the bank."

"Succor! I knew I had the best boss in existence."

"No," said Jobert, "Felix, this is just a good time to hear from you about your control schemes. Now all you Suits sit in rows about me. George, you don't fit with your black suit. You sit on the end. Dextra on the other end."

"Oh yeah. A bureaucrat like me can ask the far-out questions," said George who, often irritated by Felix, was grinning like a Cheshire cat.

"Clays are good catalysts. Could change Felix's genes."

"Dextra! a joke!" said Felix.

"A bad observation. All organic stuff here, no clay," said Spence Koch.

"Felix may disturb the relationship of the bacteria in the muck and bring about some unorthodox gene transfer." Dextra giggled like a school girl.

"It is almost worth being in this muck to hear not one but two, I think, Dextra jokes. Uh, I am sinking!"

Jobert asked, "Yes but at an obviously slow rate. Alice, how long until Felix disappears?"

"This is an enhanced experience and I realize we have some male and father-daughter bonding going on but I think I would like to get out of here."

"How tall is he?"

"Uh, I am here, Alice. I'm five ten, just right for you."

"He should disappear in about 6 hours."

"If he stopped bouncing, the rate at which he sinks would decrease." said Koch.

"Felix bounced out of the womb. He was the first true bouncing baby boy. He resonates basically," said Jobert.

"Good, let's get down to basics," said Dextra.

"I calculate the rate would be about a foot every two hours. Felix should be out of sight by about 4 PM," said Koch.

"You are assuming the sinking rate will be constant. That's not so."

"Thank you, Dextra. OK, a more complicated equation. Assuming Felix follows a negative exponential, I would calculate...," said Koch.

Jobert interrupted, "Plenty of time for some good questions and answers. Gentlemen, and ladies, let's listen to Felix describe our new setup. Go ahead, Felix. Try to be succinct. We are short of time."

"You are! I am! OK. Our sensors and sonic system insure constant conditions in the vat. The output hydrogen is channeled to a compressor where a sensor controls the flow..........."

Even in a bog, listeners can fall asleep.

"Thank you Felix. Most lucid. Sun's wonderful, isn't it? Everybody wake up. Alice, did you learn how our plant works?" asked Jobert.

"What I know is that guy is still in my bog. Why don't you get him out of there?"

"Alice, we are getting data on sinking rates of systems experts in a marsh," said Dextra.

"Dextra! Another joke! I hate to bring this up but I am getting in deeper-…"

Alice interrupted, "Nonsense. There's solid sand down there. All you are getting are rates of soddenness. Anyway he's polluting my bog. Get him out."

"I'm polluting the marsh? Help me out, Alice, and we can go walking and talking about the marsh and make beautiful music together."

"Don't do it. We weren't kidding about Felix being a bouncing baby boy. He still is," said Thor.

"Maybe I better protect my daughter. Ha. It's Felix who will need protection. OK, Dextra, you get him out. Let's go."

"I? I don't know anything about marshes."

"Consider it a problem in gene transfer. Use your ingenuity."

"Boy, that's leaving the right people here," said George..

"George, I have to tell you that those two are the brains who will make this a place to be remembered. Alice, the spill is minor. The goop will be metabolized in no time. We need time to get some more measurements. Would you give us that?"

"No! Anyway we've already reported you to the authorities."

"Don't you have any loyalty to your dear old Dad?"

"For what...tell me for what?"

"Hmm. I did pay for everything you've got." said Jobert.

"Ah money. Your God. Not since I got out of college. I've earned my own way since. More important, I think for myself now and I can see the damage your factory is doing. And I can't see what is probably far more important what your bugs are going to do to the system."

"Oh come on. Very little. You know how many jobs there are in my factory; and how many people will gain if we succeed in producing volumes of hydrogen from this new technique?"

"Ha. Gain how? To live in a destroyed environment?"

"Alice, that's a real problem for everyone, isn't it? Alright, back to work. We'll have to deduct wages for the time spent in this lovely outing," said Drysdale.

A general groan. Jobert laughed and patted Drysdale's shoulder, "Nice to know you've got a sense of humor, Henry."

∞

"Mr. Drysdale, PACMAN on the phone."

"PACMAN? oh the PCA man. Well might as well get this over with. Hello PACMAN."` Drysdale giggled, startling Jobert.

"PACMAN? Ha, ha. Yes, we have a report of a serious spill at the bog next to your plant. We would like a report as soon as possible about what happened, how it happened, what your containment plans are, what dangers the spill may entail. We are sending a field team to look over the site."

"The spill is trivial. I have had men on the job. In fact we did report. Another report by Monday."

"We are reporting to the Chair's office. You will no doubt hear from him. He will assess the penalties," said PACMAN.

"Penalties? for what?

"There may be none of course. Expect to hear from him. Goodbye."

Drysdale sighed. Damn bureaucrat.

∞

"Hello, hello. Ah, PACMAN, so nice to hear, see you. I understand you found your way to the site of the atrocity. You found no real problems, not so? What measurements have you?"

“Mr. Drysdale, we received an anonymous tip, on your stationary I might add. One of your help is not loyal. As for us we need more measurements and there is certainly a minor problem. That isn’t sugar coming from your factory. That’s lots of nutrients and we found some of your bacteria. Consequences unknown. We must talk. You must do better.”

“You found no dying plants or animals in this marsh. And our bacteria there, impossible. What’s the problem? What do we have to do?”

“That kind of decision comes from the grand poohbah himself, the Watershed Chair, Hugh Richter.”

“I have heard about him.” Drysdale’s tone expressed doubt.

“I think he gives good objective decisions.”

“That’s the trouble. And he always sympathizes with us when we have to make an impossible decision.”

“Impossible?”

“Impossible. As Jobert says, all our decisions are ethical. We have to balance: the needs of our company; profit, the needs of our workers; wages- a living;the needs of our town, good schools, a good town, a good environment and so on and on. And against ferocious competition. And against Jobert’s own daughter, a completely undisciplined rebel. I have to take account of all these people and groups when I make decisions. Let me see you bureaucrats contend with that kind of problem. Easier to do something simple like telling someone else what to do.”

“Jobert’s own daughter? Hmmn. Sorry. I prefer and I’m sure Hugh Richter prefers to use all the information we can get to assess damages and then suggest corrections. But genetically engineered creatures are a more complicated problem. He will be around as soon as all the data is in.”

“I can hardly wait.”

“Oh and be a bureaucrat sometime; it’s an experience.”

∞

“Mr. Jobert, the Watershed Chair is on the phone. Wants Drysdale. Could you take it? I couldn’t get rid of him.”

"Didn't Drysdale just talk to him? He must have some kind of bug up his ass. Sorry, Mary. Put him on. Hello, Jobert here."

"Ah, pleased to meet you. The complaints reaching me about a spill are dismissed by the PCA people as non-significant. The bacteria found are parts of the bog environment. I wouldn't have called if I hadn't heard you have some kind of bacterium from New Guinea and are engineering it to produce hydrogen. Now tell me all about that. That worries me."

"Now how did you get that information?"

"An anonymous note."

"On our stationary?" growled Jobert.

"Yes."

"The second such note! Who is our traitor? Henry Drysdale sent you a note quite some time ago about it. Hell. Bug? oh, we got the bacterium from an archaeologist who was doing some soil studies about a dig in the New Guinea highlands. Looked through the microscope and there was this humongous bacterium; he thought it was some kind of worm at first. Gas was coming from the soil. Doesn't have a name yet. We thought it would be fun to stick its hydrogen genes into our E.coli and, fantastic, it worked and produced hydrogen. The original bug did much better when we could get it to work. At ten times the rate of our engineered E.coli. We would be free of the E coli problem- you know-a bacterium that lives in our gut. And it looks as though this New Guinea bacterium, if we can grow it in volume, could take us to an efficiency at which we could make real money."

"OK, instructions. Keep that bug in a negative pressure building....."

"Oh no! Do you know the expense? You are imposing a heavy cost on our research. That may make our Board of Directors decidedly negative to this lab. Why? What for?"

"Ecological...I am not so concerned about the genetic engineering as I am about the possible escape of your bug into our environment. The New Guinea highlands are cold. The bug could be preadapted to our environment. If it gets out and spreads like wildfire from a revertant or, even as it is, every bog could potentially increase its production of hydrogen or even change radically due to this strange bug. It is the potential ecological catastrophe that is the problem, a completely new species- a bacterial Japanese beetle- loose in our bogs. There ought to be heavy fines for people who introduce foreign organisms that have not been thoroughly studied. Sorry. I know you are competent and responsible people; but people are incredibly careless. Well! We have to have a conference and need extensive ecological studies on the capacities of this bacterium. As for the engineered E.coli, we know it can't grow in a bog. Still there is the possibility of it getting into people. But that's a problem for the public health people, not us. I assume you have reported to them."

"My geneticists insist they've engineered it so it can't revert or grow in people. And very improbable the New Guinea bug could live here. Almost impossible!"

" No. You can't say that. Maybe it is a bacterium that can also live in the human gut. Found at a dig! Make bombs out of our citizens. One cigarette and boom, a flameout. Just kidding, sir, got that joke in a local bar- maybe one of your people but you must confine that thing absolutely safely until we know more about it. We'll also talk about the spill. Have your secretary set up a time at your plant for a conference."

"OK. Good-bye. Lordy, how much for a negative pressure building. Decision for Henry but why not a room? Mary, get supply to find the costs of constructing a small negative pressure room or chamber. Got that? Why did I ever agree to give room to this experiment?"

∞

"Guy Barnaby, Washington Undersecretary of the Environment is on the phone about the genetic engineering... again."

"Ah, now, Edmund, you know this pas de deux we are about to..." "Hello, Guy. Sad to hear from you." "engage in is absolutely necessary."

"Yeah, but why do you bastards leave me to make the impossible decisions?"

"Ha! I just wish we could trap you down here in Foggy Bottom where we make policies for which we are royally hated by thousands of organizations out there. Have you ever felt the flames of hatred coming from a thousand points? Like laying on a burning bed of coals. We save environment and I know you think that a good, and we use the best statistics we can lay our hands on. We have a summary of the pollutants in your area and we must see that the sum total doesn't increase as per orders from the Solons. And that nothing new and dangerous be added. We are about as good as the Fed chairman at doing our job."

"You are indeed."

"Save the irony. We must get together as soon as possible. We'll send a preliminary finding for you to react to and to evaluate when we get together."

"Then you decide."

"Right. And leave to you the decision- taxes or, better, effluents. Or for the bug, more stringent regulations. We also have to talk about your new plant in Texas. Until then."

"Yes."

∞

Drysdale groaned, "There are calls from the Pecwa Bird Club, from the Zoning Office, and from the Pecwa sewage engineer. He wants to know if his settling tanks are going to blast off for Mars. I said no."

"Henry, you should have gone into teaching or something where nobody bothers you. We've got work to do."

"I turned all other calls over to our PR man. He'll know how to handle them."

"Hello. Jobert Industries. Can I help you? Sir, Sir!"

∞

"You really think there's any danger in the stuff we're doing?" The lab tech looked worried.

"Nah, hell, I handled far worse bugs up at the U, things that can send you into the next world in a hurry. An' do it in a way as shitty as possible. I never seen better control than they got here. An' it's a good place to work. If they get things working and make money we're sitting pretty. Lotta malarky about the dangers."

Chapter 4 Grouse at the Resort

"Easy, Phenix, easy. Get this coffee into me and we are on our way." An intelligent hunting dog recognizes the start of the hunt. The wolf ancestry shows in the frantically wagging tail and purposeful trotting to nuzzle each other dog or person in the group. The cold nose wiggles-no-writhes, in anticipation of scents and scenting, the jaw drops slavering for a future bite. Phenix, padding impatiently around the cabin, glowed red, eyes reflecting the dim light, and watched his hunter-leader, alert to every move, ready to spring for the door.

Jobert stepped out, gun on shoulder, Phenix brushing by to reconnoiter the clearing, returning for commands. Jobert's face was relaxed but as expectant as the dog's. Both were immediately completely in tune, adapted to the forest. It was as though their beating hearts, thoughts, their very beings, were integrated with the trembling aspen branches, glittering sun-sparkling hoarfrost, each color of the forest, each ray of light, each whisper of air, each scent. All united to produce corresponding vibrations in man and dog until a steady symphony of harmony pervaded their souls. The dog's mind began to center on incoming odors. Phenix trotted from fern bed to clump of hazelnut, to patch after patch, all his functioning self seeking the bird, while noting the juncos, the woodpeckers and other extraneous birds. His liege, his trainer, was as well-trained a hunter, producing the right signals so that dog and man went through the forest as one organism, relaxed and watchful. There were no thoughts, no uncalled for reactions, no stupidities.

Phenix halted, tail unmoving. Edmund brushed off the safety, shouldered the gun, ready. A flick of the hand and Phenix flushed the grouse. Edmund fired. The grouse disappeared into the distance.

Missed. Could it be the steel shot? Nah, near enough. Little rusty maybe. "Go, Phenix."

They wandered the forest, leaping logs, climbing over deadfalls, walking through beds of luxuriant feather moss, deep green against the forest floor, occasionally flecked with the dark red of a nestled russula mushroom. Off-white aspens marched on all sides, interrupted occasionally by the graceful white clump of birches. The forest floor was a bed of aspen leaves blackened and shining like silver dollars. A bear grunted in the woods. Then a moose rumbled nearby. A pair of ravens croaked overhead. One flipped over and the two clashed claws, like cymbals producing a crashing noise reverberating through the tree tops.

"Lunch, Phenix." Jobert sat down back to a tree, unpacked his sandwich, tossed a bone to Phenix and wondered if it were possible to achieve this feeling of wholeness, of unity in the city. He doubted it; Tim was right. Moments of fascination, of interest, of excitement but never unity.

He leaned back to snooze, Phenix's head in lap, to awaken to a grunting sound. The moose passed by, musky, eyeing the growling dog, placid brown eye observing the odd intruder. Phenix growled again, stayed put.

"Good boy. Not a bird. Let's see if we can have better luck."

Phenix was up and hunting immediately. He halted near a tangle of alders. Edmund made sure to be free of blocking branches and shouldered his gun. A flick of the hand and Phenix flushed the grouse. Again the rifle swung, fired, this time to tumble the grouse. Phenix quickly found the bird, and brought it back triumphantly to lay it at the feet of his liege. Edmund squatted.

"Phenix, did you ever see anything so beautiful. Look at that pearly gray on the tail, and those bands and ruffs and eyebrows. Maybe we should do as Indians do and ask forgiveness for killing the bird. I do. Do you, Phenix, do you? ... let's go home. A wonderful day, eh?" A camp robber landed near the grouse. "No, no, this is not your lunch. Shoo."

Hunt over, Phenix gamboled about sniffing, snuffing, prowling, kicking up a late wood frog, nudging it along with his nose, curious, then abandoning it to catch up with his leader.

∞

"Damn! Damn!" Edmund, Phenix at his heel, stood still, aghast at the sight. Oh no. They can't do this to me. This is my hunting grounds. This is good forest, my forest. Edmund looked out on an expanse of lawn, a glitzy house with swings, bikes, and a pink flamingo. A boy bicycled down the drive. A dog rocketed out of the garage and ran toward them barking furiously. Phenix growled and eyed the creature. The dog halted, then lowered its head and fawned toward them, ending by crawling up to and jumping up and down and against the disgusted Jobert.

"Phenix, if you ever do anything like this creepy dog is doing I will lose you in the woods. Ah, you're too smart and have some character."

From the house came a man and a woman, she angry, frowning, he questioning. The woman spoke, "Don't you hunt here! There are children! You could shoot them! What if they saw the poor bloody bird? It isn't right to murder poor innocent creatures."

"Now, dear, I am sure the gentleman meant no harm. The gun didn't sound too close. But, sir, we feed the deer and grouse and just enjoy the animals and birds. If you shoot the grouse we lose this pleasure. I am sure you can appreciate that. Down, Puffy, down. He won't hurt you."

"I assure you I will not shoot near your house. I have, however, hunted these woods for twenty years. My hunting has had no effect on the number of grouse. The game people assure me that the grouse I take would most likely perish in the next winter."

"You ought not to kill animals; it's not right. We are going to demand that hunting be stopped here."

"Madam, the bird kills bugs, hawks kill the bird, or I do. This is normal, the way nature works."

"We are going to get it stopped. We don't have to be reduced to animals," she answered.

"We are animals. If you tame these birds you will kill far more than I. I see your cat hunting over there."

"He can't help it. You can."

"Cats are the greatest bird-killers we have."

"We won't discriminate against hunters; they'll be welcome here in hunting season. Now, dear. Uh, here's a brochure describing our plan to build a resort complete with golf course, tennis courts, swimming pool, horseback trails and snowmobiling. Hunters welcome in the fall. Now, dear. We would like people around here to join us in this development."

"I've got to go. Good-bye." Abruptly Jobert fled the clearing.

Gone was the oneness with nature. Now everything was an enemy to be cursed, kicked, hated. He saw nothing on the way back to the cabin.

"Damn, damn, damn. Phenix, I want to kick something, anything...you keep your distance! All those years. Why? Why here? Why these idiocies here? Why not near the city! Damn, as though encountering those people was not enough, they dump trash at my door. It's a notice. Throw it- their shit into the fire. No! Says a meeting against the resort. Who? Who cares! Phenix, we've got a cause. Join the bird-watchers. Destroy my forest, will they!"

∞

"Dammit, the Watershed Chair should be here. Where is he?"

"Got called to the Inter-watershed Coordinating Authority. Better for us. Let's go ahead. We can make points without him interfering."

"Sir, are you going to support us?"

Edmund waved the importuner away. He had thought he was well disguised; what was telling these people he was somebody? Better hide in corner seat. Shouldn't have shaved, a prisoner of habit. Maybe my posture; better slump, be disguised.

People had already arranged themselves into complicated stratified social groupings. There was an apparent redneck group, beer cans in hand, ready to jeer- but at whom? Next to them was a fall phalanx of late summer-timers, landowners each in stylish alligator shirts, duck trousers, tennis shoes, a gentleman's outfit, suitably middle class. Then there were hunters wearing game jackets and fishermen with flies on their hats (for use?), and blue collar workers; gas station attendants and car mechanics, fingernails with the inevitable grime, and store clerks with white collars and some Jobert Lab people, obvious foreigners, looking uncomfortably out of place.

The support seeker was back. Edmund looked at the ridiculously young woman. Could his aged hormones withstand being bashed by a resplendent pair of knockers and those large batting eyes? Exudes...unaware ...innocent....sex. He didn't think he had an over-endowed libido but even a celibate might be uplifted by this kind of bouncing, upstanding presentation. Better keep his eyes off 'em or she'll think I'm, is a dirty old man, or, if not, either way, she'll overuse 'em.

"Are you going to help us?"

"Won't know until I hear what you have to say," answered Jobert.

"Mister, we are holistic; we want to stop all shooting, leaving animals to live their peaceful lives. Really what we want is the Garden of Eden, all creatures living in friendly harmony. For man, we want free love and free spirits."

"Uh, remind me- was there sex in the Garden?"

"What garden?"

"Eden."

"Yes, I think so."

"Uh, I thought that was a consequence of eating the apple. Anyway, I thought this meeting was about the resort. And I am a hunter."

"You don't look like that kind of person. About the resort, yes, but don't you see. It's the use to which it will be put that's wrong, and not the idea. Oh there's the man. Think about the poor animals, mister."

Now what would a hunter look like. Some kind of beast?

A grinning lumberjack leaned over and said, " 'member me? Cut down that tree for you." Jobert nodded, "Fella gets faced by something like that- send his hormones flyin'. What's a poor guy jack-pine Savage like me gonna do? Do you suppose if I pretended to be agin hunting she'd come to my cabin for fun?"

Jobert frowned, "Don't. All innocent sex."

"Innocent sex? Is there.....?"

Another Savage, tough looking, interrupted and said, "Not for us Savages, she won't. On'y for some kinda outsiders. Thought some of you bigwigs would show up. Make money and lord it over us jackpine Savages."

"I'm not a bigwig and I just want to hear the discussion," said Jobert, irritated.

"Huh, can tell you are an outsider. Come from the city don't you? Well we ain't so dumb. Watch our speed."

"A pleasure."

"You know about that resort over to Bijacic-ain't nobody makin' a decent living over there-jest people from the cities, and not many a them, all getting a vacation real cheap. People thought they was gonna have good jobs. Din't get 'em."

"I don't care about them. Resort will be an improvement, with trees gone and all," said another Savage.

"No it won't. Could lose our woodcuttin', guidin', huntin' and fishin'. Watershed Chair says we are set to be a huntin', fishin', tree- cuttin' economy. Offered to help us get out if we don't like it. If you don't like it and stay, that's your business."

"Gentlemen, let's hear the discussion," said Jobert.

"Ladies and gentlemen, the meeting is open for business. We will dispense with other business so that we can talk about the proposed development. Mr. Monarcis, the floor is yours."

"Well! It's real nice being here with you good folk. I was told what fine people lived here but people didn't tell me half so good as I find. I am going to tell you about our plans to give you good people something rewarding, something you deserve. Our company takes pride in developing properties sure to please and to raise the tax base. When we get complete, the project will draw people from the cities, from out of state, from all over the country."

"Who wants all them outsiders?"

"Please refrain from comments until after the presentation."

"Oh that's OK, OK. I am sure the gentleman meant well. We have bought a thousand acres, option on another five hundred. The slide shows the area. There's the blacktop leading east out of town. The dirt road going north is the other boundary to our property. It's basically waste land, mosquito breeding marshes. Some popular trees."

"Popple, mister."

"Yes, yes, popple. And a patch of pines."

A forester spoke, "Patch! hell, that's a hundred acres of virgin pine."

"Save comments until later."

"Now this is an overlay showing how we plan to develop the resort. This area in green will be an eighteen hole golf course. You'll be able to play golf! Now won't that be beautiful- no more wasteland there; something, hey. The lodge will be on this hill. This is the design of the lodge-a fine addition to this neighborhood. Looks just like a Holiday Inn, don't it? Spacious rooms, beautiful pictures of deer and grouse on the walls, rugs you can sink in, queen-sized beds, and a fine restaurant open to tourists and travelers. Mostly we will cater to vacationers who want luxury and sports up here in the north woods. Notice how well landscaped the lodge is going to be, lawn and trees. Over there will be ten tennis courts and here a kiddie's playground with all kinds of slides and swings. Then there is Mud Lake-an ugly name not very attractive. Mud Lake-a terrible name- will be deepened, with a sandy beach over here for swimming. Lake Elysian we will call it."

"Lake Leech more like it. Swim and donate blood."

"Save the comments."

"We will cut a lot of the pines-give you lumberjacks some work. Then there will be a bridle path with pines along it. Now isn't that something! We estimate that the resort will bring in at least ten-fifteen million a year. There will be jobs for as many as 200 people in season. We will contribute to your tax base. Everybody will gain. New industry, new fresh blood for the area. Thank you for your attention. Glad to answer your questions."

"You have tax increment financing for this. Isn't that illegal?" asked a disillusioned -appearing gentleman.

"Yes we have tax increment financing but that will come back many times to you good people. Whether it's illegal must be settled by the courts."

"Before we go into the question session, Mr. Monarcis's company has kindly provided coffee and donuts. It will give you time to look over the pictures of the resort on the walls and to look at the brochures provided by the company. When I ring the bell, return and seat yourselves promptly. But before we break, I want to note that we have a distinguished guest, Mr. Edmund Jobert of Jobert Industries, at the back of the room. Welcome, sir."

A polite bow. A mental 'damn'.

“Knowed he was a high muck-a-muck. Acts so high and mighty.”

∞

“Gawd, that’s a relief. Damn chairs crease your behind like a knife. Can you believe that guy?”

“That would sure screw up them bogs. Ain’t no drainage here. Become sewage pits.”

“Talk against it; go ahead. You got your trees to cut; make a good living. We need jobs; all we got is low-paying jobs. Bell’s ringing.”

“Come to order, come to order! Mr. Monarcis wants to say a few words; and then the floor is open for comments.”

“Well! We are privileged to have with us the great Edmund Jobert. Mr. Jobert, if I had known who you were you can bet I’d have given you a different welcome out at my house. Mr. Jobert, ladies and gentlemen, came by my place while hunting and with great modesty didn’t tell us who he was. We were impolite because we didn’t know who he was. He deserved a better welcome. Mr. Jobert is a great industrialist-civic leader. We all welcome you. We know the wonderful work you do, your great generosity. It’s great to have a genius here. Welcome again. Perhaps we can talk later.”

∞

“Gawd, reminds me of a second looey at Salerno. A king of brown-nosers. He smeared the major with praise, practically shined his shoes.”

“Gramps, no war stories please.”

“Can’t help it, this developer is brown nosin’ so high soon he’ll be coming out of what’s his name-Job something’s mouth. Just like the Looey. There’s’...”

∞

“I’m here as part of the opposition, Mr. Monarcis. I come here for quiet and for hunting.”

"Sorry to hear that, Mr. Jobert, but we respect your view and only hope to convert you to our side."

"Mr. Chairman, this project would sure screw up the lake and bogs. There ain't any drainage here. It would be a stinking mess. Cost hundreds of millions to drain the area. And there is no soil that would grow anything not even grass. If you want grass, you gotta bring in soil," said the lumberjack.

"Listen, Olie Mattson, you got a job cutting timber, you got no right to talk. Me, I make my living, my business, with cleaning septic tanks. We'd all get some work from this project."

"Yeah, you'd haul more honey, Pikala."

"Listen, wise guy, I do honest work."

"Didn't say you didn't. Right kinda work for you."

"How would you like a knuckle sandwich," erupted Pikala.

"Glad to oblige."

The Savage, the burly nymph-ogling logger, strode toward Pikala. The Chairman waved the town cop to stop him, a command very unenthusiastically received. The row of redneck Savages sat back in gleeful anticipation.

"My money's on Olie. He's got a arm like a oak log from heistin' logs."

"Don't put down Pikala. He's as solid as a rock."

The cop separated and calmed them leading them back to their seats.

"Mr. Chairman, if I understand the new land laws, this here developer got no right to put a house where he done. And sure has no right to locate out there in them bogs. Who got paid off?"

"That's tellin' 'em!"

"I regret to say the Watershed Chair could not be here tonight. He is in Washington. Rest assured he will get a complete transcript of this meeting. He will know the law thoroughly."

"I can speak to that, Mr. Chairman. I do have a right to build a home and develop a resort there. I have that choice according to the new laws," said Monarcis.

"Yeah, but you have to pay all the costs by that same law. And you must replace all the natural land you destroy. I haven't heard a word about how you plan to do that. And it isn't possible to replace a virgin pine forest. And who said you could have tax increment financing? The Watershed Chair would say no. Anyway that's illegal now. I wanna know too who got paid off."

"Let's not have these insinuations. This Chairman requires you to stick to the facts."

"I interrupt. Here I'm developing a whole new industry for this area. I ought to get tax support. The speaker seems to assume that the Watershed Chair and the others are dictators but that's not so. We can appeal, and will, if it comes to that or, if necessary, from their decisions to the national Department of the Environment," said Monarcis.

"Yes, you can do that but you have to respect the new local Chairs or there will be chaos. The Chair is a first class expert on environment. He classifies the environments for difference uses. If the Department of Environment Undersecretary goes against him, he must demonstrate that the Chair is wrong or somehow biased. The Undersecretary will be opposing his bureaucrat's judgement to the scientific objective judgment of the local Chair whose statisticians have a mass of data on hand in their computers that the Undersecretary can't match," said Jobert.

"Tax increment financin' is against the law. You know the rules. Taxes are high enough here. These woods are supposed to be for timber, wildlife, huntin' and fishin'. Once again who got paid off?" said the logger.

"That's crazy. I don't pay anybody off. And things will be better when our project is completed."

"People already here do not run down the water supply more than they are doing now. Everybody gotta pay all costs direct or indirect. That's what the law says. And you would have to truck out your new increased sewage," said the logger.

"Mr. Chairman, I favor this development. I got a house and family and I have to keep a roof over their heads. How can I do that unless there is development?"

"There is national money to help you relocate. You belong in the city," said a well-dressed yuppie.

"The hell with you; you got everything already; I don't. I like it here. I'm gonna stay and I want development."

∞

"Hell, they could use septic tanks."

"Listen you-you got a business hauling honey. You got no right to even talk."

"Nuts. Mr. Jobert, I run the local septic tank service. Know you put one in. Call me if you need some work."

"OK. Might need you soon. Leaking tank. Oh Mr. uh.. lumberjack, uh Mattson-`that's Olie'- ah, Olie. I have a windfall I want cleaned up. Has lots of good logs. Interested?"

"Yeah. Real good pine. But you know how many widow-makers are in there? It's gonna be dangerous getting them logs out. Lotsa deadfalls. Might cost more than its worth."

"OK, look it over, give me an estimate including the value of the logs. On second thought you can have the logs if you just clean up, close off and so on."

"I'll do that. Might be better just to burn that woods. But I'll look it over."

"You started to tell me about yourself, once. How long have you been lumbering?"

"Mr. Jobert, I been a lumberjack since I was fifteen. Cut down trees before that. I remember when we'd go out through real pine, trees reachin' 90-100 feet, two feet through. That was real work. Just you and the tree and a partner. There was grouse and bear and moose right there with you. Hell, a man just glowed with health. Gulp down cold air, drink from the creek, see a eating-size trout flick away. Chop some, saw away, and crash down comes the tree. Smell of fresh wood chips, crushed moss. Team of men rassle the log onto a cart to be dragged outta the woods. Sit for supper with the other jacks tomfoolin', jokes, good humor, tired. Sleep like a rock. Didn't get rich but it were a good life. I remember when there were miles of real pines. Last of it now goin'. Wisht it wasn't, but I bin a lumberjack all my life. I love my cabin, my woods. What else am I gonna do? Yeah, I can see the end; maybe a widow-maker will finish me before that. Now we're cuttin' these sticks called trees. Hell you can cut 'em with a pair of scissors. What kinda lumberin' is that? I guess I ain't no different than anybody else sees his way of living going. Big trees going with me. Won't be nothing like that ever again. Going to grow them in nice corn rows now. Gawd! Same with the fish-most of 'em stuck in by state fisheries. Catch one- might have been put there day before. Still, they don't put them on the hook for you. Not yet. Hear Japs fish in department stores! Well, I ain't going anyplace, got no place to go. Stay here with this weed patch woods, read my books, eat my deer. Bettern fishing in a department store, surrounded by nances doing the same."

"Hell, you had it good. Crooked leg and all, I couldn't do no lumbering. So I pumped gas, guided, anythin' keep me going. Oh, I love these woods too. Popples as good as pines on'y they're even raping them now. Look like a battlefield where they clearcut. Popple come back easy, though. Them big companies don't give a damn about people, woods, anything except profit. Sorry, Mr. Jobert. Just the way I see it. What then, after they go? Gotta get people in so's we can make a living. Ain't nothing wrong with hauling; honest work, needed and I make a living. Doing something for the environment, too. We'll make it somehow."

"I'm sure you will. Both of you stop by my cabin sometime; about two miles in on my private road. We'll talk."

∞

The local planner began to speak. Clearly he knew the law and the local people. He was making sense. What he was saying was well thought out and far ranging. Unfortunately, he talked in a monotone, a soothing voice. How to stay attentive, hear his message? The audience was spacing out, each person in his own way. There was the summer vacationer, a teacher perhaps, determined to hear, jaw set, looking attentive but unfortunately no longer there, mind on something at his cabin, fishing or repairing. His wife, clearly attending only to her knitting, will ask him what the guy said. He won't be able to answer. What would the meeting Chairman say? He looked like he was set in concrete. Odds...he'll say thank you so much for that interesting discussion and 'now who's next?' Of what use a droning, mumbling messenger? Shoot the messenger might, after all, be a good rule. At least shoot droning messengers. A service to mankind. Maybe the threat of shooting would bring about an effort to clarify, make eloquent the message. Is droning monotony a personality characteristic? The soundest logic might be delivered in a deadly monotone. Was that a description of the academics, philosophers especially? Oops, a new one. No sleeping while this guy is talking. More likely to arouse the mob spirit. The local kids are already running with him; get them going enough and they will tar and feather the environment people, run them out of town.

Oh boy, a deputy sheriff, this one a real redneck. The rubber hose and iron fist are in his voice. Gets the chance, he'll give those kids a lesson in applied metaphysics. The totalitarians of this world, the right time, the right place and they can produce a catastrophe. A hot kid going to tell him off. Go, go tell him off. Oh God, an on- the- other- hander. Every view expressed with its opposite. One prays for an accident to cut off the other hand. But probably he would wave the logic of both sides with the one hand. He has no viewpoint!

Jobert surveyed the audience of lumberjacks, fisherman, hunters, resort owners, barkeeps, ne'er do wells, greens, naturists, survivors, and unidentifiables. The incredible diversity of people seemed to him to preclude any rational outcome of the democratic process. Surely there was never a majority for anything, only splinter groups, each sure that it was the way, the means, the light. Forced to vote yes or no, everyone would be dissatisfied. How from a medley of views, many totally mutually contradictory, others so complex as to present no graspable program, propositions favoring motherhood clothed as controversial, arguments expressed vehemently and angrily but often not supporting the exponent's desired result, some so simple-minded and illogical as to defy rational response, and of course the nay-sayers, how is it possible to arrive at a rational conclusion? Fortunately the new law gave power to someone as expert as possible in all the problems of a watershed. That there should be a Watershed Chair charged with gathering data and with deciding land and water use on a no-deterioration basis seemed reasonable but whoever the person, he-she must be reasonable or become a tinpot dictator, a Noriega. The way the law reads he/she is not a dictator, but also is not easily turned aside. Cannot permit erosion, water deterioration or loss, vegetation destruction, all hard tasks. Or would the constant threat of transfer or removal from office suffice to produce objectivity? Even if objective, how smart the decisions were depended on not just the data but also on the computer and on other Chairs. How smart he? Common sense better? This guy has the right to build a resort, his freedom, but with the automatic high taxes here could he make it? If not, damage here. Lots of stupid business men. With the completely free market, and that still doesn't exist, he might not have located here. Still, he is required to clean up any damage.

"That Chair he got one handicap. He got that guy, what's-his -name, from the old DNR under him. He is the dumbest bureaucrat I ever seen. Don't know anything technical, just shuffles paper," said the lumberjack.

"Ah, he's a good organizer?" responded Jobert.

"Oh yaaah, might be; don't know what good that is."

"Well, good night. Don't forget to look over my timber."

Chapter 5 Alice's demonstration

"Alice, we are organized fairly well. Why don't you drop out of the demonstration? I know you like to thumb your nose at him but he is your father and you might antagonize him."

"No, that would look like cowardice or maybe hypocrisy. I have to be there. Anyway I make up my own mind. I say what I think. He knows that. He gives me this song and dance about the voice of reason- his voice, of course, not my voice. Anyway he will only be amused. I just wish I could get to him for once. Enrage him. But that won't happen. He understands too much, damn him."

"I meant you might pull punches because he is your dad."

"Never! You know me better than that, Diana."

"Well, OK. Some people will still think you are biased."

"The hell with them. Gypsy! Put some clothes on and stop dancing! The Suits will lose their eyeballs if you keep it up."

"That's my idea, Alice," said Gypsy. "Keep 'em off balance. Stick it to 'em. Down with the Suits. ...I bet they're not watching."

"Huh. They've got a telescope on you. You're likely to get three proposals this week, one decent."

"Ha, ha. I a hausfrau. Hoo, hoo. I finish by mooning them."

"You'll freeze your behind. I'm glad the light is getting dim...five, all indecent. Advantage, Suits! I'm glad I can't hear them. Get thee clothed- here comes the crowd."

Alice eyed the newcomers. She muttered to Gypsy, "Look at them. Mostly they are fuzzy environmentalists who confuse what's good for them with what's good for everybody. A lot of 'em think animals have rights. And those kids…they just want to be part of something. Everyone of them an environmentalist oh yeah!. Oh hell! I'm repeating my dad's words again."

Gypsy asked, "Is there anyone who isn't an environmentalist?"

"Are there ever! Too many to count. There are Wall Streeters, political operators, organizers of marches and of public displays and of letters to the editors for whom 'the ecology' is just another cause to co-opt for their own re-election or their own ends and so on and on. Even this bunch is mixed. That wouldn't surprise Dad."

"Aah, Alice, follow your own instincts."

"Just what my Dad would say. Let's get started, folks."

Out of the group stepped Naomi. Alice shuddered. "Could I start?" said Naomi, "I think my plan is the most important. The thing is, never eat meat, everybody on a vegetarian diet. Then all those aggressive feelings, even wars end and Nature will survive."

A sigh went through the group. "Huh? How's that?" "Huh?"

"Even more important, if you never eat meat, only plant food, then your mucus will flow smoothly. Everyone will feel on top of the world." Alice tried to remember how this woman had entered the group. One of those casual walk-ins wanting something to do?

"Mucus?! How about spinach?"

"Oh, Charles, you must eat it...it provides the iron you need...and helps mucus production. Besides eating vegetarian helps everybody. Hello, Mr. Kraft, you are here! Well!"

"How are you, Naomi?"

"Oh yes! I'm in perfect health. You look OK but Alex and Rich ...what kind of foods are you eating?"

Rich bowed and said, "Mostly fast food; we both get our share of cholesterol and fat every day.. Makes me feel good, Naomi."

"Rich will never eat right. Well there's Gypsy. Some place for a demonstration ay, Gypsy? Bugs!"

"It's not bad, Gilbert. Temperature is just right, not many bugs. So, I've been dancing. Hello Rich and Alex. The gangs all here."

Gilbert laughed, "Should have waited for us. Right, Rich, Alex."

"And how!"

"Hello, Gilbert. Gypsy had an appreciative audience up there."

"Alice, that's not a good audience. A dance of a sugar plum fairy for a bunch of clerks."

"Gilbert, they're human.."

"The extraordinary for the ordinary. I know, I know. Just... you always wish they'd loosen up, sometimes take our side. Well let's get started. Hello, hello everybody. The name's Gilbert

Kraft...everybody! call me Gilbert. Now Naomi has your minds centered on nutrition."

"Yes. And think of all the poor people all over the world without enough to eat."

"We'll come back to vegetarianism later. We have to plan an agenda. Uh I'm shivering. Cold, isn't it?...ah, the fire is started-just in time."

Naomi said, "Mr. Kraft, I don't know what we should do. I..."

"Please call me Gilbert. We're all friends here. Everybody! Let's get started. We have to agree on a plan of action. The company has polluted this bog, has released dangerous microorganisms which could radically change this fragile ecosystem, has broken the land laws, acted lawlessly, and many other things. We need to set up committees, arrange demonstrations. 'DOWN WITH JOBERT' would be a good sign for somebody."

"Ooh, that's a good idea," said Naomi.

"But not Alice Jobert," said Alice, a bit irritated but smiling. "We've been doing some planning already, Gilbert."

"Of course. Stupid of me to jump right in. What are the plans?"

"It's terrible that they use animals to test their poisons on," interjected Diana. "And just as bad is hunting; it is an immoral blood sport. Think of the pain!"

Alice sighed; Kraft didn't bat an eye. He said, "Yes, indeed. Most people don't understand that. So their consciences aren't bothered. Doesn't affect their profits up there," nodding toward the lab.

"I'll put on my sign-'Business Plutocrats Torture Animals.'

"Mr. Kraft, if we could get everyone to eat properly all these kinds of problems would disappear. It is bad foods and the poisons produced by them in our blood which makes people do the things they do." Naomi was not going to be moved from her thesis.

"Call me Gilbert. Yes, there's something in what you say. But we get bad foods from agrochemical companies which sell pesticides and herbicides knowing the farmers will overuse them and pollute the earth with them. The companies will profit, not the farmer. And certainly not ordinary working people. What we must do is fight these companies, especially this one. Why don't you make your sign read- 'Boycott Bad Food'. That will carry your message about mucus. Now we must plan our agenda. Damn, I'm cold! Alice, couldn't we be better able to plan a strategy in a room at the college? I have some wine and it's warmer there."

"No, no. I wanted everybody to see the spill. Right now we have to decide what to do about the spill. I admit it isn't THAT big a spill, but I think we should at least picket long enough to get in the news and to get through to the new Watershed Chair."

Kraft urged, "Uh, Alice, we ought to do much more than that. This is our chance to make the local people aware of the problems the company is bringing. And we don't want to get through to the Chair, we want to get at him. They were put in there to preserve companies not people. He or she is sheltered by a tenure of ten years and can only be removed by agreement between either the Solons and the President or with the state legislatures and governors. So we can't get at him. They are insulated from day to day pressures. We can't produce results by just demonstrating; we must have confrontations. To get at the bosses and the Chair requires getting the common people on our side. And that's not easy. Companies can't get at the Chairs either."

"There was that case in Ohio..."

"Don't be so gullible, Rich. They were fined peanuts."

"Who's gullible? I just like to look at facts."

Alice wanted more, "Rich, Gilbert is right; we have to try to get through to people. Look what acid rain and the warming have done to the forests. Gilbert, if we get enough people marching, shouting, writing letters the public will learn and maybe the companies too. Now! Who will volunteer to compose a letter for our members to send to the newspapers and magazines about this spill? Who will volunteer?"

"I will but I need advice as to what to put in the letter about the spill," said Gypsy.

"I'll provide you with some sample letters. I will also be available for advising."

"Gilbert, you are a good organizer but please be factual."

"Gypsy, please call me Gilbert. Alice. I am always factual, but you must realize that this is a war we are fighting. It's not just environment. We have to use this spill to fight all the other injustices. Think of the destruction of the community from this kind of thing; think of the bribes and corruption involved. Do you think this company won't get away with this? We have to fight the money-hungry politicians, too. This is a multi-national company- remember what one of those did in India at Bhopal. Maybe you never read about that? Well, thousands of people were killed and injured by cyanide, isocyanate. Peanuts paid by the company to them. What we do here can affect the third world. Oh yes it can. I personally think we'll get a good environment once we organize the system properly."

"Christ, you are going to solve the problem of the Universe and Everything. Why not concentrate on this spill? Just tell the truth about it....keep the politics out of it. With socialism we can be successful like Russia was! Oh yeah. Nuts! We have enough problems right here. We don't need to take on the problems of the world." Rich was irritated.

"I didn't say socialism. And don't you wave the red flag at me, Rich. Let me tell you something, Rich. Politics can't wait for everybody to agree. You must go ahead. Or you'll be like Jobert all thought, no action. Socialism uh…anyway they didn't have what we have to work with. Now we must construct a just, harmonious society."

"I think Rich is right. Let's stick to our local problems," said Diana.

"You can't separate them from world problems," said Alex. "What Gilbert and I know absolutely certainly is that there is only one way to solve these problems."

"Your way. The one true way. Yeah," said Rich.

"Somebody coming."

"Well it's the lord high muck-a-muck and a toady. Who you robbing now, Jobert?"

"Kraft- you here- figures. Rabble rousing, I assume."

"Ha! raising consciousness about you, Moneybags."

"Moneybags? I prefer capitalist. Whose consciousness and what for? Nonsense." Jobert turned affectionately to his daughter. "Alice, your mother is anxious that you call her tonight; something about your brother in Europe."

"Yes, OK. Drugs again I'll bet. Hi, Tim, the Toad," said Alice in a pleasant, welcoming and warm voice.

Tim waved and croaked, toad style, "gronk, gronk."

"And there comes Dextra! What brings you here?" said Alice.

"I wanted to see your group. Hello, Tim!" said almost joyfully. Alice looked very disbelieving.

Jobert interrupted, "Alice, let me know how Bob's doing. Please! He never writes to me. I have one piece of advise for you, Alice. Don't listen to this rabble-rouser. What he wants to do is not what you want to do. The rest of you beware of Kraft's claptrap. He's always on the make. Wants you to do his thing."

"I am capable of running my own life!" Alice spoke angrily.

Kraft burst out, "That's telling him, Alice. What they don't need is your bull, Jobert. Don't listen to this corrupt SOB- any of you. He is trying to divide us."

"And how! I must tell you that the Watershed Chair has sent his men to look over the spill and at the moment they think it unlikely that any kind of work or penalty is warranted. The spill is dissipating without any visible consequences."

"Ha! Bought off again. Didn't I predict that, people?" said Kraft.

Alex spoke up, "There are still those dangerous bacteria out there. I wonder how they excused that. And as usual Jobert doesn't give a damn as long as he gains a profit."

"What nonsense. Listen, all of you! Right now we have invested a very large amount of money in this project; we hope to have a process which can produce cheap energy and to produce profit. And we are certain to solve some pesticide environmental problems; something you won't. As for profit, that is required to keep anyone, any company, private or public, in business. In fact profit is necessary for everyone, for you tonight and tomorrow, for example. If you don't gain, profit, by your demonstration you have suffered a loss of energy uselessly. All that food gone to waste! If I hunt and get no grouse I waste calories if I don't also gain from the beauty of the forest. The grouse I get is a profit. So is being in the forest. If you rabble-rouse you can't truly gain. Capital is what you fall back on so you don't go hungry. Another word for profit is survival."

"To think of a dead animal as profit is evil," said Diana.

"Another phrase for profit is gouging the poor. Socialism would correct that," said Alex. "Getting a profit is gouging, stealing from poor people. Look at the slums in our cities where people can't make a decent living."

"I don't think anyone knows how to solve all society's problems, especially people like you two. Well! Enough! I will not disturb you further. Oh... the Suits express their admiration for the mooning and, oh yes, next time get someone skinny. The effect is not insulting to them. On the contrary, disturbing."

"That was Gypsy."

"Ah. Beware, Gypsy whoever you are. You've released some instincts up there," gesturing toward the building. "Ah well, enjoy yourselves. Bye, bye."

"That SOB. Sorry, Alice, but your father is a bastard."

"What Jobert is is not that," said Tim in his quiet style.

Alice seconded him, "No, Gilbert, he isn't. He is something but not that. Well, I think we should demonstrate anyway to get attention. Chloe, you call the newspapers and tell them we are going to demonstrate tomorrow morning."

"Good idea, Alice."

Kraft looked around at the assembled environmentalists. He spoke quietly to Alex. "Alice is the smart one but she won't stick. Her old man got to her; she doesn't realize that. Watch her. She looks depressed, not herself lately. I thought it was a great thing when that Rappert guy went after her, surprised me. But the bastard deserted me anyway, and her, and was no help in getting her in deeper. Still, she was here."

"Still committed a little bit then," said Alex.

"Maybe. Is it possible to produce an intelligent campaign against the factory with nuts like some of these? Not promising material, but anyway warm bodies Get them to picket and scream at the company gates, maybe even produce a ruckus. One demonstrator injured at the gate would produce a great headline. Try to teach them about the injustice of the system but at least get them to push the right political goals and gain a greater result. The main thing, keep them united. Get them to change the system."

"Right. A good environment is guaranteed once you get a socialized system," said Alex. Alex was immovable in his ideas.

∞

"OK people, here's what we do. A couple of you climb the fence. The rest of you- well you all know what to do. Don't resist the police; just hang limp when they arrest you. Now I'd like to talk to each of you separately about what to do; to make sure you don't make mistakes."

"That's a good idea, Gilbert. I'll talk to each of you also," said Alice.

∞

"Alex, watch the socialism stuff. It won't sell with most of 'em. OK to talk to me but we don't want to divide the group."

"Yeah but I get tired of some of these nuts. To depend on people like these!"

"They're OK. We can co-opt them. They give us bodies for the demonstrating. Food fads may be crazy but we need the faddist. Ditto the anti-hunter. The profit thing should be stated as gouging. Don't start arguments with 'em. Stick to the demonstrating. Remember the goal is to get Jobert. He's a kingpin; if we nail him we can bring trouble to a lot of the industries."

"OK. Right. Later, eh? How come you hate that SOB so much?"

"It's a long story. Listen I knew him in college. Everytime I urged something he was there saying I was stupid. didn't matter what I said. he was rabid against the party. Nothing it could do anywhere was any good. OK so the party made errors same as any political system. but he wouldn't recognize even the successes. I thought he organized, planted people at meetings to jeer at me, disrupt the meetings. . And he was rich. No need to work to get somewhere, not like me. I didn't have a dime. Maybe that's why I hate the SOB everything easy; me everything came hard. But I fought for poor people. He talked a good line for poor people but never ever did anything."

"All words, no action."

"Right. Never so much as lifted a finger. He taught me there is only one way. Get the help you can. Do what is needed."

"A pure bastard."

"Ruthless. Believe me."

"You or him?"

"Goddam you, don't put me in the same box as that bastard."
"Ah but you have a lot in common."
"So do a hyena and a lion."
Diana came up to them, interrupting, Gilbert said, "Diana, you are right about hunting being immoral but the local yokels don't think that way so let's forget that for this demonstration, OK?"
"Oh, yes. You can depend on me but I don't really believe in a population problem."
"Of course not. What did Mao say? Oh yes, people are capital."

∞

"Listen, Gilbert. Population is the central problem. This penny ante demonstrating won't solve anything. As long as people increase and as long as their desire for material things stays the same, no problems will be solved." Rich was not going to let Kraft's slogans go by.
"Yes, yes, population is a problem, Rich, but we can't do anything about it right now so why not muffle it until we win a few, eh. I agree with you wholeheartedly. But we can't win without starting and this is a good place to start."
"Well I am here because Alice is here, no other reason, but I'll go along with any reasonable demo. I won't climb any fence."
"That's OK. We have some climbers. And you do lend support."

∞

Tim had stayed in the shadows. He turned to Alice, "Your father and Kraft are like those mythical beings who are condemned to struggle through all eternity. Your father thinks the way to solve things is to make systemic changes based on individual capacities. Kraft wants to change everything and have the wise rulers dictate how things will go. Those are views that can't be reconciled."
Alice said, "Funny I don't like to have my father and Kraft put into a category."
"Of course. Your father is different."

Alice frowned, started to speak but Tim spoke, “Listen! “An owl is hooting. Do you hear it, Alice, Dextra?” They concentrated, nodded. Dextra eyed Alice. Was she a rival? Tim was attractive and interesting and different. She doubted that a daughter of wealth would be interested in someone who didn’t care about power, money, social position.

“There it is, ‘ho cooks for you-all’ again. That’s the owl,” said Alice looking at Dextra. She was, Alice thought, a highly organized, engrossed scientist, a woman without a sense of style, attracted to a man who denied progress, who thought what Dextra was doing was interesting but finally just another event in the undirected chain of life. Still why all that lipstick this evening? There was also a nice scarf, a miracle. Was Dextra falling? To Alice, Tim seemed like a cool drink on a hot day. His was the voice of quiet thought, he never shouted, became obsessed with any one idea, thought he was totally right, everyone else wrong. He could be relied on to be thoughtful and dispassionate. Too bad he didn’t believe in anything, any progress. Not to believe seemed to put one in limbo, to have no bearings, no guide to the future. Could Dextra have said why she was attracted? Had she analyzed Tim at all?

“Alice, I came along with your father to see how you were getting along. Your crowd seems to be getting organized. By the way, the spill is cleaning itself up.”

“Yes, it is. Tim! Why think about organizing or spills on this beautiful evening?”

“The stars say you’re right, Dextra.”

Alice said, “Tim, did you pass the dead ditch? I heard about it from Rich. Maybe you couldn’t see it. I’d...”

“Show it to us, Tim. What is it?” said Dextra.

“Uh, yes. There’s really nothing to see this time of night. Not enough light now. Some bastard dumped a tank of herbicide in the ditch. Everything is drooping and dead, ugly to see.”

“Let’s you and I walk that way, anyway. We can use our flashlights,” said Dextra.

“OK. Alice, do you want to come along?”

“Alice has work to do here,” said Dextra.

“No, no. I can come. Everything is organized here. Tim, tell me about the Renewal.”

“We have seen it; Tim is making it beautiful.”

"Don't know about that but, yes, we've pretty well cleaned it up and now are planting bog birch and transplanting a lot of flowers. Best of all, the birds are moving back."

"Which birds?"

"What species have you seen? Ah I tripped. Can I hold onto you, Tim. It's hard to see now," said Dextra.

"Oh, mainly warblers migrating through. Here's the ditch; hard to see but look closely at that! Isn't that awful?"

"We have a solution to this problem. Our engineered bacteria can clean tanks and so prevent this," said Dextra.

"We have a pretty good idea who did it. He hates everything. His cussedness is more than I can bear. He was arrested once for doing this same thing. Ever since, there have been spills like this," said Tim.

"Why would he do it?"

"Why would someone slash a great painting or poison a beautiful oak tree? To vent his spite, his hatred of everything. It is so easy to spray and to dump herbicides or poisons or trash anywhere just to get rid of the stuff, cheap available solution. And the guy's poisoning is just the same as knocking the nose off of the Pieta, uh, that statue at the Vatican. It is too perfect so smash it. Same with the tree. It's only a tree. Same with a flowering ditch."

"Tim and I both know that what has been done here is multiplied million-folds by slobs everywhere and cannot easily be undone," said Alice.

"Still the nearby ditches must be able to supply everything that was here," said Dextra.

"No, not necessarily, this was a rich spot. Maybe the last of some species is now gone. And a pollinator or some kind of animal necessary for some other animal may have been lost, too. Maybe some interesting conundrum has been lost."

"You mean an unsolved problem? We must organize to replace them, repair the damage," said Dextra.

"You assume that we can repair the damages that we do to the environment; and that's not true. The relationships out here are more complicated and dicey than anything you or I can conceive, even how we relate to each other. The new state is always less interesting than the original. Anyway, with ever more people there will be ever more damage. So things won't persist, not even those we invent."

"So, better to just leave things alone," said Dextra.

"Right! Nature is far better than we at inventing," said Alice.

Tim added, "Nature takes longer but produces adapted and finely beautifully tuned animals and plants. Pick up a dead bird and notice the beauty, the intricacy of the feathers and their patterns. And you can't stop... there's no part of the bird that isn't fascinating. To me anyway. If only people would just not try to improve on nature or not overuse it."

Dextra spiritedly said, "I must disagree there. Genetics is progressing so fast that we can soon repair individual genes and reproduce any genetic makeup, maybe even invent lots of new species and new forests."

"Dextra, no amount of technology can do that. I have to admit genetics is great when it reduces problems to low levels but is totally incompetent when it comes to constructing organisms that can survive without help in the environment. Ah well, enough! Alice, I have to return to the lab; I will watch your crew and you tomorrow. See you both tomorrow."

"I'll go with you, Tim. Aren't the stars beautiful? Think! they are so many light years away."

Alice watched them go. Could he really be interested in that woman? Clearly she is working on him. He won't know how to handle her. He may like her but he won't be tied down- he has to be free. Should I talk to him about that? Tell him to tell her to buzz off? No, he'll think I am being mean-spirited. And I would bet she's terribly vulnerable- no, he shouldn't do that. And I may be biased- could someone with his ideas possibly make a good mate? Like Billy Rappert. Oh hell!

∞

"Worth my while to go down there, Boss? That pair of hips looked just right."

"Felix, one thing I am sure to do and that is stay out of your affairs. Go if you want. Her name is Gypsy. I don't think they'll lynch you."

"Gypsy! A sure thing! I'm off. Hello and good-bye, Mr. Drysdale."

"Where is he going?"

"He saw a female in her best clothing. Wants to make her acquaintance."

"I am sure I don't want to know more. A researcher who is a rake! It doesn't seem right somehow. But, welcome back from the bog and demonstrators. They seem to me to be terribly superficial and not to have thought out the consequences of their slogans. Did you make any impression on them?"

"Didn't expect to. And they're not alone; few of us know the consequences of what we do. History teaches no lessons; looking into the future is no better. We are, of course, slightly sure of what we see happening. They are right to be disturbed by things happening before their eyes. And to act on it. Henry, don't you think it's time we got better acquainted with the Watershed Chair- size him up?"

"He seems reasonable to me. It does seem time for us to get our letters off, seeking some permits for test sites."

"Make an appointment for Tim and me to see him. I want to size him up. We can ask for permission to use the Renewal Site or even the bog right here for testing our pesticide packets. And, oh yeah, keep it quiet until we get the permits. That bunch out there- and especially my daughter- would be sure to try to stop us. Henry, at last we make a real contribution to society and, not coincidentally, to our profits. You've done great work up here, Henry."

"Thank you. I've also sent an internal memo urging everyone to prepare for testing. It's time to get an OK from the CPA, the Watershed Chair and others."

"Remember the Watershed Chair is the one who counts."

"Yes, but he won't go against his experts."

Chapter 6 We meet with the Chair

"**H**ey, Tim, that was Gilly Lappin who just waved a thumb at us. Looked lost. Do you suppose he understands his predicament?"

"No. Always does look lost. Always is."

Jobert looked back at the receding figure. The raised thumb drifted down to join Gilly's tired, metronomic shuffle. Gilly was dressed in dirty pants, a much worn work-shirt and battered fedora, his usual outfit, and seemed dejected, shoulders slumped, head down, lost in space. In Tim's rear view mirror he dwindled in size, a sad figure emanating an air of defeat.

Tim nodded, agreeing with his own thoughts, "Hell, Gilly's a natural born survivor. Nothing complicated in his life to screw him up. He's always going to make it. He's a winner even if he doesn't see the dimly comprehended vicissitudes of his life."

"Let's pick him up. Come on, back up, Tim; let's give him a ride. We'll take him along to the meeting. Learn something about this Chair by how he handles Gilly."

"Hop in, Gilly. We'll get you home after a meeting we are going to. Free meal, Gilly."

"I like that. Real nice ta pick me up, Mr. Jobert. What meetin'?"

"With the Watershed Chair about dumping. No, no! Not about you. Just about dumpers. Where are you coming from?"

"Jus' outta jail."

"Again!"

"Yeah. Fed me real good there. Sheriff's a real nice fella."

"How are the wife and kids?"

"Huh? Ain't seen t'em since I went ta jail. They doing what they always do. Them kids're runnin' round all over ta place. That boy Dodie he's after Mazie alla time. She's got big tits. Muh daughter."

"Dodie your son? Hmm. Uh, here we are. Tell us about that later, Gilly. Oh oh. My daughter is here and that guy Pikala who wants to clean my septic tank. Now what have they in common?"

"Mr. Richter, Mr...ah...uh Pikala, Alice meet Gilly Lappin, our first apprehended dumper," said Jobert.

"I know Gilly. Are these people taking advantage of you? Fight for your rights, Gilly," said Alice.

"Naw. They give me a ride."

"Know him. Can't even spread gravel right," said Pikala.

"Glad to know you, Gilly. Uh, how's that name spelled?" Richter was friendly if quizzical.

"Gilly Lappin- evvybody knows that. Ain't, Tim?"

"No, Gilly, it's G I L L Y L A P I N," said Tim.

"Ah, Lapin." Richter pronounced the name in good French style.

"Nosiree. It's Lappin. Me."

Richter eyed the five visitors, an interesting array including one nice-looking woman dressed in jeans and throat-open red flannel shirt, sneakers, a red hair ribbon, watch, no jewelry, a clear resemblance to her father; and Pikala, a typical local tradesman with necktie (much used), a much worn suit, potato-faced and Lapin, good Goodwill clothes somehow made totally shabby, face not so much vacant as dull, looking with little curiosity at the office and the people with him; and Jobert and Mirave, both alert looking like they were ready for a hunting or fishing trip, boots, warm wool shirts, rough pants.

"I see. Well. Good. Oh. Well, I'm Hugh Richter, Watershed Chair. Have a seat, all. Ah, I assume you all know each other. That's good. You'll excuse me for receiving you all en masse but my time is short and I don't see anything confidential in the proposed discussions. If anyone objects? ...good."

"Mr. Richter, please describe for all us citizens what your powers and duties are."

"Right, Mr. Jobert."

"Whatsa Chair? People ain't chairs."

"Jesus!" Pikala had turned on a gargoyle grin.

"True, although some may be stools. Pardon me, all. After the Catastrophe, the American people, Congress, President finally agreed that environmental considerations would no longer be forgotten, or be an afterthought, or a casual part of our lives. Instead, every projected change, every usage of environmental resources would be placed under scrutiny before implementation. Pardon my pontificating..."

"I got shovels, picks."

"Yes, yes, Mr. Lapin. Important to doing things."

"Lappin. Screw tinny?"

"Close study, Mr. Lapin, er Lappin. It was decided that soils, air, water, natural areas, must be preserved. Because the watershed is a natural unit for maintaining the natural environment, Watershed Chairs were established and filled by technically competent people (I hope I am one such) whose sole task is to ensure no deterioration, and even to help improve the environment. The Chairs were to be widely technically competent, educated people and were to be constrained by rules nationally formulated by the Solons. OK? Enough of that. And by the way, we are the bosses, not our Secretary of the Environment or his Undersecretaries. Now. You have a problem, Mr. Jobert. You have to convince me the government should pay."

"Yes. I want to know more about that boss business later. Tim, explain our problem; describe what's going on."

"Mr. Richter, our Renewal Site is being used as a dump. We did agree to clean up the site as per Renewal Law but feel we should not have to pay the costs for removing newly dumped material. Midnight dumpers, I might add."

"There is real money involved, Mr. Richter," interjected Jobert.

"Yes, yes. OK. That's going to require a real discussion. Before we get into that, tell me how the Renewal is going."

Tim and Jobert both sat back, thinking about the dumping. How does one describe a dump? Looking at a dump is like looking down an outdoor toilet. Most people see a dump with gulls floating above at a distance and pass on undisturbed, enjoying the graceful floating birds. TV viewers, seeing the trash being pushed by a bulldozer or processed at an incinerator or at a dump, are nauseated and reach for the TV Remote; strangely, they rarely connect what they have seen with their own habits. The pieces of dirtied plastic, the un-namable, somehow brown-streaked whatever, scattered everywhere, are something revolting that came from someone else. We couldn't have done that. The discarded refrigerators-who owned all those refrigerators anyway?- the bed-springs-not from our beds surely? -the broken tools, the busted furniture, the old shingles, siding, roofing, bent shelving, picture frames, jammed rusty cameras and dented binoculars, boxes, boxes,

boxes, pasteboard, pasteboard, old discolored linoleum, wardrobes, and paper...repulsive paper...like toilet paper after use, all the things that fill our homes, wear out and have to be discarded when they no longer fit the decor. And last but not least common, the indescribable, all taken to the dump.

"Tim, you tell it," Jobert directed.

"Well. We removed something like a few hundred tons of trash. I can't believe that people would be so- so- materialistic. If you don't buy all that crap, I don't, then you don't have to get rid of it. It's crazy. Hell, anyone visiting a garage sale will see all kinds of things that look as though they were never used. Is there an inborn drive to accumulate stuff like a pack rat? What do people want with so many things? Why not live simply? Why accumulate all that junk, all that throwaway stuff?"

"Tim, spare us the Jeremiad; just tell us what you did." Jobert insisted on concentration.

"Dad, don't be a Philistine. What he is saying is important. We should do with less, much less."

"Maybe, but at the moment we need to get some information."

"We took out garden hoses, mattresses, car seats with stuffing erupting, oil cans, junked cars- all kinds of those- I suppose it didn't pay to haul them to a junk dealer. And wheelbarrows, pieces of concrete block, and old gas stations, I guess. And broken bird feeders, and baths, old bathtubs, boilers? -I don't know- maybe gas station gas tanks. Plastic, plastic, plastic. An archaeologist digging in there would have thought we were a kind of squirrel people gathering endless amounts of useless objects. People don't need that much stuff!"

"Only a few of us can live back in the woods in a shack, Tim," said Jobert.

"I know. Well, we hauled all that stuff to the incinerator, first pulling out all the recyclables which we took to recycling centers. As an experiment we burned much of the plastic in our muffle furnaces leading the gases through a water solution which we discarded as harmless."

Jobert growled, "Hm. How many muffle furnaces ruined? Not so smart. Tim, get to the fun part."

"Right. We discovered that the Renewal Site had some fine patches of the original vegetation- some orchids and many other bog plants. Especially there was a fine patch of bog birch which we have proceeded to spread around. It is taking. Then, unfortunately, one day there appeared fifty-five steel drums. The gunk in them was heavily contaminated with heavy metals and TCE. Those went to the toxic waste disposal center. Their leakage has put a high level of heavy metals in the peat where we believe they will stay. There is TCE in the water. We believe the bog will take care of that problem. We have enough measurements to show that that stuff is being broken down in the bog. We think the dumping of the barrels occurred after we got the site. But, Mr. Richter, our Renewal Site is being used as a dump. I have waited at night hoping to catch the dumpers. Two nights ago one came up, dumped, hollered at me, called me a (stuff your ears, Alice) 'mother-fucking shithead' and floored the gas pedal when I came up. I chased him…couldn't catch him."

"Like a movie cop, probably! Tim is a born race driver, Mr.. Richter. All of this has cost us a bundle, I might add," said Jobert. "But Tim lost him going around a curve. There is a maze of old logging roads and turnoffs back there so it is almost impossible to catch these guys. And we can't station men there all the time. We were lucky to catch Gilly."

"Can't you set traps?"

"No. There's no one good place to station a guard. And somehow they seem to know where we are."

"Mr. Lapin, how does that work?" asked Richter.

"Dunno. Ricky usta tell me about where ta dump. He got a phone. I ain't got a phone."

"Who's Ricky?"

"Ricky's Ricky. Seen him at the tavern down the road."

"So, a phoning network." Jobert exuded satisfaction.

"People allays been dumpin' there. Their right. City trucks now. They come hunderds a miles. Costs money ta take it ta that center- what's it."

"Recycling center?"

"Yeah. I took 'em some iron. Dint wanta pay me."

"Mr. Lapin, take the iron to the junk yard. They'll pay you," said Richter.

"Why don't they pay?"

"Good question. Why not, Mr. Richter?"

"They are prohibited from competing with private companies."

"It will be difficult to maintain that rule," commented Jobert. "Excuse me gentlemen, my secretary insists I talk to her."

∞

"Don't seem right they don't pay me."

"Gilly, you're so dumb. Where'd ya steal ta iron?"

"Mr. Pikala, Gilly is just making a living!"

"Yeah. Off who, Miss Jobert? Ain't but three things Gilly does. Making babies- he's good at that- stealing stuff, and dumping. He ain't good at those- keeps getting caught. Own up, Gilly, where'd ya get ta iron?"

"Found it."

"Uh huh. Stole it."

"Why don't them cyclers pay me?"

"How come they don't?" said Pikala.

"Competition. It pays to recycle, so private business is more efficient. As Mr. Richter said, government is supposed to stay out of the competition," answered Tim. And asked, "Gilly, why didn't you take the iron to the junk yard?"

"Cycling place is nearer. So I kep' the iron an' they caught me."

"Likely sign posts or bridge supports or maybe some kid's swing set. Anyway, any new babies, Gilly?" asked Pikala.

"Yeah, one onna way. County people oughta give us more money but they don't. Don't help us anymore'n before."

"Gilly, ta one man poppalation explosion."

"We get by. All that figgerin."

Jobert frowned. "Tim, what's Gilly mean 'figgerin'?"

"Gilly has to give the ages of the kids, their year in school, their vaccinations, health records, what welfare they are getting and so on. Alice, under the new rules a family with more than two kids must pay all costs (school, or other) they incur. More kids-no added welfare money. Maintenance, nothing more."

"That's cruel."

"Maybe so. Alice, the rule ought to produce a negative feedback so families limit their offspring according to what they can afford. Money telling them they've reached a limit. Automatic population control."

"Tim, you are cruel. We can talk to Gilly about not having kids, can't we, Gilly."

"They just keep coming. Ain't nothing I can do about it."

"Ha, ha, ha. What'd I tell you." Pikala smirked.

Alice scowled at Pikala who shrugged his shoulders. She looked disgusted, and asked, "What sense does that kind of penny-pinching make?"

"Alice, my sweet, it makes good sense. Adam Smith made one error. He did not make people, especially offspring, a part of his analysis. Children as well as adults are agents in the free market and should be treated as such. There should be no subsidies in the form of tax reductions for large families. That is a violation of the functioning of a free market."

"Mr. Jobert, what do ya think of this new setup?" asked Pikala.

"It just might work. Their hearts and reason are in the right place. Wonderful to have an official who can give a quick decision. Thank God he has a limited, fixed time in office. If he didn't he could easily become a bureaucratic tyrant. Still there are intractable problems. Take Gilly here- he has at least a dozen kids. The rules now say just maintain them. No extras from the government. Even so, people like Gilly are the camel's nose that could bring down the whole tent."

"I woulda said some other part. An' I don't mean the dingus. Richter is back."

∞

"Continue." Mr. Richter was frowning; he must have gotten some bad news.

"We have dumpers who come in on back roads, dump fast and barrel off into the nowhere. This is not minor; they are dumping by the ten...twenty ton load." Tim finished his description.

"You are doing what is needed. I can't fault your efforts or judgments. I think however you are stuck with the dumper problem. Why don`t you place guards around the Renewal Site? Break the dumping custom and it will cease to be a problem."

"Guards would be costly. We feel there is a principal involved. It's not just the dumping. We are being asked to pay for the cleanup of those steel drums not of our doing. There is arsenic and other metals and TCE-that's bad stuff- and other organic stuff.

The organics can be burned, the metals can't and must be filtered out. That is expensive, very costly; we should not have to pay for it."

"You can be sure I'll send your complaints to the Inter-Watershed Committee. He'll have his waste disposal people on it. I am new here and have to ask you again, why did you move here instead of into some urban industrial site? Here, you have to pay for roads, sewage, special or otherwise, all extra costs incurred by you, costs which are higher now in the country so that reuse sites in the cities would be first choices. And you must bear these costs, Mr. Jobert."

"I felt, Mr. Richter, that there would be a gain from isolation- no distractions- easy to concentrate. Also safer when storing dangerous materials. And we will bear our just costs."

"And there is grouse hunting." Alice smiled sweetly.

"Oh yes, daughter mine."

"In a city site, under the new law you would not have had to bear the costs. The laws making new owners responsible for the previous owner's dumping are now gone in the cities; in their place, there are more complex rules. The Undersecretary's legal staff will know them."

"Dumps is needed. It's where you put stuff."

"Shut up, Gilly!" growled Pikala.

"Mr. Lapin has the right to be heard," said Richter.

"Explain the new laws to us."

"Mr. Jobert, you ask too much. Even the Undersecretary's legal staff is having problems. Let me say this- neither the Undersecretary nor anyone else in Washington can over-turn my rulings; they are based strictly on evidence; they can only suggest and must suggest alternative procedures to you. Those can involve no environmental deterioration. I am the sole judge of that."

"We are going to appeal to the Secretary of the Environment for a judgment on who should bear these costs as a matter of principle," said Jobert.

"Good. I can't settle something like that. My job is to insure that water quality coming in and leaving this watershed does not deteriorate. Same with land, air, timber, organisms. I will transmit the Secretary's choices to you. I understand your arguments but part of your permission to be here is that you not decrease the quality of this environment and improve equal to what you destroy. Therefore you are doing the Renewal Site. You chose the bog rather than an upland site for renewal. You must understand that the choices we give are so constructed that they are the cheapest and the best for society, the minimum cost. Any other choice would cost more. When combined with a policy of everyone paying full costs for his endeavors and a family policy which sharply increases costs for families of more than two, this system ought to lead to an equilibrium between population, resource use and environment. A cybernetic system, no, no, a negative feedback system. We hope. We allowed you a choice and you must live with it."

"A dump ain't useless; people can hunt an' find stuff they need. It's like my culch heap where I get wire ta fasten things."

Jobert turned to look at Gilly. All stared, startled, surprised by this wisdom. Jobert returned to the subject, "We don't quarrel with your job, or the choice. I personally am in favor of the ends you hope to achieve. That the system will go to equilibrium is doubted by some of our computer people."

"I would like them to talk to our people. Can you arrange that? Mr. Jobert, Mirave, I have a meeting coming up with my local experts- that parade of characters that just passed in the outer room. I don't think we have any great decisions that have to be made, but I have to join them soon. So let's get down to you other people; what can I do for you? Miss Jobert, you are concerned about the spill and Mr. uh, Pikala about dumping 'honey' in an old landfill."

"Why would anybody dump honey! He nuts?"

"Gilly, don't talk!" said Pikala.

"That Pikala, he don't like me."

"Now, now, Gilly can speak up too. But first you, Mr. Pikala. I have to tell you the penalty for that kind of dumping is severe."

"I got a lot ta say too. That buncha experts you're gonna meet with're all air and no action. That screwball entomologist just watch the loopers, ain't disturbed a single caterpillar. They'll eat the popple to the ground before he sprays. Ain't no soil here and they got a soil expert. Ha! And a hydrologist-ain't no drainage here- what good is he? A vegetation expert, for God's sake. Ain't nobody here don't know a good tree when he sees it. Real estate man-what's he doing? He'll be damn sure to keep everybody happy, especially real estate people, lining their pockets I bet. And a farmer for Chris' sake! All we raise are ticks."

"Yes, yes. The dumping?" Richter was a bit impatient.

"Awright. That old land fill ain't lined but ain't no drainage, stuff won't go nowhere. What I dump will fertilize it-make things rot faster. Anyway that's what one a them ecologists told me. I ain't doin' any harm. And ain't adding to any creek, or sewage place. Ain't nobody comes in there except maybe somebody to shoot a bear."

"It would help the turn-over rate."

"Yes, Mr. Mirave, but what he is not saying is that the 'honey' could contain hepatitis viruses among other dangerous things. That bear hunter could contract hepatitis at that 'honey' dump."

"Serve him right, eh Tim?"

"Now, Mr. Jobert, we can't infect people because we don't like what they are doing."

"Maybe not, but anybody hunts in a dump deserves it, not so, Ed?" said Tim. Jobert nodded.

"See!" Pikala was pleased to be backed up "Dump's where I get all kinda things. Real good plastic bags. Dunna what use is a swamp. Jus' mosquitoes and weeds. Swamps a good place for dumpin'."

"One man's dump, another man's treasure, eh Tim? Now, Gilly, don't you like it when the flowers bloom in the bog?"

"Lotsa flowers along the road. Lotsa iron pipe ta sell in the dump. Made some money from that swamp."

"And should be able to. Mr. Pikala, you must take your honey to a sewage pipe in Bijacic. There will be a charge and I know it is a drive but you are required by law to do so. Next time we will take you to court. Understand?"

"Yessir. Us poor businessmen always gets it in the neck."

"The rules. Now, Alice, your problem."

"Mr. Richter, Gilbert Kraft is chief advisor to our environmental group. You know the name, of course. He says other Watershed Chairs have imposed heavy fines and other penalties for environmental misdeeds. That's why I am here. Why has there been no motion about the spill at the Jobert Research Lab?"

"Back to that. First, what other Chairs do doesn't determine my rulings, although I pay close attention to what they say. I am aware of no penalties imposed for spills such as this one. More detail-our experts have sampled very carefully, have run chemical and bacteriological tests and organism surveys and can find nothing in the way of an effect. Your original complaint implied that there were .... might have been dangerous bacteria released."

"The New Guinea bacteria hydrogen producers and the E. coli," said Alice.

"...no... that seemed a reasonable possibility. On consultation with Miss Chirali we have learned that the bacteria (E. coli) have been so changed that they could not survive in nature. They have a nutritional requirement that can't be supplied by the bog. We are sure they can not survive there. We could find neither of the lab bacteria there. In addition the bacteria that are already in the bog are masters of their environments and no engineered coliform hydrogen bacteria could compete. So we judge there was and is no problem."

"But they did spill! There ought to be a fine."

Jobert thought about the spill and asked Tim in an aside, "Would a guy like Kraft have the guts to enter the plant? Even if he did, how could he know the right room, the right valve to turn? And the closed swamp drain? Anyway, the room was kept locked. Could he and the inside traitor work together?"

Tim shrugged, "Possible. Ed, that's paranoia. He is a boil on the behind, that's all. Forget him."

"Miss Jobert, you're rich. Don't you care about us Savages that need jobs? Why don't you go back to the city and have a coupla kids? Or here would be OK, too."

"Mr. Pikala, please don't enter into this. Miss Jobert, if the spill had been because of gross carelessness or had been large we might have fined the company but no such circumstances occurred. There is still another real possibility; I am told by Jobert's staff that someone may have deliberately opened the valve. I want to give them time to try to apprehend that person. I judge the company is a good citizen; it is nevertheless using some potentially dangerous bacteria. You can be sure we will insist on complete control."

Alice answered Pikala, "Some jobs aren't worth the damage caused. And Gilly is producing enough kids for us all."

"Ha, you never needed a job. What do you know and what kinda kids?" jeered Pikala.

"Enough of that! Mr. Richter, we have some private matters to discuss. Won't take long," said Jobert. "Your back room maybe?"

"Alice, Mr. Pikala, Gilly, unless you have further questions-ah-no? You can get a cup of coffee in the Cafe across the street."

"Gilly, we'll give you a ride home. Buy Gilly a cup of coffee, Alice. Wait for us, Gilly."

"So what are you up to?" Alice was glaring at her father and at the Chair.

"If you want to stay, Miss Jobert, you are welcome. This is simply a matter of timing. Everything said in my chambers will be published and available to you. No fixed decisions will be made."

"I'd like one a them Danish, too, Miss Alice"

"Oh alright!"

∞

Jobert as most citizens, most entrepreneurs, tried to avoid bureaucrats as much as legally possible. The bureaucracy receives applications, supplications, requests but then can easily bury them in a sticky, ever more binding, engulfing tar-baby paper-chase. The struggling citizen may feel that he has been engulfed in a gulping, gurgling tar pit from which escape is impossible. Jobert had listened to Richter's words and watched his reactions to Gilly and the others and had decided that this was an intelligent, reasonable man. Mr. Richter was, however, part of a system of governmental regulations and control which could potentially constrict, even destroy his plans to launch an environmental cleanup company based on the use of bio-engineered bacteria. A bureaucrat must first protect himself. But the new system with the Chair with limited tenure might do better. Even so a thwarted citizen might attack. Therefore a bureaucrat has an unwritten prime directive either to do nothing, to pass the buck, to delay, or, in extremis, to make a decision. Time is a friend; with its passage the request, demand, may happily be forgotten, eliminating the necessity of a decision. The citizen tires, quickly runs out of money, and at last says to hell with it. Groups can be more persistent but only profit making organizations can have the man-power and cash to persist over long spans of time. Lack of money is the aggrieved citizen's or organization's loser. The advantage is always to the cash-filled, staffed business or, finally, always to the government.

Jobert walked with Tim into the back room. "Doesn't seem like another impossible bureaucrat."

"No, Tim. He shouldn't be. Richter, or rather his type of new bureaucrat- the terminal technician doesn't have to be guarding his rear all the time. He's a technical expert with an appointment for a fixed period of time. He can't be easily removed; therefore he is independent of political commands, free of all the self preservation problems and can make objective decisions. He is like a Fed chairman."

"Yeah, but he's sure to feel the heat of public opinion. And the other bureaucrats are sure to be heard from."

"Unless he does something wrong, he will be difficult to dismiss. Think of the advantages. His type of decision-making on environmental problems would also avoid the NIMBY (not-in-my-backyard) response, maybe even prevent some engineering monstrosities, and reduce pork-barrel 'growth' problems. His day of judgment will occur when he leaves office; then he will be held accountable for errors, misjudgments and stupidities. Then he has to get a job based on his performance while in office. How would you like to be under that kind of a threat?"

"Here he comes."

"Gentlemen, your problem."

"We are having some success in our research with engineering bacteria to break down pesticides. We want permission to test out our bacteria in the environment as soon as possible. We can give you assurances that these bugs cannot reproduce in the environment, only act metabolically to do what we want them to do."

"Gentlemen, such a result is devoutly to be wished. Please have your geneticists describe exactly how they have produced the engineered bacteria, your other people how they will be packaged, applied and how their presence in the environment will be monitored. Those reports will go to our national Genetics Review Board, and to our other experts. I will personally expedite this matter."

"Thank you, Mr. Richter," said Tim.

"Mr. Richter, I'm off to Chicago. Hate to leave in the late fall. Too beautiful. I hope to see you next spring with all the necessary permits at hand. We are doing some even more far-reaching experiments with bacteria for doing cleanup jobs, to say nothing about our work with our hydrogen bacteria." Jobert turned to Tim. "Tell Henry we got things started. Tim, stick with us; you can do some good with us. I know, I know, progress is an illusion... but think of the possibility that some people and the environment will be better because of what we are doing. You ought to be part of that. I hope to see you in the spring."

"Oh I like what we are doing. Nature will be a little better off for a while, anyway. Survive Chicago!"

Chapter 7 Welcome sweet springtime

"Good to be back. God how I love this country in the spring. Henry, I know you'd rather be in the city but sometime walk with me in the woods; you must learn the quality, the feeling of budding leaves and grouse drumming. After Chicago this is heaven."

"Edmund, I do understand your feeling but I do just as well with a nice garden. Anyway, wherever I am, I'm always immersed in my work so the surroundings don't matter much."

Drysdale was dressed, as always, in a gray Brooks Bros. suit, striped old school tie, black dress shoes, black socks, and seemed the epitome of the organization man. Did he ever cut loose, wear informal clothes? Even his language was gray, never a cuss word or off-color remark. Was his home, his personal behavior as organized as was his business life? One hoped not. He did have a dry sense of humor. He very rarely said anything unexpected. Would he be capable of originating something? He was a good organizer in conventional ways and kept close track of events in the research lab.

"You are a good manager, Henry, but you need to learn to loosen up a bit. Well, tell me how things have been going."

"Good news. We now have our engineered bacteria in buffered dry packets usable by anyone, even an ordinary gardener, to clean the residual pesticides from their spray tanks large or small. One just dumps the powder into the spray tank, adds the right amount of water, stirs and gives it 48 hours. And we are ready to spray our powders on spills, a little engineering added, I think successfully."

"Well, hello, Thor the thunder God; not gassy I hope."

"Mr. Jobert, I wonder if I'll ever live that down. Mr. Drysdale, someone was on the phone, wanted to talk with you. Says he saw lights in our bog an hour ago. Thinks our bugs are producing hydrogen in the bog and it's catching fire. It has to be some kinda nut. Said he saw lights flitting around all over the place. Told him it was nonsense. All our hydrogen bacteria are in tight containers either as spores or in culture medium. Can't escape. He said he wanted to talk to somebody who knew what he was talking about. I kept my cool."

"Good response. Thank you, Thor."

"Lights. Thank you, Thor. Could be my daughter's crowd, or maybe some kids from the town fooling around. Henry, there's no end of nonsense up here. Still, it could be cranks trying to cause us trouble."

"Not on a night like this. There's a good thunderstorm brewing out there. Still, you may be right; some of the stranger environmental people have shown up and may be communing with the holistic environment. They could be trying something. I'll send Ira out."

∞

"Well, Ira?"

"Ain't nobody out there-saw some funny lights-maybe fireflies. Twister weather…air hangs on you like a dishrag. Storm hits, it's going to be a doozy."

"Where were the lights?" asked Drysdale.

"Inna swamp-come on and off, moved around. Thought I saw a couple a flashlights tother side but they went out. Now what kinda nut would be out onna night like this?"

"Thanks for checking, Ira."

"No problem, Mr. Drysdale."

"Henry, who's around the lab?"

"Felix is working as usual; as you said he's a demon for work. and he's a night owl. I've come in at two in the morning and there he was working away. He was so concentrated he never heard me. He says he now has an improvement on the control methods."

"Just the right person, Henry. Well get him out of the lab; we're going light hunting. Must be some boots in the samples lab."

"Edmund, I must protest. You shouldn't be going out in this weather."

"We, you mean. Why in the world not? I've been out in far worse. Don't worry, we're tough old birds."

"It isn't that, Edmund. There's a lot of lightning in the southwest and there is a tornado watch."

"Ah, Henry, you can't live forever. Let's get boots and flashlights out and see what is going on."

∞

"There, I see a light. Did you see that, Boss. Christ, I feel like I've been swimming through a vat of beer. Only not as good. I'm so sodden I might as well have gone swimming. If Alice were here, I could enjoy this anyway. Boy, look at that light go. How in the hell can it move so fast? Did either of you ever see anything move so fast? What is it? Nothing like that ever appeared in a computer lab. Men from Mars! at last I meet Martians."

"Felix, you have a fevered imagination. Henry, Felix...let's box one of those lights in and catch it. It could just be some kind of strange firefly."

"Edmund, that's not sensible. Yes yes, alright, I know...I know...you insist; I'll go this way. Felix you go station yourself out there about thirty feet. Edmund, we'll drive it your way. I'll whistle when set. Then we'll all fall on any light that shows. And get sensible and get out of this weather."

"Good planning, Henry; we'll make a naturalist out of you yet."

∞

Why do I have to have so imaginative a boss. Why couldn't he be a financial expert who never leaves the accounting sheets, someone who would let me alone to do my managing in the production end. Still, I guess I'm lucky; he never has interfered with my work and is, in fact, always supportive. He is a good leader but must be slightly nutty to drag us out here. Dangerous for him, yes, and for me. He risked my career in that dumper chase and now out here chasing fireflies or something. If something happens to him, I will be lucky to manage a five and dime store. Ah well.

A rumble signaled the nearness of the storm. Felix stood in the bog wondering what a systems expert was doing up to his knees in this muck, risking his neck to find out what a light was. Strangely he was enjoying himself. It must have been the weirdness of the occasion. He liked Jobert and was impressed by his willingness to come out on a night like this. A real person, the boss. The rustle of air through the birches, the occasional flare of light from the approaching storm, a roll of thunder, the mystery of the night augmented a sense of being in a lonely, forbidding, enchanted place.

Henry, a practical person, wished he was at home watching the TV. He was comfortable enough; still, was his hair beginning to stand? Foolish to risk a lightning stroke. A light!

"Turn off your flashlight, Henry; watch for the lights."

Jobert was delighted with this hunt; wouldn't it be something to get some of those financial types out here. Bring them into the real world. Henry whistled; Jobert answered quickly by two responding whistles. Now to watch for a light. There was one! He ran staggering through the bog and leaped for the light to encounter a solid body, 'Mr Jobert!' with which he landed in a tangled mass in the bog. The light was gone. He started roaring with laughter, quickly joined by Felix and Henry.

"We're prize specimens; chasing nothing in this bog. Well I'm satisfied; whatever the light is, it isn't insect or human."

"Boss, dim memory tells me about Will-o-the-Wisps uh Jack-o-lanterns- lights that appear over places like this. Burning something or other. Can't be hydrogen, that's bolony- nothing to start the burning."

"Gentlemen, did your hair begin to rise then?"

"Boss, your hair is glowing."

"And yours. From the lights of the building. I think we better get out of here. Wait! that light over there is not bolony. It's a prowler. Here comes the rain; you two get into the building. I'll join you soon. Henry I need your flashlight. Run, there's a deluge coming."

Drysdale shouted in anguished voice, "You can't, you mustn't."

"Oh yes I can. And must. Go. I'll be with you in a minute." Jobert shielded his flashlight, trotted along the path toward the steady prowler light. It went out. He caught a glimpse of shoe tracks on the ground.. but no one was in sight. A blast of wind and suddenly he was enveloped in a cataract of water. He dashed for the building overhang. The white roar of rain drowned out all sound. A brilliant flash of lightning, a thump, and a roar of thunder shook the building at his back. What was that? Once he thought he saw the shining of a flashlight but it was immediately gone. Was that an automobile engine? He leaned back to wait out the rain. The rain began to slow. Felix appeared under an umbrella. They walked to the lab.

"Felix, I'm sodden, not much value to an umbrella if you are soaked already. Ah Henry, what we need is a good warmer upper."

"What do you like?"

"Whiskey and soda will do me."

"Sounds like what I need; that and a warm woman."

"Felix, you are an original," said Jobert approvingly.

Drysdale said, "I worried about you being out there so long. There was an incredible thunderclap that shook the building."

"Safe as in church. Cheers, gentlemen. I saw another flashlight just before the deluge hit; I heard and felt a thump and a rumble of thunder and then maybe a car engine."

"It's probably town hoodlums in their junk cars fooling around. Even so I'll tell the night watchman to look around as soon as the rain slows down. We have a lot of nerve calling the town hoodlums crazy. Three grown men trying to catch a will-o-the-wisp in the middle of a bog qualifies for the nut category," said Drysdale.

"Yeah but I enjoyed that; felt freer than I have in a long time. We all need a little excitement, eh Felix?"

"Right, Boss. I came alive. You have to come alive, tingle a bit, Mr. Drysdale."

"Yes, but when the electricity starts your hair rising it's time to get out," said Drysdale.

"Which we did. I'm wondering if that glow was just the lights of this building, long way off though. Felix you said a name for a glow like that. What is it again?"

"No. This is different. More like something I read about in Moby Dick-um …St. Elmo's fire. Indicating a lot of juice about to descend on us."

"How foolish we were."

"Come on, Henry- you feel more alive, don't you?"

"I have to admit I do but why risk death? And we still can't demonstrate that the lights don't come from burning hydrogen from bacteria."

"None of our bacteria there and thermodynamically impossible," said Felix dismissing the idea.

"Why risk death? Well? Something mental- if we don't face our mortality, we live a false life. I'm no scientist but ecologists tell me death is the price of life. Only if there is a cycling of matter and of people is a decent life possible. If some creature made something, say a skunk oil, that couldn't be cycled we'd very soon have a stinking environment. Too many people or mice or anything and things begin to collapse. That's what ecologists say."

"Can't refute that. I was in Pennsylvania when they were having a gypsy moth plague. I can't tell you how nauseating that was. But people fight to live no matter what their health or circumstances, and that's not reasonable," said Felix.

"Three or is it four billion years of evolution tells you, you must survive."

"Speaking of nauseating, did either of you notice that odd odor when we came in?"

"Just the usual lab stink, don't you think?"

"I suppose so. I'm off to bed."

"Also."

∞

Jobert breathed in the dawn piney air, looked at an azure sky and thanked God he was there and not in Chicago with the money men. Oh to be in the bogs now that spring is here. I picked a perfect day, week to return to my lab. June blue, June cool, June dewy. All the birds singing, the frogs piping, swifts twittering and flying in formation. Tim says that's supposed to be sex, the male defending his female on the inside from the rival male on the outside of the formation. Ha! Great to be alive this dawn. Walk the woods, smelling, listening, watching before going in. Oh dear, someone! Can't ever be alone anymore. Seen him somewhere. A birdwatcher.

"Good morning."

"Good morning. Hear that song? That's a blackburnian warbler. He's on the tip of the branch there. Want a look?" extending binoculars.

"Oh yes. Thank you. My word. The bird positively glows. It's throat is throbbing like a pulse to produce that buzzy song. All that effort for an unmusical result. Here, your glasses. Thank you again." Jobert was delighted by the sight.

"Right. All the beauty is in the appearance. Takes a female bird to appreciate the song."

"Well, thank you for that bird. I must be on my way." It had been an incredible sight, that throat putting the colors the highway people wear to shame. A vibrant color enhancing the bird's explosive vitality. Amazing to think that that glory is all in the service of utility. Produce the best for the most efficient use. No, no life is more than that. Perhaps add comprehension. Knowing and understanding as much as possible. Ah well, each day something new. Time to work, back to the lab.

"Good morning, Ira. Going off shift? Odd odor this morning. Everything in order?"

"Yes sir. A long night. Noticed the smell; may be from the dump. Everything right as pie. Here, let me open the door for you."

Jobert heard his heels clicking as he passed the empty offices soon to echo with typing and paper shuffling. No getting away from the cycle set by nature. Now let's see-report on the Renewal Site dumping. We clean it up- but who pays? Shouldn't be us, matter of principle. No report yet from the Watershed Chair. Eight months. Was he giving them a run-around? Henry would have said something; he was no pushover. Go over it with the lawyers......better go see about it personally while here. Nothing on the confidential memo sent to the newspapers. By whom?

∞

Bill, the day watchman, gestured to the departing Ira, "Hold up, Ira! Ira, something weird. Looks like another spill in the swamp."

"Oh, no! The Supremo came in at six. Told him everything was OK. My ass! I better stick around. Let's go see it. Jesus Christ! I'm a dead duck. A busted wall! What came from the plant that killed all that stuff? Ooh, dead frogs. What's that- a dead weasel- birds! I better report it. Must be a broken pipe."

"There's a hunk a the building out there."

"Jesus! outta the locked part of the building I ain't supposed to go inta-fulla poisons. I felt a thump last night during the storm. Didn't think anything of it, thought it was just a big thunderclap. You know, one of those jolting one's you get sometimes. Lots of that last night. Couldn't hear squat."

"There was kids cruisin' out there this morning. Maybe something they done. Too early but you can't guess what kids will do these days."

"Bill, you stay here. On'y be careful; could be something dangerous out here. Don't let anyone near. Wish me luck. I gotta report this to Jobert hisself."

"Why not just tell Drysdale?"

"I'm dumb but this I know; Jobert seen me; he wants ta know from me. Something like this, the Supremo wants to know personal."

∞

"OK, Ira, the milk is spilt. Your route is in here, not all over the place. Calm down. Now I want to see the spill. Let's go."

"Yessir. I'll take you."

∞

"There it is Mr. Jobert, lotsa dead stuff. And there's the blown wall."

"Unh huh. Bad news; alright, I'll take it from here, Ira. Go home, get some sleep, Ira."

"Yessir. OK. Bill will help you."

"And Ira, on your way out tell Mary to call Drysdale, tell him there's a problem and that I'm here." Jobert turned back to the bog. "Everything's dead," said to the bog. Jobert felt that heart-sickness that arises every time something unforeseen, unwanted and ghastly appears. What were the stinks? Three at least. There were dead and flopping birds and animals scattered about. Dead insects. Were the plants OK? There was a broken herbicide container- almost surely the plants would be dead by tomorrow. What had blown out of the building? What caused the explosion?

"Sir, I'm Bill, the day-man. Wow, lotsa dead birds, Mr. Jobert."

"Yeah, and Bill, those that don't look like it are too, probably. My daughter calls that leatherleaf. Looks alive but it's so thick-leaved it will take a while to die. Plants look OK but who knows. Don't touch anything, Bill; we have to be extremely careful. OK, where's the source?"

"Over here, sir. Looks to me like an explosion blew out that part of the wall."

"Doesn't seem possible. Uh, it's Bill? - OK Bill, can you crawl over those cement blocks and see what's in there. No, better not.

This is the locked part of the building where we store the bad stuff. Inside reinforced wall looks intact. Ought to be. Looks safe enough, but. OK, don't touch anything. Put your wet handkerchief; get some bog water back there out of the blast way; won't hurt you; it's sterile-uh over your nose. Crawl in there and just tell me what you see. Look for a broken pipe, containers, and anything else. In and out fast; I'll be ready to pull you out. Be careful. If the smell gets too much, or your eyes start to smart, shout and back out here immediately."

"Yes sir. Here I go...... Jesus Mother Mary Joseph Oh God, Oh God. I gotta get outta here."

"What's wrong, Bill? Fumes get you?"

"Nosir. Oh God, I gotta throw up. Sorry, Sir, shouldn't bother me. I seen worse in the war. Just have an uneasy stomach today I guess."

"Worse in the war? a worse chemical stink?"

"Nosir. Mr. Jobert there's aah...sorry, there's a body with a face- aah Jesus- ugly, bad burned I guess in there."

"A body? ! Please not, we don't need that."

"Sorry, it's a body, alright."

"Oh hell. Can't diddle when there is a body. Go call the sheriff and tell Sparky, the lab photog I want pictures of everything. Immediately! You stay with him to keep him out of trouble. I want the pictures by 5 PM. Tell him to be careful; touch nothing, pick up nothing."

"Yes sir. Ha! Call that sheriff? he's smart but clumsy as that President uh what was his name? Seen him wind a fishing line right around a outboard motor propeller so you couldn't get it out. Maybe you better ask him to call the state cops. Comes from a long line of fuck-ups. Excuse me. I'll get him."

"I guess I'd appreciate that. Sheriff seemed competent to me. Oh, and send some guards here to keep people away. That stink could be a dangerous chemical. Warn everyone. Now what the hell was anyone doing in there? How did they get there?"

∞

"Ah, Henry, I came in early to find this. Something exploded."

"Incredible! The chemists separated the stuff that could have exploded. It isn't possible. Still! Last night. Remember that rumble. We thought it was a thunderclap that shook us."

"That WAS just a thunderclap. Henry, one nasty problem. That barrel we got from the pharmaceutical house. We were going to use it as a test of our system of reducing mixed toxic wastes to something innocuous. Call and find out what was in it. Could have been something explosive and surely a dangerous mix."

"Oh, no, they assured us it was safe."

"Mr. Jobert, telephone from Chicago- something urgent."

"I'll take it in my office. When this gets out a horde of reporters will descend on us; beware of them, Henry. You and I must talk."

∞

"Sheriff, you joke."

"No, Mr. Drysdale. I smell dynamite in there. Smells like dynamite went off. Face is a charred mess but papers in his pocket show it is Kraft. Heard of 'im. Need somebody to identify him for sure but everything fits."

"Dynamite! Impossible! None in there! That room is kept locked! Only one key. Only the janitor or watchmen can get in. Kraft! ... How could he get in there? Are you sure you have the staff to handle the investigation? Or should we send for state help?"

"We'll do a good job. Why the reinforced inside wall if you didn't plan to store dynamite?"

"Some of the chemicals we thought we might store can be explosive."

"I see. But it was dynamite used in that room there. Could be set off with wires. Hear Mr. Jobert didn't like the guy?"

"Dogs don't like fleas- no personal animosity. It was an accident, wasn't it?"

"Don't know."

"Sheriff, we want to send a crew into the room and around the bog to find what chemicals, what containers and other things got blown out of our Hazardous Waste Storage Room, the Toxics Room. And to get samples and to see the extent of the damage."

"No. No, you can't do that. My men will be scouring the place. Could be wires, more dynamite out there. Don't want any amateurs screwing up any evidence. That body could be a homicide."

"Homicide! I don't believe it!"

"Believe it."

"Sheriff, I'll have to tell Jobert."

"Do that. Tell him I want to see him."

"Sheriff, some of the chemicals blown out may be, no, are toxic; better have my crew help on the job- you'll find them very able."

"Give me their names; I'll have to ask them some questions first. Marko and another of my men will go with them."

"Sheriff, I'll send them to you immediately."

∞

"Henry, there's a takeover move and a group is trying to kick me out, say they are tired of Jobert's Folly-this place. And lots of other things. Yeah, that's what they call it. I'll tell you more later. I must go to Chicago immediately. Let me advise you about the press. What they want more than anything else is a headline. Better to say nothing."

"A reporter, sir, from the Bijacic News. Asked to interview Mr. Jobert." Mary looked apprehensive.

"Already! The first, a local, ought to be easy to handle. Henry, you do the talking. Send him in."

"Ah, Mr. Jobert, Mr. Drysdale, can we take your picture? Thank you. I represent the Bijacic News. Mr. Jobert, could you tell us the nature of the spill?"

"Mr. Drysdale knows far more of the operations than I do. I'm just visiting. Tell him, Henry."

"We don't know what caused the spill. There may have been an explosion. Apparently some chemicals have been released."

"What chemicals, sir? And what caused the explosion?"

"Oh, some pesticides and some stock chemicals we were using in experiments with engineered bacteria. Possibly other materials. We won't know until my staff does sufficient testing. We don't know what caused the explosion."

"But you must have known what was in the exploded room."

"Yes, but not what got out here."

"The dead animals in the bog were caused by pesticides? Pesticides wouldn't kill birds or animals, would they? not this quick."

"Now how did you find that out? No, no we can't say what yet; any of an array of the other chemicals could have done it. Our technical staff has begun a study to determine what blew into the bog and what was likely to be affected by it. Only further work will tell us what happened. Now if you will excuse us we have lots of work that must get done."

"Why are people being kept away from the site altogether?"

"The sheriff's decision. He doesn't want people walking through the area; there could be evidence there."

"Mr. Jobert, didn't you bring this facility up here because you were going to use dangerous materials?"

"Not really. We were seeking what this magnificent country supplies in abundance, peace and quiet, a place where a researcher would surely have plenty of time to think. Uh, gentlemen, Mr. Drysdale has to get back to work now. He will be available to you tomorrow at this time."

"You won't be available, Mr. Jobert?"

"No, I have important business in Chicago. Good day to you. Henry and I have work to do."

"Thanks for the interview."

"Edmund, I started to send our people into the swamp to see what was blasted out there, but the sheriff insisted only under the supervision of his crew."

"Good thinking, Henry. Send Tim. He's a great observer- and Felix. Between them they should see anything and everything. Henry, that was a nice, no knife, easy reporter- or an incompetent one. How did he find out about the dead birds? Anyway, he wasn't trying to hang us; but he can't be that naive. TV has sophisticated everyone. Wait and see."

"Perhaps just not corrupted."

"Corrupted- a good word. Wait till the national newshounds get on our track. They'll be howling after us soon."

"Why can't they leave us alone?"

"Because we are a good target that will sell lots of papers. A spill is great for TV and so on. And in spite of all their tiresome motives, they are right. Anyone manufacturing, storing or using

dangerous chemicals ought to be watched. Good for the public, good for us. Keep us on guard against carelessness. Henry, modern industry uses some very dangerous materials. Carelessness or dumping are just not on. What a time to have to leave! Stonewall them, Henry. Oh God, the sheriff. I'm gone to Chicago. Careful with the words, Henry."

"That sheriff isn't going to like your being gone."

"Yes, I am sure that is so. Goodbye."

∞

"Mr. Drysdale. My men are ready to scour the marsh."

"Good. Here come my people. Sheriff, meet Tim Mirave. I'm told he has eyes like a hawk, and Felix Bountz, who ought to spot anything electrical and Dextra Chirali. Dextra, what are you doing here?"

"Thought I could help. That's Felix over there, Sheriff."

"Dangerous in there. But you know that."

"Yes, well, OK. Good experience for them, Sheriff and they are different talents. Now I must leave."

"Where is Mr. Jobert?"

"He had to go to Chicago on business."

"Did he now! You call him and tell him I want to see him immediately. I need someone to identify the body."

"Um-hm uh yes, well he's not here. Between you and me, I can tell you his daughter knew Kraft well."

"Marko, go get- her name Alice? - Alice Jobert- soothe her but let her know she must identify a body for us."

"Sheriff, how do you know her? Oh, the demonstration. The rest of you be careful out there. We now know there was a methyl isocyanate solution blown out, and there are other dangerous chemicals out there, so touch nothing unnecessarily. Sheriff, it can't have been a dynamite explosion; we had no such thing."

"There was dynamite. Maybe not yours. There was a little bit of fire; coulda blowed itself out. Heard that happens. Sure stinks around here; and in the swamp."

"I want to get engineers in that room to see what's wrong so we can correct it."

"Not until we go over it; could be fingerprints and we need pictures. Here comes the Doc. He's also the medical examiner and coroner. Makes a decent living that way."

"He doesn't look too well organized," said Drysdale.

"He always looks like a unmade bed. Don't let that fool you. He's smart enough. Who are these?"

"My people." Drysdale spoke, "Dextra, Felix, Tim you three understand that I don't want you to pick up so much as a leaf out there."

"Right, the only thing you do is look. You see something, tell Marko or Eric; that's them two coming. One of 'em picks stuff up. You don't. They've got bags."

Marko looked at Eric; both looked at the trio, lifted their eyebrows, groaned. Eric shrugged and asked, "Sheriff, who are these characters?"

"This is Tim, Felix, Dextra. That right? People from the lab; they're going with you."

"We are looking for pesticide containers and other stuff from the Hazardous Waste Storage room. What else are we supposed to look for?" asked Tim.

"Anything, everything that isn't swamp. Ah, you boys have your bags? Good. Go."

"Dextra- Miss- , uh, what are you here for?"

"She's useful, Sheriff," said Tim.

"If you say so."

"I go with Tim; I'm from the lab."

"Chris' sake, inta the fuckin' swamp."

"Marko, watch the language."

"Can we take notes, Sheriff?" said Felix.

"I want to see 'em."

"Alright. Your deputies used to bogs?" asked Tim.

"No. You tell 'em how to go."

"OK. No danger- uh Marko, Eric. Just going to get soggy."

"Tim. Bogging again. Do you suppose the Boss is trying to tell us something?" asked Felix.

"No. Said he wanted your sharp eyes along with mine."

"As though we could improve on Tim's eyes," said Dextra.

"Huh?" Tim spoke, "We're supposed to look for anything from the Toxics room and for evidence of interlopers, anything that might tell what happened last night. That sheriff was certainly relieved when we said we were willing to walk out there on the mat with you deputies. Felix, Dextra why don't you two walk along the edge? I'll walk about fifty feet in. We'll do a complete circle. We promised not to pick up anything- just call one of you deputies over if we find anything."

"Tim, you are noble. A great plan. Us two not in the muck." Felix grinned.

"Don't need to holler to us deputies; we'll be right with you. An' we all gotta get out there. What's a nice girl like you doing up here in the woods?" asked Eric.

"I'll walk nearer to Tim. We can talk."

"Oooh? About birds and bees?" Felix was mischievous.

"Felix, why don't you look carefully along the edge. Suits you," said Dextra.

"I'm Eric. I'll walk with you too, Dextra."

Felix eyed the trio as they staggered out on the mat, Dextra navigating after Tim. Then Tim walked further out leaving the deputy talking to a vexed Dextra. Dextra even had lipstick on, second time. Tim frowned. A problem? He saw Eric bend over and hand Dextra a bunch of feathers. She fastened the feathers on her brilliant red tam They were a beautiful contrasting blue and white. She staggered back to Tim and said, "Aren't these pretty? Tim nodded, "Blue jay feathers. Where the hell did they come from? I've got to go in the deep part; you better get back with uh Eric." She retreated to Eric.

She called to Tim, "What is that beautiful song over on the point?"

"That's a hermit thrush singing. There's probably a nest there." Tim watched her surreptitiously. Lipstick? Romance? Me! No! Still Dextra was acting like a bog person and giggling like a school girl, suggesting Cupid at work. In the spring thoughts of love and walking with one's love can eliminate all rational thought. Tim was aghast; she must have kept to the recesses of her own mind for a long time; coming out is dangerous. A night owl is blinded by the light. Someone like Dextra can suddenly be taken over by the hormones. And will do things that will horrify them when they come to consciousness again. When the mind is blinded, Mama Nature is in charge. For someone like Dextra that is extremely dangerous. Emotions are destroyers. Poor Dextra. Anyway it is a liberating experience and may even be good for her. But not for me.

"Tim, I'm going to find that nest." Dextra walked to the edge, searching and found a nest. It has a piece of paper in it, Tim."

“Thrushes will do that” Tim, objective, scanning as for a rare plant, looked with his usual watchfulness; Dextra, a useless searcher had eyes only for Tim who kept his distance. Eric watched Dextra; Felix eyed Marko; Marko disgustedly wondered what he was doing out there with this ‘fruit’. Was that dumb Eric on the make again? With a dictionary? ! fu Chris’ sake. The deputies and the lab people lived in two different worlds, each with its own perspectives, its own sensitivities. Each had standard sets of insults, and compliments deliverable in accepted ways. How do you speak to someone on the other side? How even do you ask for a cup of coffee in a strange restaurant? ‘Cup-a-cawfee’ may be too impersonal, too impudent. ‘Could I have a cup of coffee’ too formal, too cold, coffee badly pronounced. When groups of people from different levels of society and different parts of the country suddenly have to work together, there begins an immediate scanning, a sizing up. The general demeanor, clothes, behavior are absorbed much as a baby scanning its hugging parent stores data about that parent. So the strangers. Then begins a process of testing. Each response adds to a catalog of good, bad, and indifferent approaches. Eventually a code of inter-group behavior arises, with occasional new, and deletion of old, non-productive or even irritating responses. Always, there are quick flicks of the eye checking reactions to proposals, or, if the observer is invisible, a prolonged watch. One thing always transcends the divide- sex.

“Swamp. Gonna sink outta sight.. Can I hold onta ya, Dextra?” Eric had made a move.

“I’m with Tim. Just watch your footing. If you stay in one place you will sink.”

“Gee, thanks, Dextra. How you know that?” said Eric.

“She has walked over this bog,” said Felix. Guy was getting a lot of negative feedback from Dextra.

“Nice ta know. Seen a pitcher once. Showed a guy found inna bog- 1000 years old- was tanned like leather. Don’t think I’d look good that way.”

“No fear.”

Eric went back to Marko who snorted, “Eric, fu Chris’ sake, you got the hots for that kinda broad?”

“Sure I’m broad-minded. Ha, ha. I mean sure she’s different but shape and looks ain’t bad.”

"Ha. Lissen, she could freeze you in bed. An' she talks like a damn dictionary. Come on!" said Marko.

"Nah. I just thought I'd test ta see if she's loose. Maybe not. She's maybe got the hots for that guy Tim."

"Now, he seems reasonable, no side. Don't seem hot for her."

"Yeah, but a bird watcher. One way, that's trouble, that could be my chance," said Eric.

"Ha! That Felix is something else."

"I think he must be one of them geniuses; he's nuts."

∞

"Something over here, a piece of concrete."

"Coming over, Dextra. Say, you ever see the Indian drawings on our cliffs? Like ta show them to you after work."

"Thank you, but I am going with Tim tonight. Indian drawings would be interesting."

Tim called, "Marko, some plastic jugs and pesticide containers over here. And a box, got a company label on it. And a piece of insulated wire."

"Here I come. Now you found something!" And fell into the muck.

"Pick yourself outta the swamp, Marko," called Eric. "Looks like a hunka the lab wall, Dextra. Sure you don't wanta see them pictures? Would be real fun."

"No. Tim and I have a date."

"The Sheriff is waving us in; must be something up. OK everybody ashore."

∞

"A body! Ho-ho, the plot thickens. Who was it, Sheriff?" asked the reporter.

"Tentatively we think that environmentalist, Gilbert Kraft. Don't you use that name until we get a certain identification."

"The environmentalist? hoo-boy! somebody told me he was an enemy of Mr. Jobert? Sheriff, how come he was permitted to leave?"

"Routine. He will be back when we need him. He had important business to attend to."

"Wow, I better get this story in. Hottest I've ever been on."

∞

"Alice, it is Alice Jobert, right? I'm sorry to have had you brought in to the morgue and I hate to ask it but we have a body that we need identified and we have reason to think that you may be able to do the job."

"But what's it got to do with me? Sheriff, I haven't been around here in days. I'm just back from Chicago. What happened?"

"Oh. I see. How many days back?"

"What does it matter? Well, a week anyway. What happened?"

"Ah."

"Oh, OK, I'll look at the body."

"Brace yourself; it isn't pretty; just part of his face intact. Hands may help, rings on them."

"Please, I…oh alright."

"Lift the sheet, Doc."

"Ready?"

"Oh God. It's Gilbert. How awful. I have to sit down."

"Put your head down, Miss Jobert. You'll be alright in a minute."

Gilbert was dead. What was he doing? How did he get blown up. How? What was he doing? How could he be so careless? Or me. He was so persuasive. He was a good organizer but he would take over, get control, and I found myself doing what he wanted me to do, not what I wanted to do. He was always operating. I thought he was useful; he used me. He talked all those people into becoming active. He said the spill wasn't enough; we had to have a really serious incident. What did he do? What was the incident? Was it what killed him? Did I help? I'm in trouble."

"Now, who is it?"

"Gilbert Kraft. He was helping our environment group organize."

"OK, that's what we thought. He was helping?"

"Yes. How could this have happened?" asked Alice.

"We hoped you would give us some ideas."

"No, I can't. Why would he go near the lab? Look I have to go. I have an appointment with my Doctor"

"Alright. Thank you for coming in Miss Jobert. You look sick; better go home and get some rest. We'll be sending someone out for a more thorough interview later."

The sheriff watched her leave, her head down looking forlorn. Now how does she connect? Better trace her movements. Go get the boys on it right away and on old man Jobert himself- him taking off like that.

"What have you got, Eric?"

"That birdwatcher found this concrete block, pesticide cans, some papers, hunk a wire."

"Where is he?"

"Took off; said he was going to see Alice somebody."

"Ah, that's Alice Jobert."

"Damn. That Dextra told me she hadda date with that birdwatcher."

Marko grinned, "Just din't wanna associate with an ignorant guy like you."

"OK boys, good work. I'll call the library; they ought to be able to tell us the ownership of the company on the label. Boys, I bet that company name on there is a Jobert company. Could the old boy be involved? Nah. Unbelievable. Now a job for you. Check on Alice Jobert, everything."

Chapter 8 Ferrets and a traitor

"Mr. Drysdale, did you see this? The newspaper is implying we planned the explosion so that we could test our bacteria on pesticides right here outside our building."

"Pure nonsense. These reporters!"

"Sir, the reporter says he has a copy of an internal memo from you telling someone to do that."

"Oh no! Mary, what could I have written that could be misinterpreted that way? And how did they get it if there was one?"

"I can guess the memo. But who here would have given it to him?"

"Yes. Who? Hunt the memo down, Mary."

"I'm sorry, Mr. Drysdale, I didn't want to tell you- we found out this morning- the memo file has been completely erased. And of course there's been a lot of work since then.."

"Erased! Our traitor! Who is he? Who has access to our memo files?"

"We're attempting to find the person but don't know where to look."

"Somebody in this organization is trying to damage us. Who's got a grudge?"

"I can think of people."

"Very distasteful. Weren't there backups? Ah, but were they erased too?"

"Yes, they were on tape. But they were erased there too."

"Somebody who really knew our procedures. We must find who is doing this, and who used our stationary to send notes to the Watershed Chair. Let's get Jobert's Ferrets from Security in Chicago.. Mary, call Chicago and tell them we want the Ferrets immediately. We need someone to do our own investigation of the memos and the accident."

"Ferrets?"

"Jobert's name for them. You'll see why."

"We still have diskette copies; one of the secretaries likes diskettes. She erased them too but hasn't used them since."

"Mary, you are a genius. They may be recoverable. Get the computer man, the Whiz, on them. Maybe he can rescue them."

"Mr. Drysdale, the Whiz talks all the time; the word would be all over the place that a hunt is on."

"Of course. We'll leave it to the Chicago Security people. Good thinking, Mary."

"I'm not a computer expert but there is another possibility; the memo may have been copied onto a desk computer in an office and that copy could still exist."

"Or be recoverable."

"Mr. Drysdale, it also looks like we have a lawsuit based on someone coming by the spill. The person claims he was affected seriously by methyl isocyanate poisoning."

"How did he find out about the methyl isocyanate? Our traitor again! But no one was near that until twelve hours later! It was guarded. They'd have had to sneak by our guards."

"The person says we didn't prevent him entering the site, therefore it's our fault."

"People can sue for any reason, I guess. I wish we hadn't gotten that barrel of pharmaceutical gunk from Chicago. Can only be glad no one has noticed that, yet. No telling what was in it. You've notified our attorney? Good. But the area was heavy with signs."

"They say it's still our fault we didn't guard the site enough. And, sir, about the national reporters tomorrow morning."

" Oh yes. All the torments at once. The whole crowd will be here en masse tomorrow at 9 A.M. Send them to the lounge. I can handle it but I surely wish Jobert were here. I didn't do too well with the local reporters. Jobert gave me some good advice. Now what was that advice?" Drysdale walked over to the window, reviewing in his mind the problem of preparing for reporters.

Industrialists should stay out of the public eye if they can; they have few skills for handling reporters. People in the public eye (politicians) develop a fine art for answering, or not answering, corresponding to the reporter's art of questioning. They are cool, collected, wary and anticipatory. The first question is sure to be of the 'have you stopped beating your wife' category. Finesse the question- talk about the wife. If the questions in succession imply that you are something reprehensible, talk only about one of the questions; persistence of the same question is best met with misdirection. A windy question ought to be met by an even more windy answer. If the question is too precise, getting too near the bone, your answer should be as wide as the ocean. A good all purpose answer is 'no comment', or 'we're studying the matter'.

If the interviewer knows too much about the subject, imply that the subject is too complex.

Remember, they want a 'good' story. Any questioning, no matter how unscrupulous, that elicits a clangor is a success. What is unwanted is a thoughtful answer. Readers have no time for subtlety; slap them in the nose with a stinking mackerel of factitious banalities. Drysdale turned and spoke to Mary, "What is a poor plant manager to do against those sharks? Mary, I am expecting a call from the Watershed Chair. Oh yes, uh, when those security people show up, give them Toly Quist, that crazy janitor with the psychiatric history, and Glatz; they're both complainers; and any one else, even an outsider, especially Kraft's buddy, might give a lead and, I have to say it, Dextra Chirali."

"Oh surely not Miss Chirali."

"She's been acting strangely lately. Has been seen coming sneaking into the lab in the middle of the night. Yes, yes I know-research but that's not her habit. Mary, add anybody who's irregular in any way°oh that's crazy. Just let the Ferrets look through the employee roster; also, let them talk to anybody, they'll want to know everything about those three and perhaps about others."

"There goes the phone." Mary darted to her office.

Drysdale shook his head, terrible to become suspicious. When does honest, justified suspicion become paranoia, a despicable hunting for a phantom?

"Phone, Mr. Drysdale, the Watershed Chair."

"Damn." Drysdale picked up the phone, fearing what Richter, the Watershed Chair would have to say. He was greeted cordially. Drysdale launched into his set spiel.

"Mr. Richter, our research is bearing fruit. We have engineered varieties of bacteria which can metabolize some organo-phosphate pesticides, chlorinated hydrocarbons, herbicides, and even one that can chop up methyl isocyanate. Some require oxygen; others are intolerant of oxygen. We have them in powder form and methods so simple that any citizen can use them. With our provisions for their application as worked out by our own engineers, they are capable of cleaning up pesticide tanks, spray cans even in the home. We also have prepared them for environmental use in acid or alkaline environments. Oh yes, uh°we hadn't planned to use the bogs as experimental sites; they're too acid. But now we ask for permission to use our already heavily contaminated Renewal Site for this purpose and also for permission to clean up the toxics in the bog next to the lab- the explosion bog."

"Mr. Drysdale, I want to say yes, given the importance of your work. I do have questions about using so complex an environmental system for such a study. A simple surface might be better initially. But there is one other problem: the spill is producing a people reaction which I think will become severe. You, of course not you personally, are being accused of all kinds of things, deliberate spilling, murder, releasing dangerous bacteria, etc. I will be forced to react to that; the police findings will be crucial; if at all negative, I may have to require an investigation."

"I understand that; but I repeat, time is overwhelmingly important for our testing. The spill of pesticides and other toxics spill is ideal for us and will challenge our techniques. Our engineered oxygen-hating anaerobes can't reproduce and, further can't compete long term with their unchanged ancestors already there. They will work away and will be gone by the end of summer. Our aerobic bacteria will last even less time. Our tests are first class. On the surface, tests are simpler and easier. The Renewal Site is not so acid and will permit all kinds of tests. A simple surface won't do. Teddy Sourtis, one of our engineers, has invented a series of injection devices which can put the bacteria, along with other materials, where the pesticides are. We can destroy them at any depth. We feel this is very important and needs immediate attention. We might add that the acid environment of the bog is so formidable an obstacle to our success that it will give us a test of unmatched caliber. The turnover of the water in both bogs is extremely slow so any spread either of our bacteria or the pesticide is unlikely. In any case we will guarantee to remove all traces of our work."

"I am with you. I will take this plan to all my experts immediately-especially to the Genetics Council. Once again...none of these bacteria is foreign?"

"Right. They came originally from the contaminated bogs. We engineered them. By the way our New Guinea bacteria is now in negative pressure chambers. So are the hydrogen-producing gut bacteria. We are making progress with them. Both are under strict quarantine."

"Very well. We'll start discussion today. I'll need a formal request. The national EPA and other agencies will respond to my requests for critiques."

"The formal request is in the mail."

"Good. I can tell you right now I am very much in favor of giving you these permits. A lot of problems will be solved if you succeed. I have the power to OK the use of your transformed bacteria in the Renewal Site but want the EPA viewpoint. Your hydrogen-producing bacteria are still under review by the Genetics Council. That will take some time. I intend to press hard for this. I shall ask my experts to consider your problems thoroughly. I assure you they will not procrastinate; there will be lots of questions of a technical nature. Mr. Drysdale, where can we call for answers and when?"

"Our application includes names and telephone numbers of our technical experts. They will be available at any time through a call to my secretary."

"Mr. Drysdale, permit me to tell you my troubles so that you can appreciate why there could be delay. All my decisions are based on data and rules of procedure. I do nothing political. My insistence on the sequestering of your hydrogen bacteria is based on the observed fact that introduced species can and often have been unmitigated disasters not only to the farmer, but also to native communities of plants and animals and, most important, to the taxpayer. Gypsy moths were introduced into the U.S. by a 'responsible' scientist. 'Killer' bees were introduced into Brazil by a fine geneticist. Scientists in pursuit of research can be careless and, in the process, can bring destruction to native species, even eliminate them. And they will do anything, so long as it favors their work. A dog in the manger is generous, sweet, pleasant compared with the scientist guarding his lab. He has all the delicacy of a wolverine when he safeguards his research and his lab equipment against all intruders. Some of this behavior is justifiable.

"Worse are some Fish and Wildlife Services which have been responsible for many disastrous introductions and, amazingly, are still doing that kind of idiot behavior. Ordinary people, gardeners, have also contributed, as have highway departments. The latter show no signs of dropping this asininity. So far no one has tried to foul up a country by deliberate introductions but I believe the military has talked about that possibility. The worst introductions were, of course, involuntary- smallpox, HIV virus and the other diseases which have devastated populations. It could be argued that the American Indian was defeated not by troops but by disease carried in by settlers and soldiers.

"Part of my job is to see that no such catastrophes happen in this watershed. I have to fight idiot wildlife people, idiot farmers, idiot gardeners, idiot scientists, etc. As you no doubt know, I also must see that the water does not deteriorate, that the soil does not erode, that the air does not get worse. If possible, I must improve them. All of this must be done on technical grounds in the teeth of resistance by ignorant people. You will appreciate that I get frazzled at times."

"Indeed. My sympathies."

"Please feel free to call me for further information, Mr. Drysdale. Nice to have talked with you. No more explosions, eh. Good day."

Drysdale sighed; always something more to arrange.

"The chairman of the National Genetics Council is on the phone."

"I'll take it in my office. Drysdale here for Jobert Northwood Labs."

"Mr. Jobert's not there? Too bad. Well, OK. That hydrogen producing bacteria you got from New Guinea is ringing a lot of bells around here. There are a lot of genetic releases to the environment planned and a lot of medical experiments involving human genes located on human chromosomes, extracted, multiplied and now ready in carriers to be put back into sick people. This work is too important to be halted by any screw-ups. We can't afford even the hint of a problem with any genetically altered organism. And you are in the news. If some smart reporter gets wind of those hydrogen-producing bacteria getting loose, they`d spread your story even wider on the front page and down the tube will go a lot of our work. So! What's your maintenance setup?"

"None have gotten loose. We have established a negative pressure room. There's no external venting. Nothing can escape. If a vat ruptured the room would be flooded with UV. All dead bacteria. And we've got first class people in charge."

"Who?"

"Dextra Chirali and Felix Bountz."

"Ah. First class, indeed. Still there are the lower people. For the time being just shut up about that bug. Muffle any news from the vats."

"We've been doing that ever since last year's spill."

"Continue. Everyone here is interested in the potential of that bacteria. We're all with you on the value of your work. Just keep it quiet. One smart reporter and blooie, we're all in deep doodoo."

"Rely on us."

•

"Not again!"

"Yes again. Eric, if you hadn't had the hots for that woman scientist you woulda found something on the bog beside that lab box. Now you did get some wire; so get out there and get the rest of the wire and find how they set it off. It's gotta be out there somewhere."

"Eric ain't ready for this, Sheriff. He's still thinking a that broad. Wants to produce a race of Eric brats which have got some brains instead a those drooling kids like his sister's got."

"I show some signs a brains, something I ain't noticed in you, you creep."

"Cut the crap both of you. Eric, you stay about twenty-five feet away from Marko. Find that damn thing."

"Ain't you coming with us, sheriff?"

"No, I ain't coming with you sheriff. I'm going along the edge." The sheriff watched his deputies staggering over the bog mat. Good they had had that lab bunch to show them how. They would find it. There had to be wires somewheres, maybe a timer. Follow the shore; drag a hook; just might snag the wires. What it took was persistence; just keep looking; something would turn up.

It was hot. July in the bog is a Finnish sauna with myriads of deerflies and mosquitoes for swatting; and for smearing in the flowing sweat. Out on the mat the deputies became walking sweat sacks. This they were used to; both fished the local lakes and had become inured to the torment of these, the Minnesota birds. They slipped and sank and cursed and looked for anything different. Marko gestured toward the shore, toward the Sheriff.

"Looka that SOB enjoying himself. Gawd; looka that, he tripped over something."

"Naturally. Always tripping over something." Eric was echoing Marko.

"If he was out here he would have to swim across the mat. Couldn't stand up. What's he got? Looks like a length a wire. You know he could be right. Stuff ought to be on top. Won't sink though this stuff. But how could we have missed it? Your eye on that broad, that's it."

"Marko, I got it! It's one a them dynamiting things Plungers down! Wires attached. There's a tag still on it."

"Grab that paper, looks like a label, another one, over there. Keep your paw prints offa that paper, numskull. Now where are we?" Marko was elated.

"We're onna sorta little island here, muck from here to the shore; guy could creep out here like a drunk, hangin' onta these little tamaracks, set it off, stumble back to shore, be long gone. Opposite that big tamarack- can easy find our way here again. Way for us to go- get outta this muck. Walk around ta the left. There's a trail over there." Eric started off the mat.

"We found a dynamiting thing, Sheriff. And some other stuff."

"Blasting machine. uh huh! Good work boys, we're getting somewhere finally. Marko, call the FBI. Tell 'em we need help tracing this blasting machine; call it an ignition box; they might not know the name blasting machine. Get 'em on the ignition box, wires, the loose labels and the label on the box. We want to know where the stuff came from, who brought it up here, anything.. One other thing. Drysdale told me there was somebody inside the company who was unhappy. Sent out copies of memos. Told people about the first spill. Marko, talk around; see who that is. Could be the killer."

•

"Sir, the Ferrets are here from Chicago. They're the most unsavory looking people I've ever encountered. One looks like a thug, the other like the sleeziest, slickest used car salesman you ever ran into."

"Ah, the Ferrets! Jobert's joke. Ha, ha. Good joke, eh, Mary. You know the old saw, set a thief to catch a thief. Send them in, and, Mary, you sit in on this...don't worry- these 'Ferrets' were picked by Jobert, have a cushy job with Jobert Industries; they won't steal anything not labeled 'Steal Me'. Ha, ha. Gentlemen."

"Thanks, fer duh compliment. I'm Barney Gross; this guy's Red Belt, B E L E T."

"Gentlemen, we have a problem. Someone inside our organization has been sending copies of internal documents to the local newspapers and to the environmental groups. They also have sent messages to the Watershed Chair. The same person or persons may also be involved in an explosion and spill which recently occurred in this plant. A man, an environmentalist named Kraft, was killed in the blast. The local sheriff and the FBI are investigating that death right now. The job I have for you may involve that business, especially the explosion. There had to be an inside person or somebody with a key to place the dynamite. If you could find anything about that, it would be very valuable. You will not, repeat not interfere in any way with the work of the police. More important, we would like to know who is the person with a grudge against us who sent a confidential memo to the newspapers. That person erased our memo files. The memo was on our computer but was erased along with a lot of other correspondence. And we want to know any connections that person might have with Gilbert Kraft, the man killed in the explosion, or with any of our other personnel. Mary will make available all the information we have to date. I must leave. Gentlemen."

"Mary. Good name. Whatta you say we do the town tanight, eh? Must be some wild things ta do here."

"Red, Jesus Christ, the lady seen enough wild animals up here. Don't need to wrestle with a ape. Now we could go dancing; seen a nice roadhouse as we come in- could trip the light fantastic."

"Lady, whatever you do don't take that guy up. He's so polite you learn on'y afterwards that you've been done outta honor, bread, anything else movable."

"Gentlemen, I'm a very busy woman. These are copies of memos we recovered from the newspaper and the Watershed Chair's office°"

Gross interrupted, "So you got a creep. Can get fooled, don't hafta be a griper. Quiet type sits back burning can do it. Me, I'm pretty good on the computer. I'll find this thing. You got a main computer for files, right? And office PC's?"

"We think the memo might have been copied from the main computer to a PC in someone's office, printed out there and sent out. But note this: all of the correspondence files were erased on the main computer. There are also some erased diskettes which could also have had copies from the main computer."

"I need ta get on ta da main computer, and alla the office PC's. Somewheres there is a ghost file which I will raise from the dead. Ain't many people can do that. Ha, ha, at's a good joke, ay, Red?"

"Yeah, but I can do better, I can make ghosts. Me, I wanna talk to anybody can get near a computer. Twist a few arms, they sing like birds."

"We'd like it to be a little more genteel than that. Consult with our Whiz; I'll instruct him to give you whatever access you may need.. How did you get to be an expert, Mr. er Gross?"

"Lady, you can't be nice in something like this; takes a little persuasion. An' that I'm good at," said Red.

"Is he ever! Can make a bear sing. Me, I learnt my trade up in the slammer. Don't worry- Mr. Jobert, now there is a honey, hired me and told me what he would do if I tried anything. As if I would. This is a good job."

"We'll put out that you are efficiency experts from Chicago. That's not very believable is it? Anyway, uh, this is a list of the people we guessed would be most likely to do something like this."

"Don't worry. We know how to be efficiency experts. So some pigeons ta catch, possible perpetrators, Mary."

"Red eats pigeons," said Barney.

Mary couldn't help shuddering.

"Calm yasself, lady. We ain't gonna put anybody inna hospital. We ain't crude; just a little arm bending."

"There's another matter; the spill we had last year. We want to know who opened the valve. The contents of one of our vats went into the swamp next door."

"What difference that make?"

"It's against the law. We'd like to know who that was. And whether the same person was involved in the spill this year. And another thing- uh, here, this name on here is a person who is suing us claiming he was poisoned just by passing by the spill and getting dosed by methyl isocyanate. That we have that stuff is a well kept secret. So how did he find out about it? We'd like to know."

"Well, now," said Barney, "First we find the computer memo, then the person, then we see if he could get to the valve. And the cyanide guy. Then Red talks to them, him. Nothin' to it."

"Ira's our night watchman. He'll show you where everything is. Let me call him."

"Nice lookin' broad. Snow on the roof, fire in the furnace, you think?" said Red.

"I think we better keep our noses clean. An' stay away from the local cops. They'll spot us as soon as we spot them."

"We're clean and doing a job. Can't touch us."

"No, but they can slow us down and hassle us."

"Seen a tavern onna way in. Good place ta get all the local dope. Why don't I go there after we tour the joint with the guard."

"Why don't WE do that!"

"Edmund, thank you for calling. The news keeps getting worse. The only thing the papers haven't accused us of is rape."

"Patience, Henry. We're just the sensation of the moment. Glad to hear about the Watershed Chair. Confirms my impression. Wonderful to have an official who has at least the potential to make a quick decision, eh, Henry."

"Yes, but, thank goodness, he has a limited span of office. He has too much power. Of course if he errs and water, air, or land deteriorate while he is in office he could get discharged. Instant unemployment."

"As you said a well-designed office. The Solons did something good for once."

"Sir, the national papers were here this morning. I think I survived the ordeal. I took your advice. They didn't seem too irritated by my meandering."

"Good for you, Henry. Give them something for their stories and don't lie. Just omit things; they don't need to know everything until we are ready to release the whole story at our own time and advantage."

"The Chicago, uh, Security is here. Tim Mirave, I am beginning to understand, but these two are born thugs. The staff pale when they are around."

"Ha! They'll get the job done. Don't worry. They know I have them checked out from time to time. They are on notice that any hanky-panky and they are in trouble. Let me tell you they smell every angle that's workable. After all, that used to be their stock in trade. Whatever is going on up there they will find out. Enjoy them! Get a liberal education in people you've never encountered before! See how the criminal class thinks. After all, they're just perverted businessmen. Go out to the local bar with them and listen to their comments about the people in the bar. You have never thought that way or had the insights into the lower orders; they have. Still, it's not too different from dealing with these pirates down here who are trying to push me out. Enjoy the Ferrets. I'll be up there soon. My daughter will work up a big demonstration, so hunker down. Keep cool. I'll be there for that."

•

"Well, Tim. What are you doing down here?" said Drysdale.

"Oh. Yes. Uh. Nothing. Uh, just looking over the place. I was wondering how wires could get from here to the outside. The door must have been absolutely tight. It wouldn't be difficult to snake the wires through one of these wall plugs and out an outside box if there was help outside."

"Ah, I think we had better leave the detecting to the professionals, don't you?"

"Oh yes, of course, just curiosity. That sheriff was here when I came down. Seemed competent. I-uh, I've got to run. Got an appointment. Good-bye."

"Good-bye."

Jobert swears by this man but 'appointments' are things he doesn't have. He seemed flustered now. It is odd that he should come down here. He must know that there are some dangerous materials loose. Knowledgeable. Wouldn't be careless. Had something in his pocket. What? Trust Jobert's judgment usually, but I can't connect with Mirave. Don't understand him. Must mention this meeting to Jobert. What in the world was in that pharmaceutical barrel? They said it was a waste mix of all kinds of chemicals. Was going to be a real test of our on-line disposal system. Well, won't have any difficulty getting another such barrel. They'll be glad to get rid of some more. Would be a great test of the continuous flow system.

"Welcome, gentlemen. What's yours?"

"JoAnn, honey," said Red, looking lasciviously either at her badge or breasts, "We want what people up here in the north have. Us Chicago people like ta folla the rules."

"That's most anything."

"Nah. Can't be."

JoAnn looked at the newcomers. What rock did they crawl from under? She had a faint stir of apprehension. Stick-up? Nah. Anybody taking one look at this joint would expect an empty till. So what's their game? Here comes Marko, what's he want?

"Gentlemen," said Marko sarcastically, "up here on vacation?"

Instant recognition; a cop, rural type, Chicago hoods with instant smirks, heads turned sideways, eyes half closed centered on the cop.

"No, officer, we're here on business. We work for da Lab. You wanna see our papers?"

"That would be nice," said Marko. He copied names, addresses, took their printed business cards. Security! These hoods! They said Jobert didn't go by the rules. Now I believe it. He didn't like the knowing looks on their faces. Would be nice to change that. Look 'em up right away.

"OK. We like it nice and peaceful up here. No rough stuff."

"A course. Nobody'll even know we're here. Just doin' a little checkup for the company."

Marko left.

"OK, JoAnn, double shots a your best whiskey and a coupla bottles a beer. Ain't often I get ta order from a gorgeous blonde. Ain't that right, Barney?"

"Yeah, Chicago blondes turn brunette over night, air's so dirty."

"Ha, ha, ha. We'll sit at a table over here."

The door opened and in came a distinguished looking man in work clothes. He was slightly tilted.

JoAnn frowned, "Toly Quist, just turn around and get out. You had enough already."

Barney nudged Red, "Our pigeon. So why's he a janitor? Good looking guy like that."

Barney spoke up, "JoAnn, poor guy wants ta tie one on, he got a right."

"Not to toss his cookies on my floor, he don't. Or pass out here."

"Hey, we'll see this pilgrim don't do that. A shot and a beer for him."

JoAnn grimaced and slammed a shot and beer on the table. Red patted her on the behind.

"You do that again, buddy, and I'll wrap a beer bottle around your head."

"Ha, ha, ha. Just trying ta guess ya weight, honey."

"Tough broads up here. Where you work, friend?"

"Jober' Lab; they don' 'preciate me."

"Now, ain't that the way! Guy works his tail off, nobody notices."

Slurred voice, "They trea' me like dirt, keep away from me.."

"Like a skunk atta picnic. Ha, ha, ha. I din't mean you was a skunk. Heard they had a bad spill."

"Yeah, a splosion. Blew stuff all over swamp. Who gives a shit."

"On'y the nuts. What exploded? Hey, your glass is empty. Another round JoAnn."

"Ah, that's goo'," sliding to one side, pushed back by Red.

"You got a real thirst."

"Yeah. Dynami'... In where they keep the shit."

"How'd it get in there?"

Looking cunningly around the room, "Tell you a secret. I lef' door open sometimes."

"Hey, why'd you do that? Ah you're empty again. JoAnn another."

"You guys gotta get that guy out of here. Pay up." She slammed the drinks on the table.

"Don't be so hard-nosed, JoAnn. Gotta treat us tourists right you know."

"Thanksh. Glatz, snotty°snotty bookkeeper; gets stuff f'ris lawn. Screw uh ball Mirve too. Y shoul' sees his numbers- perfect like- eleg uh elegan' oh shit."

"Numbers? Aaah. He tell ya ta dump the stuff a year ago?"

"Tole you " said the janitor. "Talk too much."

"Gettin' a little woozy, huh? Jo Ann, we gotta go. Take this pilgrim home. See ya tomorra."

"Oh." To self, not if I see you first. "Take care of him."

"Sure will."

Chapter 9 Demonstration against Jobert

"That driver weaved through that crowd like a darning needle through a sock, got me through that mess. I was afraid he would hit someone."

"He drove a taxi in New York and knows within a millimeter how to miss a pedestrian."

"Ha! Henry, they were hollering something like 'Jobert murderer'. Where did that come from?"

"I called the sheriff about it. He says he thinks someone put together some wild surmises. But who, that's the question."

"If Kraft were there, no problem. One of his trainees? Ah, forget it. Pass me those binoculars. Aha, thought so! Tim with the demonstrators."

"Yes. Uh, Edmund, I still think he is a mistake; he could be our malcontent. I found him looking over the Toxic room and he had something concealed in his pocket. Left as soon as I showed up. What was he doing there? He may be our trouble maker."

"I remind you, he's my idea, Henry. I take responsibility for him. He is a wild card but he would never betray us without telling us first. I know the man. I picked him for one reason; he never dissembles. He'll sit and tell you what you are. Without a blush, directly. I'm still not sure he knows that he does that. A bit of a pain in the ass sometimes but useful. He will let us know what we are doing wrong with our personnel, with the local people, and our bad habits. I'm more afraid he'll just walk away from us. He doesn't believe in what we are doing, or for that matter, what anyone else is doing. He is an observer. To him progress is nonsense, a mirage. Strange, I'm, I guess, an entrepreneur; my life is getting things produced; but I find his view disturbing. Can he be right? I keep asking that question; don't want to, but do. How to keep him here? Like trying to nail down quicksilver...now he's talking to Alice, my Alice, and one of her demonstrators…saw her last year. Alice looks happy; maybe she's over that damned love affair. I hope so."

"Are you sure Tim is not selling us out?"

"Never. In fact if he convinced these picketers of his philosophy they would pack up and go home. In here, with our people that wouldn't work. We all think something can be accomplished. Uh, oh- there's Dextra, coming up to Tim. Who's the guy following her? I've seen him somewhere."

Henry answered, "That's Teddy Sourtis. He's the inventor of our injector. It's amazing that he's there. He's very shy." Teddy was normally a study in plainness; tie neuter, plain shirts, trousers, conventional shoes, but that day he wore a blue check flannel shirt and corduroys, practically explosive for Teddy.

"And out of place down there."

"Hello, Felix. Welcome to the observatory."

"More fun down there. Saw the mooning woman. She wouldn't even say hello."

"Naturally, self protection. Look, Dextra with Tim! and in bright clothing. What the devil is she doing? Can't be."

"Yes, it can. He'll unwind her DNA."

"You really think so, Felix? Her DNA intact till now, you think?"

"Yup. I'm an authority on the subject; when the hormones flow the helix is undone. Embarrassing. An internal governor points the way. Her hormones are producing long looks and kittenish silliness and odd ways of standing, all coming from deep inside to take over. No thinking allowed."

"Is this the voice of experience I hear? You know all about sex, Felix?"

"Yup. I'm the voice of experience. Did some of the same stupid things. I have to tell you it's not only stupid, it's dangerous. When people are hormoned, they are being run."

"No volition?"

"No. Dextra is new at this game, newborn really. She is stalking Tim but doesn't know it. Hormones. He has noticed her and is ducking. She knows that and doesn't know that. If he cuts her out, then her spirit is going to nose-dive."

"Tim is a sensitive person. Felix, he think about her at all?"

"He's aware, aware of her attention. Doesn't want it. We had to go around the bog the other day. Dextra insisted on walking with Tim out on the mat, can you believe it, in the bog! And let me tell you I have never seen any one so clumsy. She fell against him a dozen times."

"Dextra is never clumsy."

"Right. If she'd been a cat she'd have been rubbing up against him. Listen! she came awfully close to calling him Cuddlebuns or something like that."

"Oh, stop! Felix, that's just what you'd like to be called."

"Maybe, but Cupid has lain our experimenter low. You don't know the half of it. She blew an experiment the other day."

"No! That is serious."

"He's studiously avoiding her already."

Jobert frowned, "Probably feels he has to. But Dextra is terribly vulnerable. I have seen others like that commit suicide when the romance didn't work or even start. Besides avoiding, how is Tim responding?"

"He understands, is aware, but even as sensitive a person as Tim might not be able to ward off consequences."

"Felix! this is a problem. To be ignored would be devastating to Dextra."

"It is happening."

"No! but Dextra is indispensable. Any way to make her and Tim be a pair? No, impossible. What do you think, Felix? pair those two? No, no, that would make things worse. Tim and Dextra are as different as two people can be. She wants to accomplish; he couldn't care less. How can she capture a guy like that? He's too weird; she's too weird."

"Boss, don't ever underrate the genitals. There is no nerve connection between the genitals and the brain! When the genitals rule, the brain slumbers and vice versa.. Opposites like them can tie together, though they may not stay together. Marriage is the surest cure for romance as you well know."

"Felix, you are a cynic. No. You're right; won't work. It would collapse of its own contradictions. Somebody else maybe. Felix, there's only one way Have to get her a man, get her married. Felix, you are just the person to bring that about."

"You joke… me a marriage broker! Who? Hell, it's impossible."

"Find somebody, find somebody. You have my confidence."

"Sir, it is not only impossible," Drysdale engrossed by the crowd outside, had heard these last remarks, "but we should stay out of the lives of our employees."

Jobert disagreed, "No, Henry, not this time! She's our ace. We must not permit this to continue. Of all the Greek gods, Cupid was and is the most dangerous. Zeus used Cupid in his more nasty schemes to upset people's and the gods' apple-carts. We can't have that. We've got to stop this. But how?"

Felix pointed, "One possibility. Do you see how colorful Teddy is down there? She is being pursued by Teddy and she knows he is there but vaguely. He is an amateur at the game. If it weren't for the potential for things going wrong, I could enjoy this. Me, a voyeur instead of an actor. Think of the high jinks to come."

"No! Don't enjoy yourself! Teddy, I barely know. Is he a possible? Could you help the guy?" Jobert thought Felix must have all the experience necessary to solve any social problem.

"Don't know him that well but will do. I'll try to tell him some moves."

"Do more than that. Show him. Look, there's the Watershed Chair. What's he doing here, Henry? Foolish of him to come here today."

"He needs to know what the local people are saying, to get some sense of public opinion. And you have a five o'clock appointment with him."

"Good. He's talking to the lumberjack and the mooning woman. I'd like to hear that conversation. There they go... they are getting organized. My God, the Bobbsey twins are down there. If the cops see them they'll be sure we are deliberately starting a- a - a riot or something. Henry, you didn't put them up to anything, did you? No, of course not. Sorry. Come on Henry, let's get the Ferrets out of there and take another look at the spill. I want to see what it looks like now that whatever was spilled has had time to work."

∞

"What in the hell are you two doing here? Any funny stuff and I'll have you shoveling horse shit before you can whistle."

Barney and Red beamed at Jobert. Said Barney, "Hey, Mr. Jobert, we know our orders. Just here to see the fun is all."

Red added, “Yeah, an’ maybe see if there’s any available broads.”

“You especially stay away from these women. Look in the local bars.”

“We done that; barmaid froze us solid. Hey, Mr. Drysdale, we got some news.”

“Ah, obtained by legitimate means I hope,” said Jobert.

“Mr. Jobert, would we do somethin’ not legit’? That’s not nice. Anyway, we run inta that janitor inna local dive. Had a few beers with him. Says he left the door open sometimes on the storeroom. Little more booze, he says a guy by name Graltz or Glatz or Glanz sorta talked him inta it. Guy name a Mirav was in there sometimes. An’ he seen Glatz in a fight -uh- quarrel with an environment freak older guy. We took the janitor home; he talked more; admitted he opened the valve and gutters last year. Glatz saw him. Said Gratz blackmailed him to leave door open. Wanted ta do it anyway.”

Jobert said, “You guys do get results. Mirav ..oh Mirave. Hmmm. Where’s the janitor now?”

“Well that’s funny. Went out and talked to him next day, real cozy like, about he oughta get a better job. We went back later inna day. Imagine! he scrammed with all his stuff.”

“Did you rough him up?” Jobert was scowling.

“Mr. Jobert! you tol’ us not to do that kinda thing; we don’t do anythin’ you say we shouldn’t. Jis’ talk to him.”

Drysdale asked, “Did you get any other information?”

“Yeah. Other people seen Glatz inna bar with the guy what was iced...uh...Kraft..uh ..the ecology guy in another scrap an’..real deep talk. We’re still workin’ onna memo- computer problem. You want we should go talk to Glatz? The local cops ain’t too friendly. An’ they’re investigatin’.”

“No. First. Get out of here before the cops get suspicious and before any kind of ruckus starts. Finish the memo problem. Go back to Chicago. You solved one problem for us, one traitor down. Now for Glatz. No. I changed my mind. Find out where Glatz was on the night of the explosion. Don’t get in the way of the cops. Find out what they know about him first, if you can. Then, if he is in the clear, talk to him.”

“We’ll have a nice social talk, a few beers maybe.”

“No rough stuff, you hear!”

"Never. Wouldn't think a it."

"OK. Now get out of here! Henry, let's go to the spill site. Henry, that pair is too much for most people."

∞

"Henry, damn it Henry, it looks horrible. Death instead of life. And still dying."

It looked like a pad of death; bog birches with dark brown, crunched leaves, hanging, the mat grungy brown, with dead drooping flowers, rotting weasels and frogs staring into space. A quivering, shaking bird flopped about unable to grasp limbs, accenting the funereal feeling evoked by dead plants everywhere. The end of the world would look like this, not fire, not ice, just motionless, brown, brown, not even stirred by random breezes, a sight not mentioned when talking about short-lived herbicides and pesticides, depressing. True, it would in a short time be erased by decomposition, chemical reactions and then the explosion of new life. Still, it was for the time dispiriting, no vibrant greens, reactive shapes in the whispering morning, only black, brown, drooping lifelessness, staring eyes, dead. No joys of spring

"Henry, we must get this back to normal as quickly as possible. We have the bacteria to help us do that. I want permission to spray our bugs here as soon as possible. Go after Richter again, hard. Don't take no for an answer. Don't let anyone temporize. Call on me personally to talk to anyone at any level to get that permission. It will be the first test of our new technology. It will succeed."

"Yes sir, we've begun already. You can talk him into it too. You can talk personally to the Chair. I remind you, you have an appointment with him at 5 P.M."

"Good. I knew I could count on you, Henry. Let's get back to the demonstration."

∞

"You want to do it, Alice, go ahead but you will accomplish nothing."

"Oh, Tim, where did you get so negative?"

"Not negative, just realistic."

"Tim, tell me how do things get done?"

"When something forces them. Hello, Teddy. What are you doing here? You know Alice Jobert? And there's Dextra. Hi."

"Nice to meet you, Alice." Teddy turned to Dextra, "Hello, Dextra. Are you going into the demonstration? Mr. Jobert's up there with a pair of binoculars."

"Poo, who cares. He would think it funny." Dextra abruptly turned to Tim. "Tim, are you in the demonstration? If so, I'll join, too. It was so much fun going through the bog with you the other day. I found that hermit thrush nest. Had a piece of paper in it."

"Did it! Would you tell me where it is?" asked Alice.

"Yes," said abruptly.

Alice, bemused by Dextra's reaction, turned to Teddy, and said, "You are the inventor?"

Tim interrupted, "Me in a demonstration! No! Back to our discussion. Things get done not by demonstrations alone or even mainly, Alice. There are as many different motives and self interests as there are demonstrators. I grant you there are more altruisms on the line than there are in the company. But whose interest is served? How much reasoning preceded the demo? Long ago I was a demonstrator on an environmental issue but the screamers and paraders took over and I began to feel like an idiot. I vowed not to do that again. Then I began to write letters, to testify, to vote, but again I began to question- to what purpose? Why do it? Don't you see you are assuming there is progress? There isn't. You are raising a ruckus where nothing can be gained. Don't you see the country- the whole world- is slowly but surely on a downward path. Oh, I know lots of people have a better so-called standard of living. That won't last. Things go the way they want to go. No one is really leading or directing. Things don't really get better, except for pain or food or freedom, they just change. So best to relax, do your own art or bird watching as long as it is possible, be a friend to everyone you can. Don't pretend there will be progress. I concluded that a long time ago. Ever since, I've got along fine, enjoyed myself, have more friends, help people out. That's the way I feel and I've seen nothing to convince me otherwise."

"Oh come on. We can improve society," Teddy disputed.

Dextra spoke up, "Improved how?"

Tim interjected, "No, no you can't. Trying to change society is like pushing a cart with one stuck wheel. You never know where it's going."

Alice said, "That's democracy, always untidy. Why do you insist that things be tied up in a neat bundle?"

Dextra moved closer to Tim and said, "No. Tim is right. Look at history."

Teddy noticed Dextra's move and decided to get her attention. He shook his head and said, "I can't agree with that. The thoughtful people will win out. Demonstrations won't do it but yes may help do it. It just takes time."

"Wonderful! Another country heard from. OK, Teddy, it is Teddy? -tell us," demanded Alice.

"Oh. No. I'll- go ahead Tim," said Teddy.

"No you don't. Give us your argument," said Alice.

Teddy said, "Well. That cart you can't direct, with enough different people pushing it, can be directed. A demonstration, by itself, may have no effect but combined with other events can contribute a mite to gaining the goal. It is a familiar engineering problem. And I am an engineer."

Dextra spoke in a bored voice, "Interesting." She was wearing a shimmering silk figured blouse, a black and white herringbone tweed skirt, lipstick, green scarf in her hair pulled back in a bun. There was something schizophrenic about her appearance and she exuded an air of yearning and forlorn failure.

Alice turned to Dextra and asked, "You went through the bog with Tim?"

Tim interrupted, "Yes, Alice, I showed Dextra some of the birds and plants of the bog while we looked for evidence from the explosion. Sorry, Alice, but I won't demonstrate. Uh, I have to run. Ed is here. I want to talk with him. See all of you later. 'Bye Teddy. 'Bye all. Let's continue the argument some other day."

"I'm going to wander around the crowd. Want to come along, Dextra?" asked Teddy.

"No. I will go to the lab," said Dextra, voice dreary.

∞

"Why are you people comin' up here picketin'? Ain't none of your business. Go back and picket somebody in the city."

"Listen, we are working for you. Do you have any idea what horrible experiments are going on in there? More important, the things going on in Jobert Industries around the country. How dangerous they are?" said Gypsy.

"Oh yah. We can take care of ourselves. Everybody told us there was nothing dangerous here. Ain't nothin' happened. Say, lissen, I'm Olie Mattson. What's your name?"

"Gypsy Lie."

"Good name. An' a lot of us with jobs. What's wrong with that?"

"You don't understand what's going on."

"Don't we. Lissen us Savages mostly read more books'n you do. Long winters here. Ain't but two things to do, one of 'em readin'. You look in most cabins here you find lots a books. So we ain't so dumb. We know what goes on."

"So you read... but what? And what is the second thing?"

"Thought you wooden ask. I'm Olie Mattson an' I judge by lookin' at you, you might be pretty good at the second. Now if you stop this picketin' we could go to my cabin…"

Gypsy grimaced and started walking around the lumberjack, inspecting him. She said, "I wonder if the moose around here are pure-bred. Maybe your father caught up with some desperately fleeing Miss Moose. Olie Moose. Sounds right. But then there's the Miss Mouse. You could be Olie Mouse. … you are disgusting. Bye, bye Mousie. There's Alice and that Chair thing. Yoo- hoo, Alice."

"Gypsy, that's a real nice name. Ah hell, don't hurt to try. Never tell about these kinda people."

∞

"Alice, I can call you Alice? I have to ask an odd question. Do you like your demonstrators, your cohorts, so to speak?" asked Richter.

"Why shouldn't she? They're environment people," said Gypsy.

Alice looked doubtful, "Gypsy, it's a good question. It's funny you ask; I like the Savages much more. They seem more genuine.

I guess it's that ideology drives my people. They've been calling my father a murderer. That's nonsense, Gypsy."

Richter said, "There's Olie Mattson. Excuse me."

"I know that... but here's Alex. Let's ask him about that. Alex, why are our people shouting that Alice's father is a murderer? You know that can't be true."

"No, I don't. And it helps to stir people up, true or not. Gypsy, Alice, we have to get the animal rights people screaming, the tree rights people hollering, the blood sports people shouting, the vegetarians- whatever- everybody in action. Did Jobert plot the accident so that he could test his bacteria's capacity to destroy the pesticides, etc? We don't know but we know for sure we don't need more politics, we need action. So we get more politics. One cracked head is worth any logical argument. And shouts like that can move people."

"I still don't like false accusations against my father."

"Alice, you must get rid of these silly bourgeois inhibitions. If a lie will help the cause, we use it. If we go over the damn fence, it'll give the cops some work, get us in the news where we can accomplish something. I got a quote for the TV people all ready. If we got to the cages, we could release the animals;a picture of that would be worth everything. And I saw you talk to the Watershed Chair; we should never have let that office develop. Listen, people, that Watershed Chair is an ally of the moneybags. And that's the problem. He helps them squeeze the people."

"Oh, come on!" Alice was disgusted. "And what animals?"

"If he wasn't their boy, would he have let this research lab come up here?" asked Alex.

Alice refused the argument, "But that's the law. They can move out here if they pay the costs for bringing an equivalent area back to a natural looking wild area."

"Yes, that is the law, their law, their legislators. If some poor person wants to move here, they have to pay too. Just as much as the rich. For a company like Jobert's, this money is chicken feed."

"Mister, people around here get jobs, not people from some place else." Olie was back.

"Who's this guy? Buzz off." Olie bunched a fist. "Sorry. Forget it. Sorry I said that. Didn't mean it. Alice, want me to handle this thing? I've done so many of these I could do them in my sleep now. Good news, there`s the sheriff. Everybody up and parading; the newspaper people can't be far behind."

"He's Olie and he's right. There are more jobs."

"Alice, Alice, you still haven't shaken loose from your old man. Sure there are jobs but think how much higher wages would be if this lab was in the cities. Jobert is out here for cheap labor."

"Don't you dare say I'm under my Dad's thumb. Anyway, they aren't making money. If something looks like working, it will be leased out."

"Yes, to a plutocratic friend in one of Jobert's industries.. Their wages here are low, benefits nonexistent. What's good about that?" said Alex. "Well, look at that. There they are, our own helpers, the cops, here now."

∞

"Tell me again, Chief, why I have to handle these people with kid gloves."

"Because these are citizens exercising their rights. When they do something illegal, we haul 'em away. We don't want any broken bones or heads, go by the law. Only way to do it."

A demonstration presents a puzzle to the observer. The faces vary from vacant to inscrutable, from simpering to grim, from thoughtful to thoughtless. If the face is a true mirror of the mind, and it is in part, then every environmental motley contains simpletons and sages. A problem for the parader, one seldom raised or solved, is to find whether he is being used. The driving and often woolly ideas and strong emotions of the woman carrying the 'Defend Animals' sign are very different from those of the more businesslike woman carrying the 'No Poisons in the Environment', or from the man with the 'Don't Fool With Mother Nature'. Some co-opting is inevitable, an accident and necessary. Ten people, ten opinions. But co-opting is a genteel word for motivational thievery. The co-opter, often a politician, is a subversive, a liar, who steals other peoples' motives for his own end. Still, the observer would like to know that the paraders are true to the cause for which they parade. How often may that be the case?

"What in the devil are we doing so far from civilization?"

"Alex wanted us to come. For poor Gilbert. Says it's a chance to get a shot at Jobert Industries, something we haven't been able to do in Chicago."

"Yeah, and I feel loyal to Alice, she wanted this demonstration. Damn! that fly bit the hell out of me! I've given more blood to these mosquitoes than I ever have to the blood bank. I've never seen so many mosquitoes; the damn flies don't even move away when I swing at 'em. This is a hellhole; a cruddy part of the world, if you ask me. People who live here must be animals."

"So you think we are animals," said a burly local.

"I wasn't talking to you."

"Maybe, but I was listening. What the hell are you outsiders doing up here?"

"Picketing for the good of you people."

The local eyed the woman. Why don't these foreigners go back where they belong? If there was going to be picketing, his union would do it, not this bunch of airy-fairy freaks.

The woman swatted and snarled, "damn bugs". Her fellow picket swung companionably at the bugs and hit the local instead. He swung, knocking down the picket who sat on the ground dazed, shaking his head. She hit the local with her picket sign; he cocked a hairy, muscular arm preparing to knock her to kingdom come, then thought better of it. She sensing an advantage, swinging the sign again and again, backing up the local step by step. A local woman, seeing the unfair situation, moved to seize the woman's sign and the scuffle started. A fellow picket moved on the backing man to meet a solid fist. A cop moved in, also to encounter an accidental swinging hand, to which he responded with a stick to the stomach of the picketing woman.

"There's a scuffle. Get 'em. Follow the rules. Drag 'em gently. Come on, act like the police you are, let's go."

∞

Alex grinned from ear to ear and said, "Couldn't have arranged it better. Hurray for blackflies. Who says there is no God's purpose in flies. They're put here for us organizers. There are going to be some great news stories and TV pictures."

"They were just swatting blackflies."

"Right. Thank God for the flies. They made our day. Brutality by the police in favor of Jobert Industries, just right. Couldn't be better. Priceless."

"Who the hell is that going over the fence?" asked Gypsy.

"Some of my bunch. They want to go to jail."

"Don't those signs contradict each other?"

"So who's consistent?"

Police whistles sounded; cops waded in, arresting pickets and locals alike, hauling them away to be charged and released.

"We were just swatting blackflies. We didn't do anything."

"Have to haul you in. Doesn't matter why the scrap started, just that it did."

In the milling throng was a man who, summering in the area, wanted to protest the new airport being constructed near his home in a Chicago suburb. It would be right under the takeoff path. An intermittent shrieking roar would be his baby's lullaby. He believed in progress, even thought new airports were needed but wanted them somewhere else. He was arrested.

Nearby a young woman dressed in garish shirt and shorts was carrying a sign, 'Animals Have Rights. Stop The Torture'. She was having trouble shouting due to a case of laryngitis.

"I don't know what's doing it. Just don't feel well. Doctor couldn't tell me. These quacks are useless. Terrible what they're doing to mice in there. Putting bacteria in them. We must stop that."

She was arrested.

∞

"You're the Watershed Chair."

"Right. Hugh Richter at your service. Saw you before. You are Gypsy ...?"

"Lie. I'm demonstrating. Here to help the Jobert Lab, aren't you? Hi, Diana."

"No, no. I am no one's advocate. I'm just a spectator here. Glad to meet you Diana."

"Well, then support us. He's polluting this bog and doing damage to the environment all over the U.S. Jobert deliberately dumped those chemicals in the bog so he would have a place to test his genetic bacteria. Terrible danger to everybody."

"If you think that, send me a letter detailing what you know. I'll consider it and also send it to the Department of the Environment. I can only act on what is going on in this Watershed. The input to our computers from the PCA and the DNR and other bodies and my observations and conversations determine my technical decisions."

Diana said, "He mistreats animals; they have rights too. And he does dangerous experiments, pollutes, dumps and builds on this forest land. If you help us, we can drive him out of this area."

"That I can't do. I can only react if he damages the environment. Anything else is not my business. And I must have data to prove it. My charge is to review technical data and make decisions as to whether the Watershed is deteriorating or improving. Then I recommend to the other bodies procedures which can assure that deterioration does not occur."

Alex decided to push the confrontation. "Aw, bolony, you're just another toady of the power structure, of industry and the old boys. Another tinpot dictator, a capitalist monster."

"No. You're Alex, aren't you? I have heard about you. I can be removed from my job if the water, air, land of this watershed deteriorate or if the governor or the legislature together decide that I am exceeding my prerogatives or am morally degenerate or something similar. And the National Chairman can pick a new person at the end of ten years. Really, I live and die by the computer and the quality of the information stored in it. I may do nothing politically. Actually, I am here to meet with Jobert, a couple of locals, and especially a lumberjack named Olie Mattson...haven't been able to catch him."

Gypsy interjected, "He was here...just propositioned me. I don't believe it will work. What you decide will be just politics. Oh God, here comes your man, that moose again."

Diana said, "He's a hunter just like Jobert. Think of what the hunters do to poor deer and birds every year. They shoot and hurt animals which drag around in pain bleeding."

"You! back again." Gypsy was scornful.

"O-oh yaah. Sure. Hi, Gypsy. Thought you might change your mind. My cabin is nice and comfortable. Not so hot there as here. You'd like it. Diana, you got any idea how animals die out there? They get et up by ticks and mosquitoes in the summer.

Sometimes they lose so much blood they die. Ain't always that way but can happen. An' been huntin' since time began."

Diana said, "That's because you're uncivilized like Jobert. I hear he comes up here to hunt grouse. That shows, Alice, I'm sorry, but I heard that your father hunts; he is still brutal, a savage."

"Oh yaah, jist like us. Ever eat a grouse? Best kinda bird."

"No. and I wouldn't." answered Diana.

"What do you eat?"

"If it's any of your business, I'm a vegetarian," said Diana.

"Wisht we had more time jist to sit and talk inna friendly way. I agree it's terrible if they use animals to test their poisons on."

"Well! Yes, indeed. But they have no consciences. They only care about money. Look at that sign 'Business Plutocrats Torture Animals'.

"Still, Diana, you don't know what happens to deer up here if we didn't hunt 'em. They'd starve in winter. Or get killed by the wolves. 'And they'd wreck the woods with their browsing. Ever see an overbrowsed woods? Deer stretchin' as high on their hind legs as they can get after food. Not eating meat don't solve nothin'. You the Chair? I'm Olie Mattson who called you. Look, I found a place way back inna woods on an old loggin' road where somebody dumped a lotta steel drums and other stuff. It's in about five miles and you gotta walk part way."

"Let's go."

"I want to go along," said Gypsy.

"Great! Afterwards, we go to my cabin and talk over huntin' and all this other stuff. Promise not to try nothin'."

"You hear that, Mr. Richter? He's like a dog in heat. Here's Alice. Alice, can this guy be trusted?"

"With what? Olie is a nice guy."

"He told me he reads books. OK, I want to see those books. I'm going to take a book off your shelf, that's if there are books, and YOU are going to tell about what's in the book. If you can't tell me, you have to join the pickets here and shout 'Down with Jobert'."

"An' if I tell you what's in the book?"

"Don't get any ideas, Buster. You make a false move, you will sing soprano. My little woods knife can do the job."

"Let's go. First to the road to the dump with Mr. Richter. Ain't far. Be there in no time in my pickup. Then a hike."

"Go along, Gypsy; Olie has a good reputation," said Alice.

∞

"Alice, was that a good idea?"

"He won't rape her if that's what you think. He is sure to proposition her though. Sometimes gets a yes. Must be lonely back there in the woods."

"Who would want him?"

"Oh, he's not unattractive. Reads, has a sense of humor. The only problem is that you have to live out in the bogs. Who knows? Gypsy could be suitable to Olie and maybe vice versa. Could be a match made in the bogs."

∞

"You're that Jobert loaded to the gills with money, ain't ya? I can see all of 'em in there kissin' your ass. Maybe not now what with you killin' a guy. Anybody with your dough get away with that."

"Sir, I didn't kill anybody and my people in there are an independent bunch. Just like these people out here."

"Don't give me that. Can buy any of them. Look, I don't mean to insult you. Any jobs now to that plant of yours?"

"Just present yourself at the employment office. I don't know what's needed. And I don't interfere. Where'd you get that stuff about me killing somebody?"

"Heard that one guy in the crowd saying it, one that said to go over the fence."

Chapter 10 Whodunit and Dextra at bottom

"Mr. Jobert, that's a long haul in here. Eric there lost ten pounds easy. Where'd you get that jailbird down at the gate?"

"Spotted that, eh. He has a record, alright. Murder. My man now. I vouch for him. Won't cause you any problems. Enjoy the walk, Eric? A good hunting walk."

"Too far. I like to hunt from the car."

Marko sneered, "He wanted to see how the rich live."

"Hope you find it worthwhile, Eric."

Eric said, "Looks real good. Sorta like my cabin. More rooms. Windows are better."

"Yeah and Eric built it himself which means it is sure to fall down any day," said Marko.

Sheriff Jager said, "That lag enjoyed stopping us; so we gave him a hard time. Made him spread 'em, put his hands on the car. He only had the shotgun in the shack. Obeyed in good style."

Jobert was amused. These experienced policemen, he thought, had permanent expressions of suspicion as though there were a bad smell about; anyone is suspect. Built into their reactions was an instant assessing of any new encounter and especially a consequent cynical instant reaction to the felon. It is much like a dog's reaction to a cat. They know this is the quarry.

"Well, gentlemen, you didn't do that long walk for pleasure. What can I do for you?"

"Mr. Jobert, I didn't appreciate your taking off to Chicago just when I needed some questions answered. I like to talk to the head if I can but I had to talk to Drysdale. Next time clear with me. Understand!" Jobert nodded. "OK. We thought it might be useful to review our findings on the explosion with you. And, of course, ask a few questions. Now let's see...Drysdale tells me that you, Felix uh Bountz and him are out there in the middle of the bog, a storm coming up- which sounds a little insane to me- Drysdale and Bountz go back toward the building running from the rain; you take shelter under an overhang. It's pouring. Drysdale and that Felix went in, leaving you alone. Marko and Eric there, couple days later, find a blasting machine, a real antique, that's an ignition box, on the other side of the bog, wires running toward your Hazardous Waste Storage Room. Figure the dynamite was in there and Kraft. My Sherlocks think maybe you saw the wires, made a quick guess, ran out from under the shelter to the ignition box, rammed in the plunger to set off the dynamite and ran back in time to be escorted inside by Bountz."

"I would have to do that within fifteen minutes. I'll give $5000 to the man who can do that."

Sheriff Jager grinned, "Hear that, Eric. You're on, Mr. Jobert." Jager walked to the window, looked up. "Good August storm coming up. Going to rain hard tonight they say. We'll borrow your flashlight. At midnight Eric can earn himself a quick five thousand. You want to come along, Mr. Jobert?"

"No. I'll take your word he did it."

"Now wait a minute. I was gassin'. You try to run in there, you could go right through the mat. Nobody can run across a surface like that. You'd fall every few steps. An' wouldn't even be time to go around."

"Five thousand in sight and, ah, we stop the bull. So! Mr. Jobert could not have dashed out on to the mat, pressed the plunger, and returned to get under the umbrella of that guy- Felix, is it?"

"Still. Mr. Jobert don't hafta run; he coulda connected the wires just outside the building," said Eric."Or that Felix."

"Brilliant. And maybe got himself killed, all that lightening. And where's the charge?" said Marko.

"Plunger was down when we found it. Don't know would the charge last. Maybe somebody pretty dumb there," said Eric.

Jager laughed., "Nonsense. There are no capacitors would store a charge in the box. Wires connected there, plunger down somehow, Kraft connects the wires at his end and, boom, he's a memory. No. Experts tell me juice only produced if there is a circuit. Enough sleuthing from you, Sherlock. We're left with two possibilities, Mr. Jobert; one, lightning, two, somebody shoved the plunger down. Accident or murder. Anyway call and check up with the bomb squad in the city; they'll know all about it. If so, the question is who pushed the plunger and when?"

Jobert said, "There is another possibility. There was a lot of charge around that night. Drysdale said he thought my hair was glowing and his and Felix's-that's Felix Bountz our systems man-looked that way too. Maybe when Kraft connected the wires, his own body supplied the necessary charge."

"Ah, how you going to show something like that could happen?"

"Marko, it's possible. We'll have to consult an expert. Anyway, all that is nonsense. Mr. Jobert would have to put the dynamite in the room, put the wires through the door across the swamp to the blasting box. He came up here the day before. We know where he was that day and night. He couldn't have done the job. He'd have had to get the key to the room. Night watchman says the janitor had the key. And would have had to time the explosion with a thunder clap. Obvious nonsense. Still, why would anyone sane be out on a night like that?"

"Would be exciting don't you think? Have you considered the possibility that Mr. Drysdale or Felix Bountz could have somehow done it from inside?" said Jobert. He was caught up in the sleuthing.

"Yeah. Night watchman told us he let them into the main office. Says they stayed there and they didn't have the key to the Toxics Room; janitor had it."

"There. They're off the hook," said Jobert.

"Some one else coulda done it," said Eric. "I seen that Dextra Chirali inna tavern with Kraft and your daughter, Alice. A guy from your lab, Mr. Jobert, looks like a prune, was there, too."

"Glatz, our accountant," said Jobert.

"Eric, what were you doing there?" asked the Sheriff.

"Just havin' a few beers."

"Eric's love was there-that Dexter-he was after that broad. Eric still wants ta get some brains inna family."

"Ah, shut up."

"One further question. Mr. Jobert, do you have any idea where the dynamite came from?"

"No, can't say I do."

"Just thought it might have come from one of your own factories for use in some way in your work here."

"No such use. I don't see how. The Jochem plant in Chicago maintains a store of dynamite. No outsider could get at it," said Jobert.

"Would you arrange for us to send some detectives in there?"

"Yes, I will do that. But that's a non-starter."

"Still, we want to do it. The FBI is trying to run down the source, too."

"Very well."

"One more possibility; he could have blown himself up deliberately."

"Never. Not Kraft," said Jobert. "Sheriff, there's a piece of information our Security has come up with. You know about the spill a year ago? The janitor, Quist I think was the name, who cleaned the Hazardous Waste Storage Room was seen in a tavern with Glatz last year. He was drunk and told Glatz that he opened the valve that dumped the stuff in the first spill. My Ferrets say Glatz blackmailed him-he was..is an unhappy, maybe unbalanced man-into leaving the door to the Hazardous Waste Storage Room open in the weeks before the explosion. Said he needed some of the chemicals for his garden."

"So, the janitor, Quist, or this Glatz could have placed the dynamite. Who brought the dynamite to them? Kraft? Maybe you, Mr. Jobert, or maybe your daughter. Hm. You do hire some strange types, Mr. Jobert. Your Security, those two hoods Eric ID'd? Yeah I know, that's your business. Ours to keep an eye on them. We want to talk to that janitor, Glatz, and your daughter. And the Ferrets. Do you have the janitor's address?"

"I'm sorry to say my men say he has disappeared."

"We insist on talking to your men."

"They're back in the hotel in town."

"Mr. Jobert, I hope your men didn't strong-arm this guy. We don't appreciate that kind of thing up here and we even more don't like companies to interfere in police matters."

"Their instructions were to find out who was sending memos and letters from the plant. They do find out other things. They tell me Glatz was seen to drive toward the lab on the night of the explosion. But just the direction from near his house. I assure you my men did no strong-arming."

"Near his house; not much help. Wouldn't have to. Those two hoods look at anybody, they talk and scram," said Eric.

"Thank you for your cooperation, Mr. Jobert. We'll let you know what we find."

"Good. Walk slowly and enjoy the air out there."

"An' the blackflies."

"Almost none left now."

∞

"Welcome, Henry. Lovely walk, eh? Pass the cops on the way?"

"Yes, I did. They looked at me like I just robbed a bank. Edmund, who was that thug glaring at me at the gate?"

"Oh, he keeps track of people for me. Relax a bit, Henry. Ed's the name."

"Alright, ah Edmund. Here's something of interest. I found the original of the memo sent to the papers."

Memo to Research staff

With the recent successes in our pesticide bacteria research, we must prepare for field testing. This is urgent; we need to produce something that will have the potential of a profit, something for the Board of Directors. Therefore, do anything, everything necessary to get ready for field tests. Find a good site, any site. Report to me when ready.

"That's the memo. Edmund, I wrote it in a hurry. It's certainly not incriminating. It doesn't imply a deliberate spill at all. I suppose I should have been more careful in this day of any and all possible lawsuits and legal actions."

"Ah, forget it. The only thing of interest is who sent it to the paper and the demonstrators and the Watershed Chair. We have any clues?"

"Yes, I'm sorry to say. Those, ah, Security people have found an erased copy of the memo sitting in the desk computer of Curtis Glatz of our accounts department. I had thought he was just a chronic complainer, but they also found out that he had met with Kraft and, oddly enough, Dextra Chirali in the local tavern. This doesn't prove that he passed it on. Should we have that pair talk to Glatz about it? That one security man-what is he called- Red Belt- Edmund, I have to say it; he is one of the most unsavory people I have ever encountered. He said Dextra came in alone so he invited her over with him and Glatz; he thought maybe he could, to quote him, 'make time with her'. Imagine that! Naturally, she didn't accede to his blandishments. When he goes near one of the women at the lab you can see them curdle. The one called Barney said Chirali looked like she was lost. Totally out of place. Could she have been in the plot? An effect of her problems?"

"Never. Still, I wonder what she heard. Ask Felix to talk to her about it. What was Dextra doing in that dive? Glatz! I wonder what drives him. OK, let's sic the Twins on him. About the memos etc. Tell them again to steer clear of the cops. They have to find out how that dynamite got in the building and when. We must wait for that information. Then you can CAN Glatz after you talk to him. Give him a rough session. Whether or not the police come up with solid evidence, the best thing we can do is get rid of the guy."

"I've also brought a letter from Guy Barnaby. He wants you to come to Washington for a discussion of the proposed new plant in that small town, what was the name? Mitton? It looks like you will be turned down; the waste stream would be too much for the sewage plant there."

"No! I've been in Washington too often."

"I think it advisable, Edmund. Security in Chicago is reporting some interesting news. Appears that our janitor has been involved in shenanigans before. He met with Kraft at a rally at the University."

"Ah, of course. Another of Kraft's plots. Well, the janitor has disappeared. So we can forget him. If he wasn't involved in Kraft's death."

Jobert gazed in wonder, "Somebody coming up the lane. Whew. Dextra tipping to the starboard. What in the world? Now she's trying to squat, whoops, over, looking at something. Up- yes up- up- ah made it."

"Really, this is too much. Our top researcher."

"Wait. Hello, Dextra, come in, come in. Well, this is a surprise! What brings you way back here? That's a long hike."

Drysdale attempted to speak lightly, "Dextra, we have been having a long discussion about where we go from here. The research has been going very well; and as you know, we are on the verge of production of our packets but mass culture of the hydrogen bacteria is still giving troubles."

"Felix or Teddy…will…solve that problem. E'mun'… I come to visit you."

Drysdale wasn't having it, "More important, the Board is getting restive about costs and wants us to go after government help. We are opposed by many Board members."

"Jus' give lab people a little time."

"Enough, Henry. Good. Henry and I are just about to have coffee. Can I get you a cup?"

"Uh huuh... I sit down."

Dextra sort of swayed herself, collapsing onto a couch. She looked owl-eyed at Henry and said, "Think I drink too much, Misser Drsdle."

"Indeed."

"Yes. Always try too hard. Work too much, try make friends, fail, boy frien's none. I am failure. Evythin' going wrong. Come talk to Edmund. He is… is wise. Tell me why I fail. Why men not like me, why I social failure."

"That better wait until you are sober," said Drysdale.

"No. When sober…can't ask."

"Here's your coffee. On the end table," said Jobert.

Dextra tried to pull, to slide on the couch only to fall over. She grasped the end of the couch and pulled herself over, picked up the coffee cup, spilled some, sipped and dropped the cup on the floor.

"I sorry. Clumsy, clumsy in evethin."

"Dextra, how much booze have you had?" asked Jobert.

"Not.. not much. Few martines. Not use, not used to drink. Tired, up all night. First bar, then home, then here."

"Dextra, you are at bottom, aren't you?"

"Yes."

"Well, come on, you've had enough booze. You're going to bed. You can sleep in the spare room. OK, OK, I've got you. Just lean on me. Through the door. Good."

"Oh, you could be my man, E'mun'."

"I doubt it. I'll tuck you in. Go on. Couple of aspirins. That's it; down the hatch. Good."

"Want to talk."

"In the morning."

"E'mun', …you like to share my blankets?"

"Hmm. Go to sleep, Dextra. The world will be brighter in the morning. I'll close the door. Henry, did you hear that?"

"What?"

"Dextra asked whether I would like to share her blankets. That was a cry for help! She's really down. We've got to do something."

"Drunkenness disgusts me. Wasn't Felix going to use his, uh,.disgusting, uh, sexual, uh social knowledge to take care of the problem?"

"There hasn't been enough time. She is acting more drunk than she is; a cover so she could say some of those things. Lordy. I don't want to dip into people's lives but what else can we do? That 'share her blankets' bit suggests that her love could be fungible. Tim is already avoiding her, and I don't know what else he can do under the circumstances. He can't help. On the other hand, Teddy is already interested. Tim has been trying to help Teddy Sourtis to romance her but evidently without luck so far. Believe me this is a life and death operation. She is an endangered species."

"Oh, surely not. You don't believe that, do you?"

"Yes, I do. Teddy Sourtis is actually an interesting and attractive fellow. He ought to interest her."

Drysdale said, "Very able, too."

"But not in what counts now. But then I don't know what it is that draws Dextra to Tim. It's an attraction that doesn't seem reasonable. We saw Teddy at the demonstration with Tim, Alice, and Dextra and he seemed to fit right in. He's a quiet type, something like Tim, but he does hope to accomplish something. I would think that would be a plus with Dextra. Apparently not."

"May I make a suggestion?"

"Yes."

"Chirali is scheduled to talk at an Industrial Genetics Society convention in Washington. The local Chair suggested you go talk to Barnaby, the Undersecretary for this area. You have an invitation. Go and take Teddy along."

"Oh God, again to Washington. You are determined to get me there, aren't you?. I'd rather stay here, but I'll go. Dextra is important. Henry, that is a good idea. Tomorrow I'll talk to Richter."

"Ed er Edmund I'd better go now while there is enough light to see my way."

"I'll walk with you; I need the exercise. We don't often talk so informally do we, Henry?"

∞

"Tim! Thanks for calling back. Dextra is here at my cabin and drunk; she's a sad waif; she's taken a couple aspirin; she's sleeping right now."

"Ed, I'm trying to handle this. She's centered on me not because of me but because I was her first vision when she came out of her mind. First sights endure."

"She engulfed in thought up to now? Hmm. Tim, I've decided to take Dextra and Teddy Sourtis with me to Washington. Call Teddy for me. Maybe he has a paper to give."

"OK. He does. Ed, I doubt she's prepared to talk at that meeting."

"All the better. She'll have to do some hard work. Just the ticket."

"Take Felix too. He can be Teddy's coach."

"Good idea. OK. Call Felix and tell him we need his abilities. Tell him it's his duty. Teddy, I assume, is prepared to tell about his new injection machine. I have to talk to Barnaby anyway about who pays for the dumping and about costs of re-cycling. And about another plant we are trying to open in Mitton, Texas."

"Felix can teach Teddy how to kick her ankle."

"How's that again?"

"Yeah, you know. Girls mature faster than boys, so to get the boy's attention, they have to kick them. Works. Ought to work the other way. And Teddy's ready."

"I look forward to witnessing that training. Like to have you along but you'd be a hindrance."

"Happiness is staying in the woods."

∞

"Good morning, Dextra. Coffee and aspirin at your plate. Help yourself to rolls."

"Edmund, I must apologize. Oh, my head."

"Drink some coffee. Nothing to apologize for. We are going to Washington to see the Undersecretary."

"We? We are?"

"Yes. You have a paper to give. Get it ready."

"That paper is not ready, but yes, Edmund. Someone is coming up the trail."

"No. Damn. That's that septic tank guy. I invited him to come up here a year ago. Never get careless with invitations. Hello, Mr. Rikala. Good walk, eh?"

"Pikala. Too far for my game leg. Your septic tank need work?"

"Yes, I think so; think it froze last winter and it's leaking."

"I'll check it. First I gotta rest."

"Sit down; have a cup of coffee. Miss Chirali of our staff."

"Don't mind if I do. Glad ta meetcha."

"We were just discussing the way the new Watershed Chair and the Department of Environment work. Have a roll. They claim to operate on free market principles. They don't tell you what to do. They give you choices."

"Free choices, ha! What's that? County sanitarian tells me what to do."

"Oh yes, but don't you have more leeway?"

"Some. If there ain't soil I can't put in a septic tank. But it's better than it used to be. They let us think now. They let me do what I gotta do. That Richter changed his mind about me dumpin' septic tank pumpin's on that old dump. Says go ahead but put up sign sayin' it. PCA is goin' to monitor it. Wants me to keep track of whether the dump subsides or produces more gas. It's doin' that alright. Gotta bring out them water samples collected the way they say, every month. They don't pay me for the work. They do give me stuff to get samples in. Them big sanitary land fills'll last forever if they don't do somethin' like I'm doin'. They oughta spray sewage on 'em, soon drop down. Stuff comes outta the bottom, can put it on top again. When I was haulin' to Bijacic I almost overloaded their sewage plant and the creek. Richter said I could do that but woulda cost me more. My idea saved me a little money."

"So you did what you wanted to do and made more money and perhaps improved the environment," said Dextra.

"Yeah. I can do what costs more. Guess that makes me free-doin' what the Chair wanted me to do anyway!"

Jobert shrugged his shoulders, "There isn't any other kind of freedom, Mr. Pikala. It seems the new system shifts all the decision making to us, Mr. Pikala. And every decision is a moral decision and that's unbearable. Me, I feel like a bug wrapped by a spider in a million threads. Only I must construct the threads- my own winding sheet. Moral decisions were bad enough when you had to make them for yourself, your family and neighbors but God! for society too. Too much!"

"Yeah. Makes me sweat, too. I got a helper. He don't work, he don't eat. I gotta make money, I gotta dump one a the ways they let me. An' first I gotta take care of my family. Them government people have it easy. They test and measure and work up choices for me and see that I don't go off and do somethin' else. But I gotta keep us all afloat."

"Was it better when the government told you what to do? Then you could obey or find a way to obey some twist of the rules," said Jobert.

"That was the problem wasn't it, Edmund," said Dextra.

Pikala went back to the subject, "An' my idea was a good one. Don't make sense to concentrate things. Nature don't do that. You crap- excuse me, Miss Chirali, inna woods it's soon gone. Nature spreads things out, gets rid of 'em. Dump with sewage will get rid of things too. Good septic tank is better'n a sewage plant any day."

"Can't do that in cities."

"Yeah, but why run all that water through johns to the sewage plant to the river? Then they hunt for some place ta dump the sludge. Ought to be possible to have each house get rid of its own sewage- some kinda digester. Could use some of them bacteria I read you made, Mr. Jobert, in my dump. Speed things up, maybe get ridda some poisons which might last forever if we don't do that. Maybe you could inject water with your bacteria inna dump."

"Mr. Pikala, that's interesting. We could ask permission to join your little experiment. What do you say, Dextra?"

"It would be a good test of Teddy's injection machine. It could move across the surface injecting the bacteria packets. Especially where there is no oxygen it would speed up the decay process. We could put other bacteria where there is oxygen. We would have to sample to see what's there. Perhaps we could adapt the on-stream cleaning of toxics to the site."

Jobert asked, "Mr. Pikala, we are going to Washington to talk to the Department of Environment Undersecretary for this area about how things work in this new system. You have any suggestions for him?"

"No. Except keep rules down. We'll try to make things better. On'y need some leeway. We can sweat the problems, find out better ways. Ask 'em how we can do right for everybody. Tell 'em they ain't so smart. They can give us choices how to do things but them bureaucrats can't solve the problems."

"A society has to operate by laws, Mr. Pikala, and that implies a bureaucracy," said Dextra.

"Let them whatcha-ma-call-its Solons know, too."

"You joke, Mr.Pikala! By the time that collection of philosophical gasbags gets through even deciding what the problem is, I am out of business. This new system is their great achievement but it took them forever to arrive at it. There is a voice of reason in Washington but it is heard only after endless talk. Remarkable that they used the market to get to a good end. People are free."

"Yeah, well, people don't like ta be told what ta do but they do like ta be taken care of. They just want guarantees and get what they get. Them Commies told people what to do an' look what they got. Still ain't back to normal. Better this way."

Jobert smiled, "Don't you think each person ought to bear whatever costs he incurs? Or business, or any organization? Charity should be stoppable sometime."

"Yeah, my wife's brother he don't know that. He's sponged on us since we got married."

"People don't want to be the object of charity. They want to be independent, to rule their own lives," said Dextra.

Jobert disagreed, "Not from what I have seen. As Mr. Pikala just said they want to rule their own lives from within a caretaker system that guarantees their livelihood. They want to be free prisoners. Good for them but not for society."

"Thing that worries me is how them engineers and scientists, excuse me Miss Chirali, do somethin' smart but never see what happens down the road or if they do, think they know more'n us workin' people."

"You ask too much, Mr. Pikala. Nobody can say what a new-born baby will become," said Dextra.

"Yeah, but when it becomes a monster they oughta join the killin'. Well, I better stop this gassin' and check your septic tank. You on'y bein' here sometimes in winter, Mr. Jobert, it's likely, like you say, cracked. Can we go look? Need a shovel."

"Yes. Come along, Dextra. Every geneticist should get a look at a septic tank."

"Ain't that the truth."

∞

"Whew. Can work up a sweat inna hurry. You can see the crack. Could repair it but better just get a new tank. Though even the way it is, it will work. Little leakage here don't hurt. Will stink a little, on'y. People don't notice how smooth workin' it is until too many people use it. Then all of a sudden all crudded up."

"New tank. As now. People don't notice the environment until something isn't right or something they dumped or used comes back as something they don't like," said Jobert. "The environment as a septic tank! What a thought."

"People and homes as the polluters, Edmund?"

"When there are too many of them, yes," answered Jobert.

"Them bacteria do a real good job just so's you don't give 'em too much to do."

"Indians didn't do that. Made their mess, moved on, Mother Nature moved in and cleaned it up. Everything stays beautiful," said Jobert. "We can't do that now. We must take care of nature at least as well as Mr. Pikala takes care of this tank."

"Nature is more clever than we are," said Dextra.

"Can't say that ain't so."

"And nature is prompt. Mr. Pikala, you wouldn't believe how long we've waited patiently for the necessary permits for field testing our cleanup bacteria at the spill site. Time is enormously important to the test."

"I believe it. Had it happen to me."

"They say they must be certain field use isn't dangerous but our bacteria came from there! And we are held up by the Medical Genetics people. They are doing crucial experiments and are afraid we might screw things up."

"Nature is already organized," said Dextra.

"Mr. Pikala. Look it over. Give me your estimate. Get the work done sometime next summer or even this fall."

"OK, I drive a tractor in here? Gotta get that tank up that trail."

“Yes. It has been interesting to talk to you. Dextra will walk with you.”

∞

“Hello, hello Jobert here.”

“What kind of way is that to greet your wife, even on the telephone. Edmund, Alice is here. Something isn’t right. She is disturbed about something up there. Could she have had anything to do with that explosion in June?”

“No, Dear. It’s just that lousy love affair. She’ll come around.”

“Edmund, I want you out of those woods. You’ve done enough grouse hunting. Alice tracked down her brother; he’s in some kind of trouble in Turkey of all places.”

“He’s a grown man; he can take care of himself.”

“Don’t duck. Get back here. Charlie called; he wants you here too. Business problems. You’re away too much; your family needs you too.”

“October here is perfect. Shall I bring some grouse?”

“Not if you want to get in the front door. Good-bye.”

Was Alice involved?

Chapter 11 Washington

"Meetings! How many boring speakers can assemble in one place? Teddy, you were a star," said Jobert.

"Nonsense. They slept through the talk."

Felix protested, "Not all. That Brit' asked good questions. People can look asleep and be absorbing every word. There was a famous physicist who slept through talks to the dismay of the speakers and then asked the most disconcerting questions going right to the core of the topic. Somebody in your audience may have been doing the same. Boss, what does this joint cost?"

"Don't ask, Felix. Like it, Dextra?"

"It's alright," said in a tired voice.

"Ha. Dextra is used to absolute luxury," said Teddy.

"No, not," same dreary voice.

Felix said, "Teddy, let's treat the lady like a tramp. I mean the Hotel, not Dextra."

Teddy, "Why not Dextra?"

Their attempts to rouse Dextra were not succeeding. The bright remarks, the too vivacious repartee dragged with Dextra's depression. Jobert shifted the conversation.

"Gentlemen, look at that food and tell me you are going to treat this place as a tramp. How's the wine, Dextra?"

"Very good."

Felix nudged Teddy, noticed by Jobert. Teddy teased, "Pooh, if it was brown-bag plonk you'd say that."

"I might."

"Dextra, how's your dinner?" asked Teddy.

"It's alright."

"Sure, it's only veal, asparagus, funny potatoes and sauces. Dextra has had those before, haven't you, Dextra?"

"Teddy, why don't you shut up!" Dextra had been reached.

"Come, come, let's have civility. Those may be the ingredients but there's a first class chef here, I think you will agree. Saying it's only those things is like saying one of our packets is only a bag of bacteria. In fact, we have added a great deal as has the chef. Taste that salad dressing; it's got a real piquant flavor, doesn't it?"

"Boss, how would you go about calculating the cost of the products of a high priced chef like this one?"

"Felix, since when did you become mercenary?" asked Teddy.

Jobert interrupted, "No. It's an interesting question. Not much of this food is going to go to waste, so low garbage costs. Then he chose the best in the first place, so no waste there. He supervises a gang of cooks all well trained, so overall, a high priced chef and staff and kitchen with few additional costs. To really know how much cost to add to the kitchen product we need to compare this place to any greasy spoon. More grease, more waste, more trash scattered over the landscape which must be gathered up. So greasy spoons have a much higher added cost to the product. Formerly imposed on the public, I might add. Here less."

"So, high basic cost, low added cost, Boss?"

"Yes and vice-versa in the fast food joints."

"If forced to pay the costs of their trash they may go broke."

"Aha, Dextra is with us. And right as usual. Such costs are now being added to the basic price of products and are required. Felix and I are going to talk to Guy Barnaby about that and some other things. What are you and Teddy going to do?"

"I'm going to do the touristy thing. Go see all the monuments. Dextra is going with me," said Teddy. Dextra roused, eyed Teddy, tossed her head and sank back into her torpor.

She mumbled, "I am? Why?"

"You'd better Dextra, Felix and I have to get to an appointment. You go first to the Hirshhorn; the building is beautiful! Then the monuments. Last the Smithsonian. Last because when Dextra, and you Teddy, get in there you won't be able to tear yourselves away. Now! Who's going to pay the bill?"

"Boss, it isn't fair to strike terror to the hearts of us poor working class people when we have full stomachs."

"Ha, ha, ha. Mr. Jobert, you have a great sense of humor. I hope. I've got just enough cash to get Dextra around to a joint I've heard about over in Georgetown."

"You do? Who said we were going there," asked Dextra with some irritation.

"I think that calls for another bottle of wine, Boss," said Felix.

"A very good idea. Everybody must drink a toast to success."

"To what success?" asked Dextra.

"Ours," said Teddy.

"Yes, and to our achievements at the plant," said Jobert.

A young woman had approached the table, "Sorry to interrupt but I'm Mandy Boult, Mr. Barnaby's assistant. I am sorry to say he has been called away. He sends his abject apologies. He insisted I look you up. I am fully informed on the topics you wish to discuss. You could talk with me or make a new appointment."

Jobert answered, "Please sit down. Glass of wine? We'll talk first then maybe make an appointment. Now this is my systems expert, Felix Bountz. He may be some help in our discussions. We wanted to find out the status of our applications and, not incidentally, get a lot more information. Teddy, you and Dextra can tune out or, if you like, go touristing. Feel free. Miss Boult, could we meet with Mr. Barnaby later today?"

"I'm afraid not. He will be before a congressional committee all day. Believe me, I am fully conversant with your applications and can answer all questions."

"Very well. First, can that Texas Chair, Slocum was it?, his decision denying a permit for the Mitton plant, can it be overturned? We thought our proposal was a good one."

"No. Our experts say it would produce problems. So we can't overrule him. Everything said here is, by the way, confidential. Mr. Jobert, we have a set of alternative suggestions."

"Let's have them."

"To put your plant in Mitton would surely overload that community's sewage plant. So that's no go. An alternative suggestion- we have five- is to use the site, in the same watershed, to be found at Tyron."

"You joke. We looked at that site, dump. There had been a gas station there. It is now defunct but left leaking gas tanks and oil dumped everywhere. There was once a junkyard with everything from PCBs to creosote to lead lying all over the place. And a metal cleaning plant now closed. The ground is soaked with cleaning agents, all toxic. God knows what else. We wouldn't touch that place. Lawsuits, cleanup requirements and so on. Is there any pollutant that isn't already in or on the ground there?"

"Our PCA people asked the same question. It seems doubtful. But don't rule out the site until you hear our proposal. You must know that you can buy that land at a song. No one is interested in it. If you bought it, we would be willing to sign an agreement with you exempting you, the new owner, from extraordinary clean-up costs, providing that you, as part of your construction work there, build a series of holding ponds and swamps leading in an almost U-shaped arc down to the river. Your waste water would flow into the first holding pond and gradually flow through a series of cattail swamps."

"There would be redwing blackbirds then," said Dextra.

Jobert looked quizzically at Dextra. She had absorbed some natural history from Tim. Teddy looked and wondered if Felix's advice would work. The effect of Tim was still apparent. Felix cocked an eyebrow.

"Teddy, with that thought, we must go," said Dextra, "before we are totally bored."

Teddy was up immediately. They left. That Dextra had initiated their departure surprised Jobert. He and Felix watched them going, hoping things would work out.

Felix spoke to Jobert, "My plan is fool proof; it will work," and changed the subject, "Confidentially, what are you doing tonight, Mandy? I can call you Mandy, can't I? Always liked that name."

That simple question instantly changed the atmosphere of the dinner table. Mandy shifted her position, seeing this man more easily, keeping track of his body movements and expressions. She unconsciously smoothed her hair and adjusted her blouse and skirt to a possibly more attractive arrangement. Jobert also turned a bit to see his lieutenant, the better to keep an eye on whatever it was that he was up to. His mental set now included not just the business at hand but also Felix's ploy whatever it was. A touch of humor and irritation and resignation played on his face. Felix had already changed his social gears and was centered on the attractive assistant. Felix was also aware of his Boss and his reaction to himself, to Mandy and hers to his Boss and both to him. Felix's proposal was like a wild card in poker, fraught with unanticipatible consequences. At play were multiple potential responses. All three were now alert for anticipated but unknown consequences. Being social may be the most complicated thing in the universe.

Jobert spoke abruptly, “Felix, hold the courtship until we’ve finished our business.”

“Courtship?” asked Mandy. She gave Felix a wry look.

Felix smiled back and said, “Yeah, OK but I need to know about tonight.”

“Felix! Later!”

“Oh, I don’t mind. We can talk afterwards about embassy hopping.”

“Good way to start.”

“Fine. Could we get back to business,” said with asperity by Jobert.

“Of course, Mr. Jobert. First we would want remediation- you could use your own bacteria- and some plants that can glom onto metals. But you know all about that. To continue: we are interested in the capacity of a series of such constructed swamps to clean out not just your pollutants but also those from the old contaminated soil. You would have to bulldoze out these areas on the contour, line them with clay, cover the clay with the contaminated soil now mixed with good soil and mulch from the city leaf dump. Then you would have to plant cattails and other swamp plants, in effect establish a new aesthetically pleasing landscape for your building and that part of the city. The flow will end at a weir emptying into the river. Our interest is the measurement of the output from such a system. How much cleaning and degradation of the toxics can the swamp and your bacteria do? We expect you to keep track of that output, especially your own pollutants. The PCA will be measuring the other toxics at the weir and in the swamp soils.”

“Given the variety and potency of the toxic materials there, could that possibly work? I doubt it. Would anything grow on that stuff?” said Jobert.

“We think so. The addition of some passable soil and mulch we believe will do it. We are betting that the landscaped surface will quickly develop a luxuriant growth. Our interest is in the limits of such a system.”

“Mandy, you said that beautifully. Do some of the night spots too? What time can we meet?”

"Felix, I brought you along to do a job but not on me." Jobert was becoming irritable.

"Boss, I have to make my move when I can, when things look right."

"Complete your date now. Then we can stop annoying Miss Boult."

"See. I have the best Boss in the whole world."

"I don't mind. At the end of this meeting out front. Mr. Jobert you have said that you will also have an arsenic problem from your plant. We will set a Cap on your arsenic emissions. We will then provide tax credits on the arsenic outflow. Any reduction of those emissions will make those credits salable. You can make money by being an efficient controller of your output."

Up to the table came Guy Barnaby accompanied by a slightly disreputable, odd-looking character, shirt tail out, hair askew, an appearance irreconcilable with the surrounding dining room elegance and its posh diners.

"Hello, Edmund, hello! Great to see you. A miracle, I got away from the hearing early. They just got tired of me and, anyway, had too many other things to do and adjourned."

"Glad to see you, Guy. Waiter, drinks for the gentlemen."

"Meet Ken Oikl, my ecological consultant. You've cleared things up, Mandy?"

"Not really. We were just about to go into costs in more detail."

"Exactly what Ken and I were talking about."

Oikl collapsed in Dextra's chair, slurped her wine and started talking, "Yeah. It's weird, this cost business has me talking like Adam Smith. Me Oikl, a world class socialist, sometime biologist! A buddy of mine, an economist, and I were gassing. And I suggested that if cycling and recycling costs were added and no supports and there were no other controls, there could be a completely free market where everyone could find the lowest costs, (for the family too), no costs concealed from the user, and the whole system would come to an equilibrium. That got a loud raspberry."

"From me too," said Jobert. "Explain that about the family."

"What I figure is costs must be born by the doer. And most fundamentally by the family which must pay the full costs for its members. You have one kid you pay a base tax rate for schooling, water, services, etc. Another one will result in a doubling of service taxes. And so on."

Barnaby said, "Let's talk about practical things."

"OK. Us ecologists spend a lot of time on cycling. Nature cycles, spreads everything around. In fact, if anything cycles very slowly or not at all, or is used in one place and ends in another place where little used, huge strata of the uncycled disused material can occur. For example, diatoms use silica to make their shells at the top of the ocean, then on death the shell drifts to the bottom there to form over time thick thousand foot thick layers of strata."

Jobert said, "Can't say I ever got past production. Making something good and useful, that's fun. Getting rid of it bores me even if it is necessary and useful."

"Boss, that covers the stiffs in graveyards, not? An attempt not to cycle. Now what is the limit on graveyards and stiffs?"

"Felix, the wandering of your mind is disturbing."

Oikl accepted Felix's remarks as reasonable, "Except where there is lead, they will cycle if slowly. So no limit. The diatoms and other plants formed huge pools of oil, uncycled energy. Would have cycled to carbon dioxide and water if there had been oxygen there."

"Plastics won't," said Jobert.

"No. Not most. In the dumps they just sit. Like some ghastly, indestructible shit," said Oikl. "Excuse me, Miss."

"An oxymoron. A treasure trove for future archaeologists," said Felix. "I'm no nature bug but when we were at Mitton, Boss, I hated to see those shreds of plastic blowing over the desert. Not just blowing but getting caught and hanging on barb wire and on those little trees we saw down there."

"Mesquite," said Oikl. "We shall soon be up to our armpits in this plastic fecal matter."

"Barnaby, your ecologist buddy here has a gift for disgusting metaphors," said Felix.

Oikl responded, "The subject calls for them and for foul language. Imagine a plastic which, flipped on the mulch heap, would rapidly decompose to cycle through all the organisms as does true ordinary manure."

"So the ideal product could be dumped on the mulch heap?" asked Felix. "Do you know more ecologists like this one, Mandy?"

"Yes. Some are even more strange," said Mandy.

"Boss, ecologists aren't down to earth, they're down to shit. Sorry, Mandy. Got carried away."

"Naturally!" said Oikl. "There is a Swedish ecologist who specializes in counting the droppings of caterpillars in forests. The world's expert on caterpillar crap. Imagine!"

Mandy suddenly shoved herself down in her chair, leaning to hide behind Felix, and said in a strangled voice, "Oh God. Here comes Senator Verlicht. Hands-on-Hans."

Barnaby chided, "Now, Mandy, he's sincere." That started Oikl chortling.

"So is a rapist! If he puts his hand on me, I'll... I'll..."

"Hello there, Guy," said in a booming voice, "And the lovely Mandy."

"Hello, Senator." Barnaby was trying to sound enthusiastic.

"Hello," croaked Mandy.

Barnaby asked, and knew instantly that he had asked stupidly, "What can I do for you, Senator?"

Verlicht placed a huge kneading hand on Mandy's shoulder. Mandy turned to stone, her face paling and flushing alternately and in spots. She started twice to speak up only to be interrupted by Verlicht "Well now, introduce me to the eminent Jobert."

Felix who couldn't resist, said, "Senator, I am Felix Bountz, Mr. Jobert's systems man. How do you feel about us feeling people?"

Barnaby rolled his eyes up and grimaced. Mandy let her muscles relax and swallowed all the unladylike street language that had accumulated ready to gush forth. Mandy smiled. Felix was making a hit with her. She looked forward to an interesting evening. Verlicht registered only the tiniest flick of annoyance, the response of an elephant to a fly settling on its rump.

Barnaby hastily introduced, "Edmund Jobert, meet Senator Hans Verlicht. The Senator is much interested in developing energy resources."

"Mr. Jobert, we are one hundred percent behind your hydrogen from bacteria energy project. We won't let any of these nutty environment people get in your way. You will have my full backing. Excuse me, Guy, but I must say it as I see it. Growth is what we need and must have."

Oikl had enough: "Hell, if you didn't keep adding people the growth rate would be halved."

Felix, simultaneously, no ardent environmentalist, was impelled to speak, "That's what cancers say, do."

"Halved? Huhn?," grunted Jobert.

Oikl gulped more wine, "Well something like that. An' then ya gotta grow enough to repair roads, bridges, slums, all that stuff. Match the degrowth you know."

"Oikl, have you ever thought of studying economics?" asked Felix.

"You want me to listen to economists showing why other economists don't know what they are talking about?" Oikl laughed.

Verlicht, disgusted, grimaced at Oikl, sat down, poured and gulped half a glass of wine, beamed at Jobert, ignored Felix.

Oikl, seeing that Verlicht was going to spout, interjected hurriedly, "Do you people recall the time when Canada sent a gunboat to stop a Spanish fishing boat taking turbot? The fishery was badly over-fished as shown by the turbot being reduced to nothing but miniature specimens just barely large enough to be caught. In fact they caught the fish only because they were using illegal small-meshed nets."

"Free enterprise, my weird friend," erupted the Senator and turned to Jobert to begin a peroration. "Still, we shouldn't let those foreigners fish in our waters."

Oikl, self-cut hair standing up askew, bristling like a porcupine on defense, wasn't going to let that get by. "No, never free enterprise, that's the last thing it was. There was more to it than that."

Barnaby nodded and said, "Right. The Spanish government subsidized those boats. And all the other boats out there were government supported including the American boats That support helped produce a depletion of the fishery so bad that fishermen could not afford to go out for the low catch they were likely to get."

Oikl nodded, “The gov’ support was screwing up the market producin’ fishies nobody wanted.. And worse, more fishing boats.”

“Far worse, the fishery deteriorated. The Spanish-Canadian imbroglio was the result of government interference in the market, producing a form of madness. The fishery was being destroyed with help from the Spanish government, not that the Canadians and us Americans were any better.”

“Right,” said Oikl. “When we shet, set two hundred mile limit, our own gov’assisted fishermen prom’l uh prom uh promp’ly fished out the same waters.”

“Nonsense! There are just as many fish now as there ever were.” Verlicht persisted with his one note refrain.

“That’s because we stopped the over-fishing with a true free market,” said Barnaby, Oikl nodding his head like a bobbing manikin.

“Nonsense again. The fish would have come back anyway. You are peddling socialist propaganda.” They were treading on Verlicht’s code of reality, irritating him.

Oikl hiccuped and ignored Verlicht, “Funny shing... thing is we know perfeckly well how fish fisheries f’rever, forever. Caw, called ‘optimal yield theory’. Or fish prices, fish prices,” Oikl was getting confused. “uh economic yield. Is lower take of fish.”

“It’s only a theory,” said Verlicht with positive assurance. Oikl leaned his head in his hands contemplating Verlicht as some kind of insect requiring pinning and classification. Verlicht looked with loathing and disgust at Oikl, a creature surely from some subversive country. Oikl started again, “The problem was that fishery was Hardin’s Commons. Eve’ybody got all the fish he could get. To hell with the other guy, fisherman countries. An’ as Hardin would’ve predict’ more boats and more fish taken so fish numbers go way down.”

Barnaby moved the wine away from Oikl who immediately rescued it. Jobert winked to Felix who was enjoying Oikl. Barnaby glanced at Oikl and tossed his head, and said, “In various ways, all the other boats were government supported including the American boats. Someone suggested that nations get together and agree not to subsidize the fishermen and instead to establish a totally free market and an optimal yield policy, the yield determined locally by fishermen and fisheries experts. The

Spaniards then could not compete with the Canadians because of the extra costs of crossing the ocean and at the same time taking a limited number ,a quota, of fish. It was cheaper to buy from the Canadians than to cross the ocean. An accompanying requirement that any fishery must adhere to an optimal fishing policy was passed. Since there was no government support, the Canadian fishermen were then able to take only an optimal yield, fishing according to ecological and economic rules and continuing in business forever. Think of the result. With a life-time guarantee of a good supply of fish each year and therefore, a good job, forever, the fishermen became highly competitive and made damn sure no other fishing boat overfished, an efficient market. Ditto other fisheries around the world. All due to a totally free market in the oceans, scientific rules and no local government support. Another good thing, fishing became a local affair again. Upkeep and oil and pay for workers and all the things required for crossing the ocean to a distant fishery no longer paid."

Oikl admitted, "I used to believe we ought to have a soshlist…" Verlicht pressed his lips in exultation "Hah I knew it!" … "viewpoint. Shet, set regulations and do things for common good. I thought people were altruishtic but it ain't so, not in the market. Free market worked, I am convinced. Invishble Hand produshes code. But that's not all. Gov'ments rig markets, gov'ment gains and chosen people, too. All starts with shub,shub, subsidies for the family. Ends with the dead hand of state laying-hic-hic-clammy--hah ha fish influensh--on evvybody's head. Always damage to nature from gov, government money.. Envi'ment improves if no market riggin'."

Verlicht sat up and said, "No. We set rules and subsidies so that industry does well, and as a consequence society does well, everybody does well." He ended nodding in agreement with his own words.

"Nuts." Oikl had decided to start a fight with Verlicht. "No such thing. Evvy bird-watcher ought scream for free market, no shu-shu-shidies."

Jobert was amused, tried to help, "Subsidies. Businesses are just as bad as individuals whether they are farmers seeking tariffs against sugar imports or support for their crops or water at below-cost prices or support for exports. The sugar result is higher prices for the consumer and, incidentally, a gratuitous impoverishment of our Latin-American neighbors, and, also a recipe for the destruction of the Everglades National Park. Worse, communities cough up huge quantities of cash hoping to attract new industries or ball teams. Now that is some kind of perversion."

Oikl now leaning to Port insisted, "More environment preserve' by total free market 'an any other available way."

Barnaby said, "That may be true. Market-distorting subsidies do damage the environment in numerous ways. Whether the totally free market will remedy that remains to be seen."

"Are effecks. Shubshidies for families (tax reductions for each child), for lumber companies uh fire sales of lumber from national forests, the raising of prices of land in sugar beet country, and other shubbidies for all kinds of produc's an' indushries, damage envi'onment." He added, "Evvybody has to pay freight; then system will pusserve nature, stabilize system."

"There you go too far, Oikl."

"Shtay where am," said Oikl leaning far to the starboard.

Verlicht gave a little hop to the side of his chair closer to Mandy. Mandy, watching him like a bird a snake, hopped to her left, placing her left buttock half off the chair. Felix to her left edged to the right to give her support if necessary. Verlicht eased his capacious butt back to center, followed by Mandy. Felix stayed right.

Suddenly Verlicht sat upright and said, "Now! Just say, 'Simon says no limits'."

Felix hesitantly asked, "No limits?"

"You lose, whoever you are. You're out," said Senator Verlicht.

"Simon says stick your finger up your..." Felix was becoming malicious and about to unload on the senator.

Mandy smiled gleefully and started to say, 'ass'.

Barnaby interrupted, "Mandy was about to say 'up in the air'. Now back to growth, Senator. By law, that's not our business."

"Simon says that was a gross mistake."

"A gross mistake?"

"You are already out of the game, Mister. Stay out. Simon says there is no such thing as too many people."

Felix grinned wickedly, “Didn’t Chairman Mao say that too? Or maybe it was ‘people are capital’.”

“Young man, you are out!”

“There are already too many people,” said Jobert.

“You didn’t say Simon says, Mr. Jobert. You lose. What are you doing, young man? What kind of help do you have, Mr. Jobert?”

Felix was banging his ear as though to get rid of water.

“Felix has ear problems.”

“And how! I’ve been hearing weird things lately.”

“Some people say us bureaucrats are anti-growth, but we don’t have time even to think about that.” Mandy felt she should contribute something, anything to the discussion.

“Mandy, dear,” reaching over and putting his hand on Mandy’s knee, “You’re out, too.”

Mandy once again flushing, livid, reached for the water carafe, and said, “You take your goddam…”, interrupted by Barnaby who said, “Ha, ha. Poor Mandy doesn’t know the game. Mandy, why don’t you and Felix go. You’re due at the British Embassy, aren’t you?”

Felix was up instantly, helping the internally roaring Mandy toward the door. There, before some stately matrons, she let loose a string of expletives normally heard only in covens of children or street hoods. The ladies looked properly startled and offended.

“Mandy, you have a good vocabulary. I just learned a few new ones. Now cool down. Let’s walk so you can let off steam.”

“There’s a nice disco place not far.”

∞

“Mr. Jobert, if Guy here, or any of his weird crew, get in your way, let me know. We still have power in the senate even though they’ve tried to make us into a bunch of high school debaters. With more energy we can support more people at higher standards of living who will in turn provide more resources for more people in an ever upwards spiral.”

Oikl made a moue, “No, won’t work. Too many, peoplesh deshtroy nature shuburbs evvwhere.”

"Won't happen if they pay full costs," said Barnaby. "Population growth, I mean."

Verlicht entered the argument, "That is not a problem; there are more old people all the time. Will happen everywhere."

Oikl burped, "Yesh an' by zhen evyythin' wrecked."

Jobert paused, eyed Oikl, tuned back to Barnaby, smiled, a sardonic expression on his face, "You should meet a family we have, a fellow who reproduces like a rabbit. Spends little time thinking."

"That is still an unsolved problem. We have to train people."

"Suppose the person is untrainable. I know, I know. Nobody is untrainable. My own words." Jobert was amused.

Barnaby expanded his ideas, "Let's get back to costs. Your Watershed Chair imposed a cost for recycling your products, not very much in your case since only the container does not cycle naturally. That adds an expense which could be eliminated by cyclable packaging. Recycling is an unnatural process which will always cost more than cycling. It is one of the jobs of our cost section to estimate and add costs so that cycling materials are favored."

"All this is very interesting but what kind of bureaucracy is created? I don't need any more imperial bureaucrats," said Jobert.

"An unkind cut, Edmund. Let me draw you a diagram of our setup. Our Okeanarky. Tablecloth. No. Waiter wouldn't approve. Who's got a piece of paper? Nobody. Well, let me describe the arrangement. At the top of the inverted hierarchy are the Watershed Chairs, one for each major watershed in a state. They have the power, are the technical experts, highly trained in the sciences, and their word is law. They all report to an inter-watershed Coordinating Authority whose sole task is to make sure that events in one watershed are not negating the work in the neighboring Watershed. Below the Coordinating authorities are the Undersecretaries of the Environment who report to the Secretary who reports to the President, the keel of the ark, the steadying influence who in turn reports to the Solons. It's the local Watershed Chair that counts from day to day."

"OK, I see the structure but what's an Okeanarky?"

Oikl who had been guzzling wine like water arose, "Forgot one thing. No shubshidies for Cold War spies. Shpies now in fishing countries to see, shee they not shub uh shubshidize fisherman, secret; 'scuse me, I've got to go." He pushed himself up, staggered, nodded to all and swayed through the diners like a Chinese junk in a hurricane passing amid an elegant scatter of becalmed yachts.

"Weird. Ecologists are an interesting lot. Spies. Nutty. First part- just the word ocean- which means great river- goes back to when people thought the oceans were a river around the earth. Notice that I'm describing a boat, ark. An ark, could float, good name for us, don't you think? 'Arch'(ark) means 'rule' of the great river, of course. The ballasts in the Ark, what were they in the original ark? are the USFS forest service, SCS-soils, BLM-national lands, DOE-only the nature preservation parts, FWS-fish and wildlife, EPA-you know, OSM, and Corps and abracadabra and others I can't think of. Us Undersecretaries, the keel, can call on them for technical help, but above are the Chairs, who rule like the old Fed chairman. Left behind in the original departments, at the bottom of the ark, are the functions of development, and progress."

The senator who had been staring across the room was disgusted, "Imagine! people listen to that Oikl type of jerk."

Jobert decided to speak up. "I don't know how good an ecologist he is, but I can guess he is dedicated. And his research is important. Enough of that! Guy, we need some financial help; we believe we are on the verge of producing something which will be of enormous help to the nation."

"We must arrange aid, financing, government support," said the senator.

"We can't do that, Senator. You know that the free market demands that, whatever the cost of producing a cubic meter of hydrogen, the manufacturer must pay it. Not the government, not any city or other citizens but the manufacturer. Those are the rules, Senator Verlicht. If what you are producing has value, the market will support it."

"I'm developing a completely new technology which may change, even improve our energy sources. That is a great value to any society; why should not society contribute to its development?" Jobert wanted to extend the argument.

Barnaby wanted to oblige, "That's easy to answer. If we contribute to you, why should we not contribute to the farmer, the small business man or any citizen who says he is making a contribution? No, Edmund, that way leads back to support for the insupportable, back to the old society."

"That was a good society! Better rules than this one!" said Verlicht.

Jobert expressed disagreement. "No, it wasn't, and I don't want to revive it, but you will have to agree that if I go out of business, society may lose something important."

"That's possible but then, if it is really possible, some other entrepreneur will do it. Sorry, Edmund. No sale. Costs must be paid. A society in which all costs are localized to individuals, corporations or other single bodies will not have unnecessary costs imposed. If people pay the true cost of the water they drink, if they pay for the waste and the sewage they produce, you will have an efficient society. They must also pay for each child. No child costs concealed from the child producer concealed by subsidies. Possibly charity for the first two children, for none thereafter; only true costs from there on. No bolony rights, just political rights."

"Isn't that disgusting. Not to take care of every child, not to plan for a glorious future for each child! Insupportable! Simon says they are capital."

"I'm out of that game, Senator. If numbers are automatically controlled then no one is to blame. Arguments about population control are moot."

"Well, I am still in it. That Inter-watershed office never responded to my call. What kind of treatment is that of a Senator?" Verlicht was indignant.

"Senator, all he does is coordinate. That office has no command and can't really tell you anything. Call your Chair or us. We make the plans, get the data on sites. Our computer can cough up dozens of sites for specific purposes. We take account of input and output and site problems before we return recommendations to the local Chair. The proposer can take his pick or advance others which we then check. Notice that the environment is first, not last. We believe this will be the cheapest and most advisable environmentally. I repeat, the whole thing is like a boat; we call ourselves the Ark."

Said Jobert, "Fitting, very fitting."

"Simon says the Ark will sink us."

"Senator, I refuse to play your game," said Jobert. "This scheme ought to simplify governance, maybe even change people's behavior so they do what they ought to do."

"Never! Well, gentlemen, this has been most interesting but I must leave. I see an important constituent over there. Very nice to have met you, Mr. Jobert." Verlicht wove through the diners, patting a shoulder here, bussing a cheek there.

"Guy, is the Senator mad?"

"I think so, but if so, there's 'method in his madness'. He is a formidable opponent. Have you heard the Verlicht plan for the garbage problem? He says the mountains of garbage are a national treasure. Says pile it up, put on gravel and soil, plant grass and make a ski slope outside Chicago. Eliminate flatland. Every state, mountains!"

"Marvelous. Verlicht Mountain. Wow. Imagine the Chicagoans going out there to see the sunrise in the east. They could be droning mantras to the sun."

∞

When coming out of a traumatic period of one's life, everything is somehow gray and tired looking. At the same time one is vulnerable, searching, seeking one knows not what. Dextra walking with Teddy looked at the Hirshhorn Gallery with dull eyes, seeing only another building, not even noticing the grace of the building or the children enjoying the fountain. She felt herself in limbo but was aware of Teddy's attempts to please her. Teddy was delighted to be with her and determined to present himself in a favorable light. Of course, he over-talked, over-joked, and over-pleased. Finally, Dextra uncharacteristically said, "Teddy, stuff it."

Now standing next to the reflecting pool, Teddy felt only a sense of pleasure at the elegant building swathed in a glow of late evening light. He was at peace with himself and the world, his girl beside him. He said, "How beautiful! Don't you think so, Dextra?"

"It's alright."

"Alright! Dextra, damn it, look at it before you speak. Show that you're alive."

"Don't you talk to me that way."

"Just look at it."

"Alright, it is beautiful but what does an engineer know about beauty?"

"Ha. Any machine, any tool that does a good job is beautiful. A hardware store is full of beautiful things. And some junk, of course. Come on, we'll go over to the Smithsonian and I'll tell you how we know that the earth rotates from the motions of a pendulum."

"Why do I want to know that?"

"Because you are with me. OK, you don't want to do that so we're off to that joint I told you about."

"No."

"Yes." Teddy took Dextra's arm and off they went.

∞

"Teddy, my feet hurt and my head is whirling."

"You shouldn't have drunk so much." he ducked her blow. "Missed me. That's the British Embassy and there's a do going on. Here we go."

"We can't. I'm tipsy."

"You'll fit right in; the Brits can swish it down with the best of them. Yes, we can. There's a guard checking. Look official." He spoke to the guard, "We represent Jobert Industries."

"Do you now? Your ID's please. Ah indeed. Jobert Industries eh? Got a card? OK, OK." The guard looked with amusement at the tipsy Dextra who was petrified at their brashness. He looked them over and waved them in.

"Teddy, this is crazy. We aren't diplomats."

"Glass of wine, Miss, and you, sir?"

"Yes for both."

"Thank you." Dextra relaxed and looked at Teddy. He had surprised her. More to him then she thought?

"Hello, I'm Guy Pargally, science attaché here. This is plonk, isn't it? And the wondrous Chirali." He looked at Dextra but directed the question to Teddy.

"You must have slept through my talk. I'm Teddy Sourtis, Jobert Industries also..."

Pargally interrupted, “The Chirali! I’m in luck. Be a good boy, Teddy Sourtis, and go over to the horse’s ovaries table and fetch us some goodies. Dextra and I are going to have a tête-a-tête about producing hydrogen from transformed bacteria. We’ll be over in that corner.”

Teddy growled, “I’ll be there with the speed of light.”

Dextra giggled.

∞

“First you walk my feet off; then you get me into that- that dive in Georgetown, and fill me full of martinis, then we crash that embassy and I have to talk genetics to that attaché when my head is swimming. When I at last was comfortable, enjoying myself and that attaché, thinking I belonged there, you insisted on getting me out of there. Then more walking, another bar, more martinis and now all the way to this reflecting pool. Teddy, you made me eat, you told me what to eat, then you kept the booze coming. Are you trying to seduce me?”

“Never. What would I want to do that for? Who wants to seduce a molecular geneticist? Might as well seduce a robot.”

“Teddy, you have finally irritated me too much.” She giggled and reached toward Teddy who was attempting to walk on the edge of the reflecting pool. She stepped on a vagrant stone and, twisting her ankle, reached for support from Teddy and instead pushed him. Teddy fell in, to come up spluttering.

“You pushed me in!”, and reached to pull Dextra in.

She sprang back, emitted a groan, and favored one leg. Teddy stepped out to lend dripping support. She shivered from the soaking cold water she absorbed from Teddy. Then they both felt a pleasant, disturbing body warmth.

“Did you hurt yourself?”

“Do you think I am pretending? Yes, I hurt myself. I turned my ankle.”

“Oh no!” Teddy began laughing. Dextra, puzzled, soon joined in.

“What do you mean, oh no? I did.”

“How am I going to explain this to Felix?”

"People sprain ankles all the time. That doesn't need an explanation. And why Felix? Teddy, you are weird."

"It's just I feel responsible."

"For me twisting my ankle. Teddy, what is it they say? 'you are a few bricks shy of a load.' Again, did you get me drunk to seduce me?"

"Of course not. Never."

"Why not?"

∞

"Here they come. It can't be. Dextra's limping. Boss, do you suppose?"

"He can't be that literal-minded."

"Maybe it's the only thing that worked."

"Dextra's laughing. Nice to see that. Felix, you may have accomplished something. Don't let us laugh; look solemn. No! Laugh. Teddy is dripping water; he's sodden."

"Well! This trip was useful."

Chapter 12 Decisions and Consequences

"Edmund, Charlie here. The Board of Directors and a bunch of investors is after your scalp. The list of complaints is multiplying. Edmund, they think you are weakened; it's a case of the pack closing in on the wounded deer; it will only build. And, Edmund, I think they have the votes."

"Yeah. Naturally. Once these things start they can snowball. Who do they think built up this company, made it profitable, a world leader! I can give them a bloodletting battle they won't forget."

"You could but they do have the votes. That bastard, Volter, called me to let me know he was after your scalp. I guess he didn't know I was your friend. Said he was calling you to account. You wouldn't believe his tirade. He's screeching in my ear: who the hell do you think you are playing around with our money, shareholder's money; who do you think you are to surround yourself with murderers, sleazy con-men, bird watchers, ne'er-do-wells, and assorted riffraff and environment nuts! Unfortunately, he is representative of an important faction."

"Yeah. Let me tell you- that lab in the woods is going to produce a profitable product."

"Edmund, you don't have to convince me. And Volter knows that. But he says the work could have been done down here. Let me give the rest of his garbage. You are wasting company money. Profits are way down."

"He hasn't heard that there's a recession?"

"Not a weapon for him. Says good people are quitting. Says we need reorganization, rejuvenation, and removal of that guy up in those damn woods together with that stupid lab of his."

"The last person in the world who could do a successful reorganization of this company is him."

"Right. Just a griper, nothing more. He's not original; a lot of what he says is coming from other people. He says you are a relict of the past, that you are personally absorbing the disreputable traits of your hanger-ons. I told him how you keep track of things; he admitted that but says you let the headquarters' staff grow out of bounds, claims it could be chopped to a tenth of what it is now. He's quoting someone; he never thought that through himself. Says he's going to mount a fight to drive you out. He thinks you were only lucky to be at the right time and place. Then he says if it weren't for that you'd be a broken-down plant manager at some second-rate place. We know better. That you support these Chairs who he calls a bunch of bureaucratic dictators with their bolony about using the free market to get good environmental decisions. Says that's crap. He calls them little dictators. He complains about your kowtowing to those environmental freaks. All that environment crap. And so on and on."

"Why in the hell did he call you?"

"I wondered too. Maybe to get the message to you indirectly. And I'm doing that for good reasons. He may be a creep but the things he is saying are going around."

"I never liked that guy. He's honest enough but always on the make. He hates me for my success, I think. It is people like him who bring disrepute on industry. Your simple-minded- just manufacture it- won't work today. Industry is a part of society and must take account of environmental problems. Screw the environment won't do."

"Right. If it were only him, I wouldn't have called you, Edmund. But there's a group, more serious than Volter. If you fight them, you could also hurt the company. They ask some of the same questions. Why in God's name you put that lab out in the middle of nowhere. Wasting money on those bacteria. Where will the payback be? Yes, I know you've heard this litany before. Still, let me give their spiel. Leave the environment problems to others. We manufacture useful products. Paying all that money to so-called geniuses who can't find their way to the toilet. Putting up a building that will be unsalable when the whole useless project collapses. The place won't even pay back the costs. Edmund, these people care only for present profitability. They say you mollycoddle the help, keep on superannuated people, hire weirdos, don't fire staff who should be long gone, some of the same crap Volter pedals. That financier- what's-his name says the staff could and should be chopped by at least a fifth, the companies are too fat. Must be where Volter got his line. The Jochem plant, the

Boston and Dallas plants should be shut down. They are outdated. Close them down and fast they say. And I have to agree."

"Those are people working there, Charlie. They've been with us a long time."

"Heart is something these people don't have. They'd just chop. Edmund, I have to say they are right. Company profits are deteriorating fast. We could be in serious trouble soon. They say you should be fighting these Watershed Chairs all the way for exceptions and against the costs they are imposing on the company."

"They're barking up the wrong tree there. This new setup won't sacrifice environment to anybody's profits and rightly so. At my lab we have solved one problem which will produce profits and help the environment. That's the way to go. That's the only way to go. Make profits by making environmentally good products. Just requires a little ingenuity. No costs imposed on the environment. All prices including all external costs."

"They spotted that success. You can be sure they'll follow up on that. They want to pull your best people down to the Chicago facility; they have great plans for what's her name- Chirali, and the other good people up there. But they insist the hydrogen thing cannot and will not be successful. And is draining money away from more important projects. Edmund, I hate to call you with this bad news. I repeat; the opposition has the votes. They're going to kick you out one way or the other. Edmund, you could bargain for the hydrogen work; make your research lab into a working test plant up there to see if it can be made commercial. You could demand a furloughing scheme for all those old-timers. That will be a graceful way out. Edmund, I never thought I would say this to you. I'm your oldest friend and I hate to be the messenger. Why don't you quit? You've made huge contributions. Why suffer these bastards or the tribulations that are sure to come? Go up to your cabin; enjoy life; shoot some grouse."

"Charlie, I've battled these money pinchers all my life. I'm used to being at the decision end. And I enjoy being there. Profits have dropped but that's just temporary. I don't know. Why the hell should I quit? I can go down fighting."

"Think about it, Edmund."

"Alright. Damn it to hell."

"Edmund, you are there up in that icebox! The weatherman said it was twenty below and five feet of snow up there! Are you crazy!"

"No, I'm not crazy. The snowy forest is beautiful! Anyway, I was checking the progress at the lab. They are doing well."

"Well you get back down here and start taking care of things! More important, our son is still in prison in Turkey. You get him out of there, you hear!"

"Do you realize what the boy is charged with?"

"You knew! What does it matter what he is charged with! Get him out!"

"It does matter. People aren't sent to prison for nothing."

"They said he was carrying drugs. I don't believe that."

"He's done it before, here. I do believe it."

"Get him out of there. Now!"

"I'll get to work on it."

"Edmund, I demand you do something about our boy. Prisons there are terrible. God knows what kind of perverts and murderers are in there with him. You saw in Lawrence of Arabia what they do to prisoners in Turkey."

"Movies have nothing to do with reality. Darling, I've already gotten him a new roommate. He doesn't know and I hope won't find out that his new roommate is a bodyguard. A little cash placed him with William until his release."

"Until he's released! Are you going to let him rot! Don't you care what happens to your children!"

"My dear, he's not a child. He's a grown man who was caught carrying drugs. A couple of years eating Turkish prison food and experiencing the brutal discipline of that prison could make something of him. It's time he grew up. You were and are much too easy on him. Sorry, forget..."

"I-I! - was too easy on him! Where were you! You didn't discipline him; you weren't there. You showed up now and then but that wasn't enough."

"I didn't mean to blame you. Sorry. What matters is that we change him. I'll offer him a job again when he gets back. But we can't change the past."

"No. I won't accept that. If you can bribe them so can I. And will. Things are coming apart at the company, I hear. Charlie is hunting for you; he says they are ganging up on you. Get down here. Now!"

"Charlie got to me already. Don't hang up. Aaa," Jobert sat back, got up, opened the cabin door to a reflecting, blinding snow-covered landscape. The pines were heavy with piles of snow. A band of ravens called hoarsely in the distance. Had the wolves killed a deer? Were the ravens collecting to take advantage of the kill? Was he, Jobert, the circling wolf or the dying deer? Most likely deer. He looked up the trunk of a white pine noting the graceful clusters of needles, the symmetry of the branchlets, and then the tree. The aspens were bare. A grouse clucked on an aspen limb and went about the business of eating buds. If the bird survived the winter and the hawks, there would be hunting in the next fall, a year ahead. Surcease! Vagrant clouds turned the sun's rays on and off to produce a parade of shadows on the snow. All was right with the world here. What did all his troubles finally matter. Still, love of the power of decision, with the capacity to bring about products that could finally make people's lives better, more leisurely, more interesting, more fulfilling, had been intoxicating. Why quit? It could be an interesting fight. His decisions were still producing up here. Hard to close those plants that were once world beaters. Especially hard where so many people would lose out. Come from a very well-to-do family, but a not really rich background.

He tried to place himself in the shoes of a fifty year old accountant, lab tech, who found himself on the street, frightened, disoriented and once again having to search for a living. He had never had that problem, never been seared that way. Still, no social setup, no political system could afford to keep useless plants open. People had to be hurt; must help them. They must help themselves. No! Don't quit until that is resolved. The tormenting phone trilled again.

"Edmund, Charlie here. Back again. I bear bad news. The Jochem plant has been struck. Those crazy people are demanding that we give more health benefits, more vacation time and a raise. And they want you to stop the environment stuff. They say it is costing them money."

"And will cost them and everyone else money in the future. They must be smart enough to know that a raise isn't in the cards. Can't they see our problems?"

"No. No, they can't. They just know the past when you were running the place and it was all bustle and everyone knew they had a good job with a great boss and everything going for them. They want overpoweringly and, against reason, that everything be right, be like it was then. This stupid strike was started by dimwits but a lot of our people are supporting it. Lots of them, maybe most, know the company's days are numbered. They even know they could be on the street any day. Our problem now is how to close the plant when it could look like a lockout against the strike and might look inhuman. Edmund, we can't wait; no matter what, we must close the place. Money is flowing out like water."

"If there was ever a decision I didn't want to make, this is it. OK! We must. Go! Close Jochem down. There is nothing else to do. I'm on my way down Monday. See you then. I'm outside to get some fresh air."

"Wish I could join you. Step outside and what I get is a whiff of exhaust."

He opened the door, looked out at blue sky, the snowy woods, breathed deeply, leaned against the cabin wall, soaked up the warm sunshine and thought again of retreating to this place and forgetting the outside world. The phone started ringing again.

"Mr. Jobert, your daughter brought the dynamite from your factory."

"Sheriff, I can't believe she'd be that dumb."

"Sorry, but your daughter did visit your Jochem plant in Chicago. The detectives there backed a guy against the wall and he admitted he gave her - he thought - two sticks of dynamite. Said he thought she was real cute. And anyway the big boss's attractive daughter. The FBI traced the stuff to the same place. So no doubt where it came from. We got a reasonable date on that. Then she brought it up here. She passed a package to that guy Glatz in the local bar.

"Hell, she didn't really know Glatz. Must have been something else."

"Maybe. May have been the dynamite. She won't say what was in the package. If it was the dynamite, he must have passed it to Kraft or maybe that janitor direct. We haven't found him yet.

Bringing it up here and passing it in a bar seems the dumbest thing she did."

"Ah, dumb yes but she was being run by that SOB Kraft. A loud mouthed SOB like that attracts young people; he has, had simple answers to complex issues that rational people have trouble formulating even partial answers to. And did you ever notice he spoke with enthusiasm and exuded a messianic thrust guaranteed to get people to the lynching bee. I shouldn't be saying that. De mortuus nil nisi bonum. uh nothing but good about the dead."

"Right! Yeah, we got one like him out in a swamp. Comes to town now and then with a complete plan for revamping this boondock into a Chicago suburb. Still, your daughter is responsible. We're going to arrest her. Stick her in our jail. Let her think about her answer a bit. I have to tell you, sir, that our DA filed charges against you. One of the Chicago detectives said you had picked up the dynamite. Turned out to be a false lead but our ambitious DA thought he had a golden opportunity for some real publicity. Charge is now dropped."

"People will think I used pull to get it dropped. The truth will never catch up. Oh well, let them believe what they will. Any danger to my daughter in there?"

"Only the food. Could be worse; could feed her nothing but lutefisk and Norwegian goat cheese. Ha, ha, ha."

"She'd think it was gourmet cooking. No perverts, no psychos?"

"No. Female section could get a female drunk. Smelly but harmless."

"I'll leave her there for the time being. Don't let her out. What kind of sentence would you predict?"

"Hard to say. She did get the dynamite but then what? Wasn't there the night of the explosion. She was seen looking miserable with that Gypsy Lie woman in a bar. Ah, your company not pressing, she might get thirty days in my jail or a suspended sentence and community service. Indians need help."

"Something good for her. She'd love it. You have a policeman's welfare fund?"

"Sure do."

"Well now. I'll send it a nice contribution."

"That will be appreciated."

"Take care of her. Good-bye."

"Bye."

What to do? Leave my daughter in jail for a little while. She'll be OK. My wife, no, she'd know it was me, would skin me alive. Still. Let her stay.

∞

"Edmund! Now our daughter is in jail! What kind of children did we raise!"

"The kind you can these days. Don't worry; jail will do her some good."

"Edmund! you get her out of there right away! Do you realize what could happen to a young woman in a jail? No! you're up to some of your tricks. Probably already knew she was in there. I'll get her out."

"Not up here, Dear, Dear... hung up. Damn it. It is the right move. Better call the sheriff."

∞

"Sheriff Jager here."

"Edmund Jobert on this end. My wife's going to try to get our daughter out of jail. Don't let her. OK?"

"Didn't intend to; law is working its way now."

"Good. Good-bye." Jobert put on his snow shoes and started through the woods determined to blank out Chicago.

∞

"Jobert here."

"Sheriff Jager. Mr. Jobert, we got a possible real problem. Your wife tried to bribe me and did it with Marko standing there. Bribery is a serious offense up here. Marko is stupid but ambitious. Unless your wife is clever, could mean your wife in jail."

"Ha, ha, ha. Oh my God, my whole family in jail. That's too much. When did she do that? It's just two days. I wonder what a few days in jail would do for her? Now there's something to think about."

"She come in fast, left fast. Mr. Jobert, one thing I know, stay out of domestic quarrels."

"Oh, I won't involve you. How could she be so dumb? Couldn't you at least scare her?"

"Not so dumb, Mr. Jobert. Any smart lawyer could say we misinterpreted what she said. Didn't have Marko there, I`d forget it. I expect the DA might say that."

"Sheriff, she is smart; if her offer wasn't clear you can be sure she intended it that way. Sheriff, don't get the wrong idea. We've been going our own ways for years. No real warfare."

"Same here. It's how I survive."

"Sheriff, come out to the cabin one of these days. We'll discuss who's to blame. And have a drink."

"Will be there. Never have understood anything. Bye."
"Bye."

Once more the phone rang. "My cabin; some retreat," said to the wall. "Henry, I don't believe it."

"It's true. Glatz was more than a griper. He became a saboteur. He deliberately damaged our accounting system with a virus."

"Ah, did he lift any cash?"

"With me there? Never! When I fired him, he said he was going to sue, then he went to clean out his desk. He must have put the virus in then."

"Henry, a sharpy can steal right under the best manager's nose. I know you would be vigilant. Who discovered the problem?"

"One of the accounting clerks couldn't find a set of files. There are a whole set of missing accounts. Called in the Whiz. Files were gone, alright. He began to check the control program and discovered the virus. It's cleaned out now. And we have back-ups. I'll have to notify Chicago. I'm afraid my name is going to be mud down there."

"No. I'm going down there in the morning. I'll see to it that doesn't happen. They will use it as another mark against me. Any weapon will do now. They are already referring to me as 'That Jobert and His Woodland Frolics'. But I am going to make them eat their words with your help. Henry, write up a description of our successes. Emphasize that the plant has produced a potentially profitable product. They know that, but we have to rub their noses in it. On the hydrogen; I am going to force them to give you a chance to make it pay. I will pressure for the financing to upgrade the plant for hydrogen production. You've got a great challenge.

If you make it work you are on your way. You'll never get a better opportunity. As for me, they're after my scalp."

"Sir, I'm a production man and we have had our differences but you never failed to support me. Will these people do that?"

"Henry, if I give them my scalp, they will."

"Don't do that. We are two very different people but I would like to say how much I esteem you. I've enjoyed working for you. A few too many bogs but I've even learned something there."

∞

"Nice that you call me, Dear. After that last exchange, I thought we might never speak again."

"Oh nonsense. The grapevine has informed me that you are about to get booted by a group of directors. They're after your hide. And I am with them. Edmund, it's time to quit. Come down here to Chicago and be a philanthropist. We can go to all the events- money-raising for the symphony, for the art museum, for all the cultural things. There are so many dinners, so many soirees I don't get to because you are not here. You could be a lion in our social circles. And you would have more time for your children."

"I give them as much time as they want- which is very little. I already help The Nature Conservancy and that's all the socializing I need. I don't need or want the social circle. I like people who do things and people who don't do anything. I won't quit. I'll give them a fight they won't forget. They'll have to kick me out."

"Damn you! You are always selfish, always doing things you want to do. You…"

"Look, I promise I will be there for any important things you come up with. Why don't we just forgive each other and live reasonably harmonious lives?"

"The hell with you. You quit!" She hung up.

∞

"Edmund, Henry here. You remember that suit by the fellow who claimed he walked through the explosion area and got contaminated and then very sick from the methyl isocyanate? His lawyer called and said they were going to court unless we make a settlement. He's got doctors all set to testify about how dangerous that stuff is and what happened to his poor client."

"Henry, how did the fellow ever find out about that stuff?"

"Guess who? those- what did you call them? -the Bobbsey Twins, the Ferrets, could link him to, yes you guessed it, Glatz. But only seen in the same room. Anyway, the question is should we settle. Our lawyers say settle; the amount is small and we don't need the publicity."

"Give up to a stickup artist! No! Let me think about it."

∞

"Sheriff Jager here. Got some more on Glatz."

"Go on."

"Mr. Jobert, we know that Glatz met with Kraft in a local bar shortly before the bombing. They had met there a number of times. Chirali wearing that red tam with the blue and white feathers, came in and Kraft asked her over. Glatz and Kraft had a heavy conversation after Chirali left. Chirali we think was just a casual encounter. So far we can't prove when or how the dynamite got into the Hazardous Waste Room. Your daughter now admits she passed it to Kraft."

"Now that makes sense. That package, what was it? "

"From there to who? Glatz denied having anything to do with the bombing. And so far we can't find the janitor. Glatz is a first class liar. Wouldn't trust him to change a dollar bill. There's no good evidence he was involved in the dynamiting. But he could have passed the dynamite to the janitor. We are still searching for him. Got some addresses...just a matter of time. We staked out Glatz's house and that helped us. Noisy damn jays in the tree there. Kept Marko awake early evening anyway. Waste of damn time. We're still watching Glatz but I doubt we get anywhere."

"Sheriff, our security people sweated the janitor. He did receive the dynamite end of the chain maybe. He was involved with Kraft at the University in Chicago- at demonstrations."

"Your security- those two hoods that were around for a while? We talked to them; they confirmed that Glatz was the one sent the memos out. We really need to get that janitor. No wonder he took off. We do appreciate the information from your security but, again, don't get in our way."

"I assure you we are cooperating and don't want to hamper your work. It would be nice if we could close the story. But we can see the outline now and that is satisfying."

"I have my doubts. We're still working on Glatz but I suspect we won't get anywhere."

"Sheriff, we appreciate your efforts."

∞

"Dad, it's me."

"Honey, it's nice to hear from you."

"Dad, I just got out of jail. Of course you know all about that by now. Dad, I made a bad mistake. I loved getting that dynamite and bringing it up here. It had me tingling all the way. Does that make sense? I didn't think any real harm would come of it. Nobody dead anyway."

"Kraft get you to do it?"

"Damn it, Dad! Yes, but only because I wanted to make a gesture against you. You are overpowering. You must know that."

"Yeah, it's been hinted."

"Anyway, Kraft wasn't as bad as you think. He assured me there wouldn't be anyone really hurt or the building damaged. He did have a cause."

She still has to learn that people with causes can be dangerous. "I know. And people need causes."

"He wanted a better world. You are right about one thing. Environment was just an end for him. He was captured by his ideas so much that anything that helped his aims would be used. I've learned. I'm through with demonstrations but I'm going to keep on supporting environmental causes."

"Hon, I'm headed for Chicago Monday. The Board is after me hard. I'm going to give them my head after they agree to treat some people right. Snowshoe in here today. We'll snowshoe the woods together. We'll enjoy nature until you see what the DA is going to charge you with. Later on I can help you get a job; something you will like."

"None of that. Don't try to manage me. Oh, the hell with it."

"Don't hang up. Damn. Don't tell her what to do, you nitwit." "Hello, hello."

∞

"Dad, I'm back. I'm going to take you up. Don't turn the heat off."

"Of course. I wish I weren't going Monday. Well, anyway, we'll get a day of snowshoeing the woods the way we used to do."

"That will be wonderful."

∞

"Volter here. We've got the votes; you're out; thought I'd let you know so's you wouldn't be shocked.."

"Real generous of you, Volter."

"Damn it, Jobert, face it! You're past it; happens to all of us. You're out. If you don't believe me, check with your buddy, Charlie. Best for everybody."

"You , you… I'll have you..." Volter hung up."

Jobert looked at the phone in his shaking hand and slowly, carefully, replaced it. He had reached a limit. He walked to his gun cabinet, grasped some cartridges and his deer rifle, unused for years, and strode to the door, seized the knob and almost leaped onto the porch. The pines seemed to shake in sympathy. There was the usual deer feeding at the edge of the snowy woods. Blast something? Shoot that deer to show that I am indeed free, in command? He had hunted only grouse in recent years, preferring to walk and watch but now he was desperate, distraught, going to kill a deer something he really didn't want to do. Let the wolves eat them. Really ought to shoot someone; then he would really be free, show beyond doubt that he was able to decide the big decisions. But maybe he was just at the end of travails, doing what he had to do. No! That deer! in the hazelnut patch now. Good! He could defy law, the hunt, himself. He lifted the rifle, slipped in a cartridge, lifted the gun, sighted on the deer's calm eye, lowered the gun, lifted it again, snuggled the stock to his cheek, slid the sight toward the deer's heart. No. Better the head, more free; he shifted to aim at the gentle eye slowly squeezing the trigger. The deer arch-jumped through the deep snow, struggling to get away into the woods. No shot, too late.

A chorus of chickadees settled on him shrilling for sunflower seeds. He jumped, startled. The chickadees flitted to the cedar, dee-deeing frantically for food. Any food source is besieged in the north-woods winter. "Little bastards. I am not your feeder. God damn you for bothering me. I owe you nothing. Yeah. I tamed you, fed you; doesn't mean you too have a lien on me. Yeah, it was my idea but you wanted it. I don't owe you. Shut up. 'dee dee dee dee' Shut Up! Alright, you asked for it." He swung the rifle, pointed it, the chickadee flitting before the rapidly, repeatedly re-aimed rifle. A chickadee landed on the end of the barrel, chickadeeing frantically. It was right in the sights. "You little son-of-a-bitch, get up in that tree where I can shoot you." He swung to aim at a chickadee on a limb, the barrel chickadee staying in place. The twig chickadee was now directly behind the one on the barrel. He again began squeezing the trigger only to burst into laughter and collapse on the ground roaring, half laughing, half crying. He reached into his pocket, stretched his arm, opened his fist, now full of sunflower seeds. Two chickadees landed, each seizing a seed and darting to a branch to hammer open the treasure. He screamed:

"Who the hell is free? How many threads are tying me down! You have to obey the goddam rules. Only God, the universe is free. I'm free to obey the rules, that's all. Necessity! Necessity!" The birds fled. Exhausted, down-spirited, he slowly returned to the cabin to pick up the phone.

"Charlie, Edmund here. That bastard Volter called. Said they had me."

"Not yet, they don't."

"Good. But I am taking your advice. I will give them my head but they are going to have to pay. They upgrade my Folly plant for a trial production of hydrogen. The staff in place is good and must stay. I insist on a reasonable trial period to see if all the bugs can be worked out. Henry Drysdale and Felix can do that. I want the profitable things we have produced put on the market. Charlie, if you can get them to agree to that, I'll agree to quit."

"Edmund, they'll agree after I talk to them. About Volter. Nobody likes him. We'll ease him off the Board. After this is all over, how about coming down for a poker game like old times?"

"Eventually, Charlie, eventually."

Chapter 13 Jobert philosophical

Jobert walked meditatively back to his woods cabin. It was a good day to be alive. How wonderful to be out of the city, the grimy, ghastly city. Ten months of it! How can you- what was it Felix said? 'vibe' with today's cities? People scatter food for the pigeons, or ducks; that's nature in the city. No extravagant adjectives come to people's minds in praise of nature for there is only crowded ugliness about them. Well, maybe some praise for landscaping and for some lonesome thing sometime in the parks or for a nice shrub against some really well-designed nicely landscaped complex of buildings. Imagine a whole world of decayed cities! There was nothing for people to resonate to; all was dispiriting. Would it be possible for those Ark people to return some nature to the cities, to everyone, enough so that each day there would be an occasion to say `how beautiful!, how enjoyable', 'easy to vibe with'? It was to be hoped! He stopped to contemplate a glowing ribbon of sumac along the dirt road; a patch of yellow button tansy heads bordering the sumac. He watched a young moose amble across the road into the woods, free. Free? The year calf was skinny, should be fat going into winter. Not free, bound to its food, to the earth, by iron necessity. A redtail screamed, soared, sailed free across a cloud, only momentary freedom in the service of the mouse law. Find that mouse or starve and no more redtail. But no foresight and therefore free. No foresight? That old redtail in the tree looked miserable and, yes, old. Maybe some inkling of death. No, no foresight. Well, maybe some foresight but certainly no degradation of the spirit. He looked at the patterns of the leaves and turned as a flight of waxwings settled in a mountain ash. This was the home of his spirit, a place to shed all worries and tensions, to become a sentient, maybe unthinking, creature like a grouse or hawk. He looked up the trail towards his cabin, to be frightened by the sight of his little girl sitting on the porch waiting to go on a hike with Daddy. He recovered, realizing it was Alice in a blue frock much like her childhood dress.

"Welcome home, Dad. You look shocked!"

"Home? Yes. You know that. Yes, for a moment there I saw you twenty years younger back when we walked these woods together."

"When things were better between you and Mother. What happens to people, Dad?"

"I don't know. Too many compromises so that you are in a labyrinth with no exit. You construct an unspoken set of rules about when and how to do things. Then there's just being married. Whatever you do, though, don't construct a marriage with legal specifications the way people do these days. Won't work; it is an attempt to write the indecipherable. Take the problem of your brother. I still think leaving him in that Turkish jail was the right decision. Your mother got him out. Maybe she was right and I wrong? ...decisions! Either way it will rankle. Who is at fault when the child goes wrong? Was it my being away, too busy, so much of the time, she being too indulgent, William's collection of genes, his personality?"

"Dad, he just got into the wrong crowd. They all had too much money. His friends went bad faster than he did. Some of them should be in prison. But they use pull to avoid the consequences of their actions."

"That may be so but a boy needs friends. I suppose he got them by chance, some just the products of a decaying society. Hon, finally it isn't resolvable. I wish he had gotten interested in the environment problem; maybe he'd have gone right. Enough of that. Tell me your plans. How long have you been here?"

"Since we were here last winter. I've been going in to work with Indian children every day. Still do now and then. This is home for you and for me, isn't it? I'd like to hike like old times."

"So would I. Hello, Tim."

"Hello, Ed. Thought you'd show up sometime."

Tim, bird glasses in hand, stopped to watch a distant hawk soar. He put the glasses down and looked gravely at his old boss. He spoke easily as to an old friend.

"I just heard the wonderful news. Now you can enjoy the world all the time."

"I didn't exactly decide to do it this way."

"What does that matter? You should thank whoever pushed you. I'm sure it was necessary. Get away from all that stuff. And that's what I did. I'd had enough regular hours. I decided to quit. I never belonged in a production factory. And especially I didn't belong in one where you were not the boss."

"Don't think that way, Tim. You could have been a help to Drysdale."

"No. You know better than that. Drysdale was glad to see my tail go out the door. I am your friend, I hope."

"Always. What are your plans?"

"I saved a lot of money from my captivity in the lab and I'm sort of going to go around the country looking at the hunks of good environment that are left. Alice is coming along. Oh oh. Look who's coming. Dextra with Teddy- success, success, success- Felix did it! I'm into the woods. Ring the bell when they go."

"Hello, Edmund!"

Dextra waved joyously, resplendent in her feathered tam, a wide smile on her face, to be quickly joined by Teddy Sourtis. There was a connectedness, a freedom about their movements, a lightness that told Jobert that all was well.

"No demo, Alice?" asked Teddy.

"No..no. I'm trying to help Indians now."

Dextra spoke, "Edmund, I`m sorry about the way things have turned out for you. When I heard you were quitting, that was the end of my stay here. Mr. Drysdale is a good boss but I was always here because you were here, Edmund. I need a someone who listens to my ideas and suggestions and tries to understand what I am saying. Edmund, you backed me when I needed you in the Lab. It is just that, Edmund, you and I think in complementary ways. Did you know I was once in love with you? Don't shake your head."

"Oh, nonsense."

"Yes, it's true."

"I knew it. I've been there," said Alice.

"Oh Alice, no. Dextra was just- just what?- infatuated. You had a need; it was a projection of your need for companionship. We all want that."

"That is not so, Edmund. I would come to you with something I had invented just so I could talk to you. You were kind but never noticed. If you had responded, I would have been deliriously happy! But you put me off, gently to be sure. I recovered. I worked hard but something inside me was bursting out. Then I saw Tim. He did not have ambition but he was like you in so many ways. Then I began to reach out to Tim and you understood that.

When I moved toward him there was an observer inside who knew this was ridiculous."

"But there was also another party in there who was determined to pursue Tim."

"Yes. Calm yourself, Teddy. I had a divided mind. And then I realized he was avoiding me. At the same time, I was aware of Teddy's approach and wanted to respond and didn't want to respond. Is not that madness? I reached a low point and you, and Tim? and Felix? began to scheme. I didn't think Felix was that°ah° sensitive. I thought Felix was from another planet. When you took us to Washington I knew, I didn't know, what you and Felix were doing."

Teddy said, "I kicked you in the ankle according to the prescriptions I got from Dr. Felix and it worked."

"I knew unconsciously that was going on. When Teddy finally broke through, it was as though I had been freed from some evil spell. And, of course, I soon found that Teddy was just right for me."

"And you know a lot more about people now," said Jobert.

"Yes. I wish we could stay and talk but we have to leave immediately. When we go, tell Tim to come out of the woods. Give him my love, the love of friendship, Teddy. Teddy and I are off to the Chicago laboratories. They have promised me a first class laboratory. I do not belong in a production place. What I do is basic genetics. Teddy is taking a job there too."

"Yes. I think I can improve the sequencing machinery. I shall work with the basic people while training Dextra in the fine art of taking care of me. And of course I shall take care of her. I'm a good cook, you know."

"Didn't know that, Teddy. And how are you as a lover?"

"Edmund! Teddy and I get along well."

"Yes. I am making a human being out of her. She is no longer just an experimental geneticist. We are going to work on some things together. Some genetics experiments."

"Teddy, you will pay for that tonight. Edmund, this is good-bye. We hope to see you in Chicago. It would be terrible to lose all our Laboratory friends. We have grown to like these woods and shall vacation here and come to see you, Edmund. If you are here. I have to kiss you this once, Edmund. And, please, get Tim out of the woods."

∞

"Hey, Tim! Oh Tim, yoo-hoo. Ah there you are. Come down here. Dextra insisted I get you out of the woods. And sends her love, sororal that is."

"Ah, I appreciate that. Fine woman. Teddy is lucky. Ho, now Drysdale is coming up the road," observed Tim.

"Will you get lucky, Tim?" asked Jobert... "Well, what induced you to come all the way in here, Henry?"

"Nice to see you again, Alice, and you, Tim. It is a sunny, perfect day and I felt that you would want to hear about the hydrogen work. Most important I wanted to thank you for your support; especially for getting Felix Bountz to stay with me after you lost your battle. He is a jewel. I don't understand him but he works night and day to make things work. He is there because you were there. I am pleased he doesn't dislike me but you were the one to get him and keep him. I have something to learn there but I fear it is a matter too deep for learning. I am grateful to you for pressing him to stay. I rely on him. We have been working night and day to solve problems. A big test is coming up. If we don't show that we can produce at a competitive price, I'm sure the take-over people, watching us like hawks now, will issue pink slips very promptly. Well, my main reason for coming- please drop by to see what we are doing; I value your opinions and advice."

"Henry, I'll do that. It would be nice to see the plant again. Just thinking of it gets me to prancing like an old racehorse seeing the track."

"Are you going to consult? Your experience would be invaluable to many a manager."

"Well, I don't think I am just an old geezer sitting here in the sun. But no. If I can't manage, I'd rather do something else. I'm going to try to understand how ecologists say the world works. I want to understand, too, how genetics works. I'll write Dextra for answers. I really most would like to get some idea of how mind arises from matter. It must be in the genes, but how? That will keep me happy. And, oh yes, my wife is lining up things that I should do to improve the city of Chicago. Ha!"

"Symphony and art museum and civic do-gooders and endless well-meaning bores. Interrupted, of course, by coming up here to chop wood and hunt grouse and just watch," said Alice.

"Alice, would you like to come in and work for me?" asked Drysdale.

"No. No. I'm a little like Tim, I'm afraid."

Drysdale nodded, accepting, understanding, "Edmund, I shall be eternally in your debt. Whatever happens to this work you can be sure I'll use your training wherever I am."

"Mr. Drysdale, I wish you luck," said Tim.

"Tim, I thank you. I am sorry you quit. No, no, I speak the truth. We are in many ways far apart in our view of life but I think we could have gotten along."

"Probably. Still, that young kid ought to take care of your Renewal Site well enough."

"Edmund, Tim, Alice, I must return. We have an important test going on. Hope to see you soon, Edmund."

∞

"Sit with me; we'll soak up the sun. And save energy." Jobert leaned back against the wall.

They sat against the cabin wall, warming luxuriantly in the sun, feeling somnolent in the autumn afternoon. Each arrived at that comfortable state when the mind is suspended, drifting, in a warm, enveloping cocoon. Each swam out of the suspension to hear a steady irregular putt-putt, then an insistent louder continuous putt-putt. Tim surfaced to ask, "What is that noise?"

"Dunno."

"Some kind of motor.. Look at that."

An antique front end loader was approaching, behind it a cart with a large cement object, and seated on the end Sheriff Jager and Olie Mattson, the lumberjack. Pikala was driving.

"Finally, my new septic tank. Well, gentlemen."

"Mr. Jobert, read about your fight in the papers and knowed you wouldn't be here most a the time but figgered you'd be here to grouse hunt this fall. So I brung your tank. I'll put it in inna next few days. I'm sorry I brung them two but wasn't much I could do. Helluva thing to do ta you. They just climbed on. If they'll just get their asses off I'll put the tank where it belongs."

"Pick, next time you drive this piece of junk, I'm going to arrest you. It'll take me an hour to shake my bones back in place."

Olie said, "Pick, we'd been better off walking. Thought I'd drop by, tell you about the windthrow cleanup, Mr. Jobert. Going good. Had a close one. Pulled on a cross-stacked bunch and one of 'em swings to finish me and I jumped fast. A widow-maker headed at the wrong guy; thought I was gonna meet my Maker. Reminded me of ...of..."

"Olie, what we don't need is to hear about everything happens to you in the woods," said the sheriff.

"OK, OK, anyway...we'll have that windfall cleaned out. Gotta say it's gonna be profitable. Mill's licking its chops for the logs. Seemed like old times ta handle real logs. We gotta talk about the split."

"We agreed you get the logs. They're yours. I expect you to clean up, eliminate your road in, and then block off your track so no one follows it in."

"Olie, I need me a hand gettin' the tank off. Gonna set up a better site, Mr. Jobert. Back inna while. Leave you inna custody of the Sheriff." He giggled like a school boy.

"Pick, I'm gonna drop that tank on your toes," said Olie.

∞

"Mr. Jobert, I doubt we ever find out how Kraft died. The Chicago police turned up that janitor just by chance. He was living on the streets, just another old bum walking, mumbling, swinging his arms, and talking to everybody and every garbage can. They tried to interrogate him. So did we when we got him up here. His mind isn't the best, wanders. We got an admission, for what it's worth, that he put the dynamite in your Hazardous Waste Room. Also got a real garbled mess about it was his idea, about connecting wires the wrong day, all this while talking to the wall and anything else. Both him and Glatz weren't in town that night. We have witnesses. I think Kraft blew himself up, maybe with a spark from his own body or lightning and all with the help of a looney. Experts say both are possible. Question is what to do."

"Best to forget the whole thing."

"That's what Mr. Drysdale said. Way our DA wants to go. The janitor under drugs; really ought to be in an institution but they don't do that these days. We, maybe, could hit Glatz on passing the dynamite. Drysdale said let it go."

"Right. There would be no gain putting him in jail. That janitor bothers me. A man like that walking the streets undefended, mad as a hatter."

Pikala and Mattson walked up. "Not a bad way ta go through life. Don't reely have ta pay attention ta people's crap," said Pikala.

"No, Pick. No! I mean No! Us cops have to pick them up, sometimes. They are miserable most of the time. Now your daughter there- hello, Miss Alice- she's real popular with the Indians now. I think maybe you have learned a lesson, Miss Alice."

"Alice. I have. I was stupid to let myself be run. Sheriff, I feel like cooking up a storm. I want you and Mr. Pikala..." `call me Pick'... " Mr.. Mattson" 'Olie here' "to stay for supper. OK, Dad?"

"Fine. Tim will help."

"Will I ever! Alice, did you know I was one of the world's great cooks- hamburgers a speciality?"

"Sure would be nice ta eat here but I don't need no bachelor cookin'."

"Me neither," Olie.

∞

"Miss Alice, you have the makings of a fine cook. Could sure use another cup of coffee. Sheriffs are forced to drink so much bad coffee that finding good stuff is a pure luxury."

"Ever regret going into the law?"

"Sometimes. You begin to wonder if there are limits on what people will do. Whether anything is simple. Gets wearing. What I'd like to be is innocent again, totally innocent. That seem strange?"

Jobert answered, "No. Tim here has managed to preserve some of that naivete....some of the boyish responses....some of the spontaneity of the instant let's-go spirit. Maybe we'd all like that."

"Speaking for myself, I avoid repartee and backbiting because it wears down your own spirit. Still, the years have produced a kind of armor on me," said Tim.

"Not very visible," said Alice.

"Me, I wish I had back the big pines. Could watch the young fellas be men and not these nances you see now."

"Me, I'd like back my good leg. Was once a first class athalete. Always wondered what I coulda done things were different. Ah hell, you play the cards you're dealt. Which brings to mind. Don't suppose you kinda people play poker- say a little nickel- quarter game? Know that ain't money to you but."

Said Jobert, "Well."

"Of course you do, Dad. Mr. Pikala- I mean Pick, I think that's a wonderful idea. Don't start until Tim and I get there. I'm a card shark; you didn't know that, Dad?"

"I'm not surprised."

"Miss Alice, you know how ta play?"

"Alice. Just a little. Enough."

"Haven't played in so long, I've forgotten how. Five cards to each," Jobert was dealing.

"Yeah, and we each ante up a quarter. That includes you, Sheriff. It's the law. Ha, ha. Evvybody in?" said Pikala.

" Money hungry bastard. Sorry, Miss... Alice."

"Now let's see. You can have up to three cards?"

"Right. Me. I'll take on'y one."

"One? Pick, you're not one of those people who draws to inside straights?" Jobert was recalling his college days.

"How long since you played, Mr. Jobert?" asked Pikala.

"Sure he does. And other dumb moves," said Olie.

"Quarter to the pot."

"I'm in."

"Ed, how did the Washington talks go last year?"

"Dextra was a star. I'll raise that. Now Pick. You raise again. Of course you do. Hm..I'll call."

"That Dextra, wonder where she got them nice blue feathers. Looka the nice straight. Lesson there, Mr. Jobert."

"Indeed. Tim, we got into a discussion about cycling and recycling."

"Dextra must have found the feathers. Funny. I sat up in my cabin reading Henry Fourth again and came across the line, `A man can die but once; we owe God a death', and I thought, more than that we owe God a cycle, for only a bacterium can live forever. They bubble along and produce no fine form, no brilliant solutions, just exist and reproduce." Tim was a Shakespeare fan.

"And keep my septic tanks in good shape. An' around them too."

"Might a known that with Pikala here we'd talk about something real interesting like outhouses. OK, Pick, pony up. Get your ante in. That Shakespeare, Tim?"

"That Shakespeare musta been a smart guy. Me, I owe God that death now for over thirty years. My buddies paid theirs."

"I'll have ta raise that bet. Now, Pick, you'll have ta learn a lesson, maybe."

Tim continued, "We have the fine solutions, great eyes to see birds with, hands that can take a tree down in no time if Olie's doing it, plans that can replace a septic tank easily and quickly, if Pick does it, and so on, but those abilities cost us a death, ours. That cost is paid by every creature which has aspired to be different, i.e. birds, bugs, jellyfish, almost all of life. Costs, you see, start with being different. We've been here a few million years and for at least ninety five percent of that time, the costs of our existence have been borne by nature."

"Are you death-centered, Tim?" asked Alice.

"No...no just reality... I think."

"An' Nature is stoppin doin' the job?" asked Pikala.

"Well, no, just changing fast. We left our dead bodies, our emanations, our sticks and clam shells, our shelters behind for nature to cycle, change and dissipate."

Alice, exasperated, said, "Do you guys have to get so damn ....morbid, philosophical on us? Get your money in the pot."

"Why not, Miss Alice? Something interesting. Now evvy-body get their money in there. It's my turn ta win. Need a fat pot," Olie smiled.

"Olie's sittin' there with a full house. Can always tell. Ain't Olie?"

"Like you said, you want ta know, you pay."

Tim continued, "But, Ed, we got too clever and learned to support too many of ourselves and to produce materials and goods from molecules never found in nature."

"Ain't that the truth. So many things screwed up. Still, we oughtta be able to solve them," said Pikala.

"You could and I could but can society?"

"Time out. Have to gulp some air. Come on everyone."

"An' poor Olie sittin' there with a fistful."

"They won't melt away."

∞

"Look at the stars! It's an astronomer's night."

Tim looked up and said, "Do you suppose there's a planet out there where people are watching nature die? The way we are?"

"Tim, you should have heard about Senator Verlicht's scheme for garbage. Just pile it as high as you can, say 500 feet, put gravel and soil on it, plant with grass. At the top, he wants a restaurant-Verlicht Vista." Jobert enjoyed the memory.

Tim glowed with joy, "The Restaurant at the End of the Garbage Dump. Gourmet Food and Downhill Skiing and...and See the Sunrise over Chicago."

"Stop it, Tim."

Tim was unstoppable, "surrounded by ski slopes. Ski right outside the city! People would come out to worship the true dawn's early light glowing in the east. We could abolish flatland. There would be mountains outside Fargo, Kansas City, Odessa. Vistas everywhere. Now isn't that a vision? I wish I had been there."

"Enough air. Back to the game. I want my pot. Gettin' late."

"Not them people down to the cities. They won't solve nothin'," said Pikala.

"OK, I'll call and raise again," said Alice.

"Alice, I know you ain't used to this game but I been bettin' real hard. Don't you think you oughtta drop out?" asked Olie.

"Call me if you think so."

"OK. I call."

"Straight flush."

"Ha, ha, ha. Olie gets taken again by little Miss Innocent. Learn your poker Las Vegas, Alice?"

"Tim, take the advice of an old lumberjack. Don't play poker. Little Miss Innocent there has cleaned you out, nd me. Alice, anybody plays poker so good deserves to be my wife. What say?"

"Get a proposal from Olie sounds like askin' for a cup a coffee."

Alice asked, "Whatever happened with you and Gypsy? Don't answer if it's embarrassing."

"Ha, bound to be embarrassin'. Anythin' Olie does with women is gonna bring a blush to any decent young lady. Olie don't know the difference between females, moose or human. Anyway, let's hear it. Bound to be funny. As if I didn't know."

"Took a book off my shelf. Only one I never read. When I couldn't pass her questions, she left. Just a joke, Pick. Still. She talked so sweet. Real nice. Just too far back in the woods, I guess. Ah well!"

"Tim, did I tell you I found that hermit thrush's nest that Dextra found. Had a torn piece of yellow ledger paper in it, with words 'ene' or 'ema' and beautiful ornate numbers on it. 'Ema' a town maybe."

"Ledger paper?" The Sheriff frowned, looked thoughtful, then shrugged his shoulders.

Tim pointed out, "Thrushes often put strips of bark or paper in the nest."

Tim asked, "Pick, how did that bear dump work out?"

"Good. Dump's workin' real good. Gas comin' off, stuff growing on it now so it's hard to get in there. Helped a guy up the road sink a pipe. Took gas to his house. Worked. Bad connection. Lighted a cigarette and blew himself right off the toilet. Yep. Workin' fine...."

"Olie stop shuffling. Wearin' out the cards."

"Olie has to have a perfect cycle- I mean shuffle," said Alice.

"Gettin' late. Got some work to do tomorrow. Time to go."

"We have to get jolted again or walk. Last hand," said Olie.

"Now what have you got, Pick?"

"Olie, you ain't improvin' with age. Ed, you want ta know that, you gotta pay. It's a rule. I heard you say it. It's the price of life.

∞

“Listen... the barred owl is hooting in the pines. Some mouse will pay the price,” said Tim. “and things will cycle.”

Chapter 14 Verlicht's mountain

Jobert craned his neck hunting for his daughter, for Tim and their brood. He spotted them sitting on the steps of the capitol and immediately started walking to them and thought how attractive they were. "Hi, Hi Tim Alice over here." Jobert beamed and spread his arms for the kids who overwhelmed their grandfather, then clinging to him.

"Tim, Alice we are in luck. The Solons are going to orate. They're supposed to be a truly deliberative body, almost a collection of members of Plato's Academy and not legislators. Only with more common sense. Our chance to hear that hope realized. Want to listen?"

"Let's go," said Alice seating her daughter on her shoulder. Tim nodded yes, took Eddy's hand as they walked up the stairs. He said, "Yeah but people vote. It's too much to hope they will pick more knowledgeable, more thoughtful people, much less more philosophical types. And common sense that's a vain hope. Uh oh wait! The sign says old Senator Verlicht is speaking. Now why did they ever let that happen?"

Alice giggled, "Well we're here. Let's listen to what he has to say. There's a rumor he has more common sense now that he's gotten old."

"Believe me Hon, age adds no common sense. I'm evidence of that."

"Now Dad."

"Verlicht talking. Chance to hear the old coot once more...and he's going to talk about Verlicht Mountain. Really we can't miss this."

Tim swung Eddy to his shoulder, "Ed, to hear about Verlicht Mountain imagine that. Ed, that's a privilege."

"Yes. OK. Don't worry folks, we'll still tour the sights. This is a good chance to hear the crazy old coot again. It will be historical; the kids can say they were at a unique event."

"Ed, maybe he'll talk about the working of the Invisible Hand in nature."

“He doesn’t understand its working in society much less nature. If only Adam Smith had been a bird-watcher.”

“Where have I heard that, before. “Adam Smith, Bird-watcher.”. Would that it had been so.”

"Maybe so but there are questions requiring thought. The Solons have the task of reconciling social with environmental requirements- imagine how difficult that is to craft. There, there over there, some good seats we can hear and see well from there. You young people grab it. I’ll get there eventually.”

The chairman scowled at the lackadaisical way the members were assembling and decided to speed them up. “Come to order! Come to order!” To himself, Damn I broke another gavel. Well I'll give the bastards the siren. That gets ‘em. “Gentlemen, take your seats. Before we get to the problem at hand let's hear the minutes for the last meeting. Tom.”

“Mr. Chairman, the description of chaos is not easy. There isn't even the order that arises from mathematical chaos.”

“Mr. Chairman, direct the secretary not to editorialize, just read the minutes.”

“So ordered. Continue.”

“Mr. Chairman, that is not possible without reprising the entire meeting.”

“Of course, go on- present your précis.”

The secretary noticed a disturbance in the hall. Verlicht was entering. No, the hell with the minutes; thought the secretary, the old coot has to give us his piece. The sacrifices I make for the good of this body. O Morpheus find me. Aloud, “Our speaker of the day has entered. With your permission I turn the meeting back to the Chairman who is scheduled to give a brief review of the whole system of Chairs and the rules by which they operate. Mr. Chairman.”

“Yes, I had better give my summary so that we may turn over the meeting to our distinguished former colleague, Senator Verlicht. I will be brief. Because in a growing society the quality and quantity of land, water and air is constantly changing it is not possible to develop simple consistent rules governing their disposal. In a steady state society on the other hand, a single individual, technically capable, backed by phalanxes of computers filled with data could keep track of changes and by simple rulings of a technical nature ensure the constancy of the kinds of land use.

It is the assumption of the need (goodness) of a steady state society that permits such a Chair. He (she) can be charged with the maintenance of the quality and quantity of the water and land in a single watershed. Subordinate to the Watershed Chair there will be a regional Chair (collection of watersheds) and finally a National Chair charged with coordination and setting overall policy with the advice and consent of the Solons and President. Decisions by the local Watershed Chair are based on data and technical matters and theory but are subject to review by higher levels only in terms of coordination and the general good. To bring about the desired equilibrium in land, water and air use, Chairs are empowered to require the taxing authorities to 1) raise or lower taxes; 2) control water use - setting levels up or down; 3) control water quality by imposing heavier and heavier taxation as the quality is lowered. The Chairs are empowered to increase or decrease use of property, water etc. in their charge via taxation if necessary....................."

∞

"Now then, that is the end of our formal session. We have the honor of hearing from retired Senator Verlicht who will address us on the progress of his mountain near Chicago, bringing us up to date on improvements achieved in more recent years. We all know the honorable Senator, and I will forthwith turn the podium over to Senator Verlicht." A low moan was just apparent over the background sound. "Solons, ladies and gentlemen, visitors, you have the privilege of hearing the wisdom of Senator Verlicht; Senator Verlicht you have the floor."

"My fellow Solons and all you lovely visitors, citizens all of this great nation...."

"How long can he lay it on like that?"

"Longer than our tolerance. He's still a total main chance politician."

"He looks to me to be doddering and tottering."

"He's in his second nonage."

"Patience- that mountain may be crazy but it's fun."

"Shh!"

"They will not; they will not put houses on my mountain. They will not!" all said in Verlicht's quavering aged voice.

"He has aged, hasn't he Felix."

"Yeah. So have we."

"That glorious mount constructed of trash is now one of the great tourist attractions of Chicago. You! every one of you, is welcome to come to walk the winding trails through fall leaves and prairie grasses, to stop and view the blue and white asters and gentians up on the hillsides. You can sit on Mt. Verlicht.

"always wanted to do that"

"and there's those red, red sumac and you can see the skyscrapers of downtown Chicago; or at a different bench, look at Lake Michigan stretching out, way out. Or sit at another comfortable bench and watch the sun rising from Indiana or on the opposite side sit and look on a vista leading out to the limitless prairies. My friends, Verlicht Mountain testifies to the vision of your predecessors who helped establish this beautiful monument. We fought for progress and here it is, a memorial for my fellow politicians who had the foresight to vote for this mountain to be constructed out of trash."

"More like it was a payoff, maybe to get him to shut up."

"Tim, is it possible to be as mendacious as this guy?"

"Probably not. But listen on, he's singing our tune, now."

"That's what I mean; what he's saying is different from what he used to say."

"That's normal with politicians. Anyway he's senile and that makes it easy to do what politicians do all the time, revise their histories and say with conviction what they have always railed against. His neat mental eraser has wiped out all the previous convictions and substituted the new stuff. All the things he was wrong about have been banished from his ugh mind. Like that guy Walleye. Remember? And his ego has produced a jewel and he thinks he did it. For the first time ever I think Verlicht may be making sense. He's not just mad; he is just now seeing the true light. There's method in his madness."

Verlicht continued "The late Catastrophe has concentrated our real talents upon solving our environmental problems. There's physicists, chemists, biologists, meteorologists, climatologists and all the 'ologists you can think of bending their minds to what's needed. People do this cycling now so there's less trash. So not so much recycling. Still some products must go to a land fill of which almost all are about to go out of existence Therefore we need to shift more to cyclable materials, stuff that can decay real fast and become humus. We are all grateful to the geneticists who have developed bacteria capable of all kinds of fabulous deeds. But so far they have not given us the totally renewable recyclable tree house."

"Hurrah for tree houses. Great place for squirrels."

"What is that you say?"

"Wait, listen."

"Mount Verlicht is now two watersheds. Some of the rain drains to Lake Michigan, some to the Illinois River and the Mississippi. The local Watershed Chair, I tell you, is a martinette who keeps close track of the quality of the water coming off the hill. He insists on upgrading the entire system. With some success I might add. He has my full support, my full support. They tell me there are whole areas now which look like what the prairies used to look like. And my bird watching person- hee, hee, hee, she tells me there are meadow larks, something called horned larks, and Verlicht Pond, yes my very own, now has upland plover whatever they are. Anyway it's nice.

"The mountain is now a park and they say is attracting too many people. They want to set up rules so that too many people do not enter each day. Seems hard. They have what they call a feedback system: too many people on the hill, the number entering is reduced; if too low automatically increased. Major problems are the religious sects. Now I don't say anything against religious people but they demand access to the Visitor Rest Area so they can worship the sun. This problem was settled by requiring them to take the shortest easiest trail also used by the physically challenged people. Still they want to wander everywhere. This is prohibited."

"Tim, little Eddy change your mind about growth?"

"No. Just about the future. I want beyond all else that he see something naturally beautiful, beyond words, only to be felt in the depths of one's soul."

"Amen."

"I fear most a nature which is reduced to back yards or degraded parks crawling with insensate people looking for the next 'troglodyte' or wonder, a Chinese landscape. I am told it will take a long time for Verlicht's mountain to even approximate a natural environment." Tim started into a peroration. Alice frowned. But he was unstoppable, "According to Verlicht it's already there. Not so. It's true, it's true it will take a long time after my time to become incomparable. They will have to enact strict rules, rigorously enforced and will need lots of thoughtful people like us, and responsible volunteers, to bring it to that state. But it may come. I ask will there be that epiphany when Eddy or Alice, lying on a wet stream bank reaches into the clear depths of a burbling crystalline stream, rising hand attempting to enclose a radiant trout, when the world stands still and nature is perfect? for Eddy or Alice, will there? The thought that such might not be possible can reduce me to bottomless despair."

"I also. What was that he said? He's off again."

"The trail starts at a parking lot and switchbacks up the mountain. The wild flowers are patchy, placed in good virgin soil but all will be similar soon."

Jobert listened to Verlicht's quavery peroration, holding off sleep, eyes closing.

hotel air cloying, heavy drift into cool Cool Charley yeah don' breath too deep.

Sir! coffee? right, Charley black cafe and good coffee
phantoms grumbling hawking in own misery nowhere
night man drearies over coffee please else? no
hot yeah here allays
let's go Charley yeah streets deserted dismal echoing
whew trash peeking through grass

my kids warm sleepy Up kids gamboling on glowing green grass flowers

bevy of monks saffron pleasant Tibet?
sit kids rest
monks seated in amphitheater face East
oom oom oom.......
oom oom oom sea of smiling monks

free market free market free market monks frown questioning looks laugh oom oom oom

kids say nature
nature nature nature monks laughing
sun rises
meadow lark э/////\\\\\ э////\\\\\ э////\\\
monks oom oom oom
kids nature nature nature all together

me free market free market free market.

Jobert awoke with a start to hear Verlicht droning on, grasped the child too hard, awakening her. "What is it Daddy?" "Go to sleep Honey," And she did. He picked up the thread of argument and tried to make it into something sensible. His mind wandered again.

The Invisible Hand, he thought, will work in nature just as in society if all the subsidies affecting nature that distort economic systems are eliminated. For example, eliminate the tax support for children, special tax reductions, eliminate tax increment financing for business and industry, subsidies for commercial fisherman or amateur, for mining, for forest lumbering, for grazing, water, air, anything and the market and nature will swing toward a steady state. All misshapers of reality. Too, eliminate state enterprises, these are the rogues which will destroy fisheries, natural areas, and finally societies. Needed only are regulations, enforced and directed by highly trained experts, a system in which choice is offered with a societally favorable option; Other choices can be and often will be stupid, an outcome permitted by free will.

It is the subsidized fisherman who by inexorable force of economics fishes the Commons to extinction. Unsubsidized, the fisherman would be forced out of business before the fishery is destroyed. It is in part the failure to adhere to Adam Smith's free market and the Invisible Hand that accelerates the destruction of nature. If there were no subsidizing of fish production whether commercially or in the wild there would be no destruction either. Again if there were no subsidies, crazy insurance, tax increment financing, etc. there would be no building on fore-dunes and therefore no destruction there. Ditto for lake and stream side and summer housing; there would be far less destruction there also. Eliminate subsidies for lumbermen and forests would be better preserved. The purity of air and water would be best served by removing all support for the utilization of lake-sides, river-sides, ocean-sides. Result: clean air, clean water. Remediation of brown fields would result in the repair of roads, the rebuilding of slums, the civilizing and gentrification of the slum dweller. Need societal rules for natural areas.

He eyed the surrounding solons blearily. Some were draped on their desks, others stared at the ceiling; a few dutifully stared at the speaker, apparently listening transfixed. There was too a bored, puzzled row all diligently doodling Kilroys, giraffe necks, triangles in triangles in circles, and pornographic angels. How many meetings like that!

Tim repeated, “Ed, we have to get the Invisible Hand working to preserve nature. Old Adam Smith, must have been a Bird-Watcher at times. He must be on our side.”

Grumpily, “Right.”

The End

About the author:

He is a long-time teacher of genetics, ecology and evolution, a naturalist seeking a solution(s) to the problem of growth versus environment and a long-time proponent of saving natural environments and their plants, animals and glory. A conservationist produced by a succession of good teachers, he has saved 35 acres of prairie, helped construct an oak opening and has helped preserve and improve some local nature parks. Observation of the progress of conservation efforts has led him to conclude that the process will fail because individuals (families) finally act in their own self interest. Having lived through the period when the state-run economies (e.g. USSR, Mexico etc.) produced failing economies and environmental destruction, he has concluded that solutions to environmental problems must somehow arise from interactions of the free market (the system that works) and self-interest in the cause of environmental preservation. Trial and error will (must) show the way to a new free market steady-state economy. Given the complexity of the environment-economic interaction, you the reader may very well be as likely to invent an improvement as any 'expert' economist or ecologist. You out there, you! You can help solve these problems.

To see a sample chapter and description of book and its thesis, go to Website: sonic.net/~nielj/nomecos.html

Order: to order a book or books any of the following methods may be used:. **Note**: don't rip out page.

Postal orders - are filled at
Nomecos Publishing,
P.O. Box 382
Northfield, MN 55057

Note: orders for large numbers of books must be accompanied by a bank reference and name of bank manager.

E-mail orders
from address: pjensen@microassist.com

.

The following arrangement is useful in ordering by any of these means:

Please send _____ copies of Adam Smith, Bird Watcher .to the following address
Name___________________________
Address_________________________
City____________________________
State_______, Zip______

Price per book $11.95. Add shipping charge of $1.75 for one book. For each additional book [up to ten] add 60 cents. Beyond this number postal rates plus ten percent for handling. Minnesota residents add 6.5% sales tax to price of book.

If any physically damaged book should sneak through our inspection, return it to the above address and your money will be promptly refunded or a good copy sent immediately.